THE THIEF, THE HARLOT
AND THE HEALER

THE THIEF, THE HARLOT AND THE HEALER

M.E. CLEMENTS

First paperback edition 2023

978-1-80227-957-3 (paperback)
978-1-80227-958-0 (eBook)
978-1-80541-081-2 (hardcover)

CHAPTER I

✦ ✦ ✦

She could not escape the jolt of the horse's gallop, the smell of the man's filthy body, his hot, ginger whiskers pushing down on her head. She ached to loosen the grip of terror in her heart. And the rain poured down, soaking the leather sheets binding her to the chest of the intruder as he raged through the storm. She could hear his malevolent, iron heart, pounding like a warning to humankind that great evil staggered in his wake. The other riders followed. His band of robbers, eager to share their booty, laughed at the chaos they had caused back in the city. They rode hard along the shore of the lake, borne onward by the great, gusting madness of the storm. She could hear their cries of delight and the trees groaning under the weight of water and heavy mist. The lake was gleefully malevolent, leaping and dashing against the thin line of stone lining the tiny road to Theims.

As they rode beneath the jutting mountains, the landscape seemed to heave and shudder like the water on the lake, beneath the moonless, opaque sky that had eaten the stars and removed all hope of daylight. The sun had been quenched by this night of tears, and she had no hope of ridding herself of the terror of her abduction and the fearful sounds of her mother and father screaming for mercy. The man's stench, his leering crudity and his vile breath crushed her. She was but a child. Under his enormous weight, she had been violated with a fear only the warrior or the martyr should suffer. Her youth had been despoiled, her tenderness unsheathed and replaced with a crude kernel of congealed pain forming like a septic scab over her whole body.

Now the mountains danced and jeered, the whole earth coalescing into a watery mass. All that had once been perfect was now smashed and blended into a senseless mass of pain.

The horses began to slow. She panicked. A light appeared in the darkness in front of a long, low building with a flat roof. All the windows were barred or shuttered, the white walls gleaming like a ghostly presence in the gloom. A woman wrapped in scarlet, her face painted white and her eyes full of scorn, appeared before the intruder.

'What do you want of me?' she howled, fighting against the buffeting wind.

'Take this child and keep her safe. When the time is right, I will come for her,' yelled the intruder, throwing the child down at the woman.

'Boataz, I can't do this… I just can't. I don't want to be involved,' protested the woman.

'Do as I say or my men will stay the night!' roared the intruder.

'This sheet is covered in blood! What have you done? I'll have no part in this.'

Boataz the intruder, the villain, the robber, the murderer kicked her in the face and she fell hard, with the child, into the mud. The rain was intense, and they were nearly kicked by the horses that galloped off into the darkness. A single figure appeared in the light of the building's main doorway. She was young and slender and dressed in white. She rushed out to help the fallen woman and the child.

'Rachel, pick the girl up,' commanded the older woman, holding her face and dabbing her bleeding nose.

Rachel, panting, reached for the child and lifted her, aghast at this cruel twist of fate. Boataz had snatched her own child, Anna, many years ago, and her motherly instinct made her bring the young girl to her chest and hug her. In the eye of the storm, in the rage of the moment, despite everything set against her, Rachel determined to hold onto this child and protect her. Drenched and filthy, she carried the child across the muddy road to the house. The child looked back at the world dancing in madness: the weeping, laughing waters, vying in the mist to claw down the sky into their maelstrom grip, the mountains sliding back and forth as the trees bowed in the wind.

'What is your name?' asked Rachel, swaddling her with her sweet-smelling headdress. The child said nothing, but in the woman's arms, looking at her kind face and bright eyes, she fainted.

The house, with its thick stone walls, did not shake. It had withstood many decades of winter storms even worse than this one. It was a white-painted prison that was impossible to escape.

There were eight women in the house of Thamina, the keeper of the brothel, who prided herself on running a neat, tidy and clean establishment. The brothel could easily masquerade, when required, as an official-looking house for destitute women, allowing it to escape the attention of the authorities. A single long dormitory with nine beds filled the space before eight silk-curtained cubicles, bedecked with ornate pillows and scented veils, where the women were forced to work in the evenings into the early morning.

Rachel laid the child on her bed and worried about what had happened to cause so much blood to saturate the girl's expensive dress. Boataz had attacked someone very rich. The child's clothes were immaculately stitched and of fine linen. Rachel tried to remove the dress and wash the girl,

3

looking for signs of cuts or bruises, but found nothing. She dressed her, as she slept, in a coarse cotton chemise. She laid the child on her side beneath the bed clothes where Rachel, too, lay down and listened to the storm.

Rachel thought of the nightmarish dreams that the pair could share as they lay under the passage of a storm that cared nothing for their circumstances. She recalled her own abduction, when she had been a child, the confused pain of being taken from a loving home, then incarcerated in the brothel, wanting every day to escape its disgusting impact on her life. She remembered, too vividly, the night her daughter, Anna, had been taken by Boataz, and she wept.

She cuddled this strange child of the night, pulling her into herself, and hoped that she could help her escape the fate that she herself had endured at the hands of the monster.

The wind howled, and the stars were obscured by the ferocious collision of bloated clouds pouring a torrent of tears into the basin of water that was Lake Gennesaret. A single mouth at the north of the lake, a break in the ragged terrain, allowed the warm air from the sea to flow down into the colder depression of the lake and create a maelstrom. The stern winter months robbed many families that fished the lake for a living of their loved ones. Further up the coast, the larger town of Magdala was peppered by a myriad of lights as the fishing community set its face against the perverse overtures of this stormy night.

'Godless,' murmured Rachel as she thought of how she had been imprisoned in such a terrible, lonely and abandoned place. Who could she shout to? Who would even bother to rescue her? Boataz and his men had murdered her whole family and stolen every resource in her homestead before setting light to it. She tried to sleep, but here, in her grasp, was another vision of her daughter Anna – her childhood, her destiny – lying in her arms, far away from anybody. She vowed to escape with this child, to rescue her, and wept at the thought of one day being free to be with this child in a safe place.

Godless? Or had God sent her this gift of retribution to punish her with further failure? Or was she, indeed, a gift of redemption?

How many times had she been let down, brutalised and tainted by a misfortune that seemed immune to the edicts of God? Finally, Rachel slept with the child in her arms, their dreams intertwining into a golden braid of resilience. The younger's fearful slumber flowed into the steely resolve of the older woman to once more attempt an escape with the child.

Rachel stirred in the night. Thamina had a coughing fit, waking some of the girls lying in the long dormitory-like hall. In her half-slumber, she reached out and moved a hair from the young girl's face now illumined by moonlight shining through the skylight. The storm had eased, and skeletal branches reached out to grasp the sliver of silver light hanging in the sky. This place hated loveliness and beauty – but here, shimmering in moonlight, lay the child in white linen, like a bright light shining in the darkness. Rachel folded herself around the child and hugged her into her body, talking softly to God of a bargain to be struck before the moonlight ceased.

'Let me bear her wounds, great God of the sky, the wind, the earth, the stars in the heavenlies. Let me be sacrifice enough to satisfy your wrath!'

The canvas over the window waved and then flapped shut, obscuring the moon and returning the room to darkness. Rachel mourned that she had become a poor sacrifice – a prostitute chained to the service of Boataz through his hard task master, Thamina. Whatever value she had once had had been taken from her by the clutches of men of every shape and size: bad men, good men, rich men and poor, all had visited this vile house

5

for relief, only to allow their burdens of sin to enter her like a scavenger worm, searching for the treasure of her precious soul. The last shard of dignity lay deep within her, the single determination not to lose hope, and this was all she could offer to God – her last hope in exchange for an escape for the girl.

Morning came in dull, grey light as Thamina coughed her way through lighting a fire, then lifting the shutters. Eight girls queued to wash in the cistern, some hoping the storm would deter customers for the coming evening. Most were beyond caring for anything but the slight warmth of now.

It would be late afternoon before the first customer appeared, riding up from the fishing town of Magdala. The girls were free all day to amuse themselves on their beds or walk down to the lake and gather wood for the fire. The earnest would fish from the shore, eager to supplement their diet of bread and dry salted fish with fresh flesh.

Only Safa seemed interested in the girl, whom they left to sleep. Rachel stood with her in the queue to wash, looking back at the sleeping child.

'You are a fool, Rachel. Let the mistress care for her. Don't get involved; you have had enough trouble...' whispered Safa, a young girl of nineteen, pulling on the older girl's fingers.

'But what if?'

'No, Rachel, no, that is too much,' whispered Safa through gritted teeth.

'But what if Boataz has returned Anna to me? What if she is my daughter?'

'No, he has stolen her for a reason, and Anna – she is lost, Rachel; you must face this.'

They looked at each other and remembered the night Boataz had taken Anna. Nothing good came out of Boataz.

'I will not lose this one – I will save her from losing her innocence,' declared Rachel.

'You do not know what has happened to her – that may be too late.'

'She is a child!'

'Boataz is a demon,' whispered Safa.

'What is going on?' growled Thamina, combing her hair at her table.

'Nothing,' cried Safa.

'I want to look after the child...' declared Rachel boldly.

'Look after the child, huh!' scoffed the madam. 'You can't look after yourself.'

'I will pay her board. She will not have to work here; I will pay for it all.'

'Hmm, stupid girl, it will cost you a pretty penny, but if you can pay me a deposit of ten denarii, then you may look after her until she comes of age and Boataz does what he wants with her.'

'She is a child!' protested Rachel.

'That is between you and a cruel man, Rachel. In the meantime – I don't want her hanging round here when the customers arrive. You can lock her in the storehouse during working hours. Keep her out of my sight. We have a business to run; we are not a charity for foundlings.'

Rachel smiled and bowed politely. That is exactly what we are meant to be, she thought, ruefully remembering the name of the school painted above the door of the large two-story house: 'Theims School for Lost Girls'. A cruel joke for many of the girls who were bought there under false pretences. Once a month they were visited by Magdala's rabbi, the delightful old man Simeon, who was oblivious to the true nature of the girl's captivity and spent a day teaching them the Torah. He always complimented the madam on the stillness and obedience of her charges, not for one moment understanding the threat of death that hung over their heads if they were to say a single word out of order.

Boataz had killed Helga, with a single blow of his bronze staff, for doing nothing more than asking the rabbi for access to medical care she was willing to pay for out of her own meagre savings.

Rachel saw the child stirring and drew swiftly to her side. The girl was about fifteen years old, and her large, brown eyes opened in terror at the memory and then the realization that her nightmare was, indeed, a horrific reality. She began to weep, drawing the attention of the madam, who looked around for a switch to strike the girl.

'Come, shush, shush,' whispered Rachel, lifting the girl and taking her out of the house into the dancing wind. The thin body trembled and wilted, twitching uncontrollably, as Rachel put her hand over the girl's mouth and slipped into the small, square storehouse. She closed the door on a grey gloom that seemed to momentarily calm the girl.

'You are in great danger. You must do everything I say – do you understand?' said Rachel, holding the girl's face in her hand.

'Look at me. I am the only friend you have in the world. Now, eat this, and stop your crying, or they will beat you.' She let go of the girl, then backed away from her and placed the flattened bread on the floor.

'They killed...' wept the girl.

'Eat,' whispered Rachel. 'I am so sorry, but we were all taken, all the girls here, by a monster. The past has gone, child; the past has gone, and you must accept a new way of life until I can think of a way of rescuing us.'

The child wept in great sobs Rachel could not stifle. She locked the door from the inside and stared out through a slit at the cold, white light shining on the worn pavement between the storehouse and the old house.

She jumped as the madam suddenly peered back at her, growling through gritted teeth.

'I will give you an hour, and no more, to shut her up, and then I will teach that brat what to really fear!'

'Yes, Madam Thamina, that is understood, thank you,' said Rachel. The older woman laughed and then spat on the floor, cursing Rachel and the child. 'She will be the death of us, mark my words. Boataz has overstepped the mark this time...' she muttered.

Rachel sat next to the child, who kept forcing Rachel's arm away from her as she cried inconsolably with great gulps of air.

'My name is Rachel. I am here to help you, but you must calm down. Calm down, little one.' She reached out her hand and touched the girl's head, causing her to jolt away further into the gloom. Inch by inch, Rachel closed the distance between them until they were sitting beside each other.

'You must not upset that woman, Thamina. She is cruel and selfish. She will thrash you viciously if you upset her. Come, cease your crying. Fortune has thrown us together for a reason, my little one.'

Once or twice, Rachel inadvertently called the girl Anna, causing much confusion and more crying, and she bit her lip and scolded herself for being so stupid. At last, the crying stopped and the pair sat in silence. Rachel moved opposite the girl, their backs against the wall. Rachel wanted to cry too but fought back tears, curled her hands into fists and pressed them to the ground.

'My name is Mina,' whispered the girl in the darkness. 'Will that man come back to kill me?'

'No, he will lie low until the commotion has died down. I dread to think what you have suffered. Did he do anything to you?'

'He killed my mother and father, and then he beat me and tied me to himself. Then we galloped off into the night.'

'Were your parents rich?'

'I don't know what you mean...' The girl sobbed quietly, her face crumpled by the enormity of what she had witnessed.

'Are you Jewish?' asked Rachel quietly. There was something about the dress the child had worn that was unusual.

'Yes, but we are Roman citizens too. We settled here with my grandparents some years ago. We are both Jewish and Roman.' She pushed her face into her hands and wept silently, paroxysms of grief rocking her body.

'Dear God,' said Rachel. Boataz had never killed Roman citizens before. Thamina was right: the Roman authorities would scour the countryside for evidence of the murderer and crucify the fiend and all his associates when they caught him. If Boataz could be caught, they could all escape and be free.

CHAPTER 2

✦ ✦ ✦

Rachel spent days gently encouraging a new way of life into Mina, and she began to win the child's reluctant trust. Once or twice, she had taken a lashing from the madam for the child's attempts to run off down the road, or surge out into the sea, where she and Safa would have to retrieve her from the depths of the cold waters. All three of them would then be left in the storehouse to suffer the bitter cold of the night in damp, clinging clothes. Rachel would hang all their clothes on a temporary line over a makeshift fire while the three lay together between bales of hay, covered in filthy hessian sacks, waiting for the sun to rise and warm them. Safa liked the child, who warmed to the younger girl and allowed her to cuddle her and fuss over her while they were locked in the storehouse. Food was meagre and rank, brought by one of the older girls, Rajah, who would poke a wooden plate of stale bread under the door, muttering about outlandish and pitiful punishments that would await them when the madam told Boataz of their misdeeds.

At night, Safa and Rachel were summoned back into the main house, bedecked with warm lights, curtains in rich fabrics, a blazing fire and warm beds, to entertain and meet the needs of the customers who came up from Magdala smelling of fish and stale sweat.

At three o'clock in the morning, Rachel lifted the child into her own bed in the warmth of the main house, and the two slept beneath the wind of evil dreams that sometimes leapt in the dying embers of the fire to afflict the girls' minds with terrible nightmares. At dawn, cold and exhausted by the night, Safa, Rachel and the child would join the procession of broken women as they searched the sea shore for wood for the fire to warm the breakfast. Summer's dawn was a distant memory, but its colour sometimes flushed the horizon with a clean yellow stripe, squeezed between a dark canopy of swirling clouds and a distant rim of sunlight streaking the skyline with diagonal shafts of white light. The beach shingle held the stain of night, coloured in dark greens and turquoise. Seaweed festooned the remnants of the high tide, and sea shells glistened in patches of silver sand. Mina walked in a daze, like a body devoid of life, stumbling in the mud of the shoreline, unable to do anything but be pulled along by her arm. Terns wheeled over the thin line of mud flats, oblivious to the aching heart in the party of women scavenging for firewood.

The girls wrapped their faces in silken scarves, protecting their ears from the biting cold, searching the banks of pebbles for anything that would burn. After an hour in the freezing wind, they had enough to light the fire and warm the little puddings of meat, which they ate alone on their beds. Safa and Rachel sat on the bed, Mina lying between them, covering her head with a blanket. They tried to get her to eat, but she barely ate anything, occasionally sipping from a wooden cup of water. The other girls, led by Rajah, were hostile and wanted to know who was paying for the child's keep. Rachel simply shook her head and said she would.

'Why are you getting involved with this child? It is the responsibility of the madam,' growled Rajah.

'This is bad business. You can tell by her clothes she comes from a high-ranking family,' said Laila, the second-eldest girl who very rarely spoke, preferring to keep a distance from the other girls. 'If the authorities come, we should have nothing to do with her. The old woman must take the blame; they will pass it all onto you, Rachel, you idiot.'

Gamil stuttered into life. 'If she is paying for the food, that is all we need know.'

'Rachel has earned us more beatings than I care to remember, forever escaping and causing us trouble. What stupid dreams she still harbours of a life outside of this hell hole – and now she has this child, God only knows what she is planning. She will get us all killed by implicating us in this latest abduction – she can't keep out of trouble, the stupid woman!' shouted Rajah.

To Rachel's surprise, Mina looked up at the woman and let out an awful screech. She ran and hurled herself at Rajah, biting, scratching and pulling at her hair. Mina was, of course, no match for the stronger woman, who flung her to the floor and started slapping her with her hand. Rachel tried to restrain the older woman, but Rajah drew out a small knife and threatened her.

'Just leave her,' Rachel said, ignoring the blade and going to help Mina to her feet. Rajah skillfully whisked the blade across Rachel's face, causing a thin line of blood to appear across her cheek. Rachel winced and dabbed her face with the back of her hand.

'Do what you want with me, but leave the child...' Rachel said softly but with determination.

'What is going on? What is going on?' The madam was at them all with her switch, whipping the girls across the back of their heads and their backs.

'This child will ruin us,' bleated Laila, taking the switch from the old woman and throwing it onto the floor.

Thamina sat on the bed, looking exhausted. The girls went back to minding their own business.

'You three come with me,' she said, raising her tired frame.

Rachel and Safa pulled Mina out of the house, across the wind-swept yard and into the warmer storehouse, followed by the madam, who was swearing and cursing the day she had been born.

'Sit down,' she ordered, and the girls sat on the bales of hay in the gloom, looking up at Thamina lit by the cruel white light in the doorway. She was always dressed in a gold-coloured smock under a fur coat, her grey hair covered by an ornate studded bonnet. Inside the gaudy attire lay a shrivelled, miserable woman who had aged before her time. Her face was gaunt, and she trembled as she spoke.

'So what do we know of this child?' she demanded.

Rachel and Safa said nothing, bowing their heads in silence.

'Come on, out with it. What trouble is afoot for us all?' Thamina was getting angry, and the girls knew it would be best to try to assuage her anger.

'It is too early to question her,' said Safa.

'Where do you come from, eh? You!' shouted the madam, pointing her crooked finger at Mina.

'Say nothing,' whispered Rachel, covering her face with her shawl.

Mina shrugged her shoulders.

'Can you ride?' the madam asked Rachel. 'Come on, girl, out with it! Can you ride a horse?'

'Of course I can,' replied Rachel.

'I have an errand for you. The three of you can go – give me some peace. Three miles up the mountain, you will find an old woman; her name is Amal. Deliver this message for me and spend a while there before you return for work.' The madam gave Rachel a tattered scroll sealed with wax.

'And mind you tell no one of this. Take coats and bonnets.'

Rachel looked at Safa, who shook her head and opened her eyes wide as if to say she had no idea what was going on.

14

Very rarely were the girls given coats and bonnets for fear they would escape. They dressed themselves, and then Mina, in warm outer clothes from the main house and walked out along the shoreline until they met the single track climbing up a crag in the mountain wall.

'Three miles! That will kill us if it's all uphill,' moaned Safa.

'Mina, are you warm enough?' asked Rachel.

'I want to go home,' she said, starting to cry.

'As long as that monster is alive, there is no home for any of us,' replied Rachel, pulling the child closer to her. 'Come on, let us see what this Amal is about.'

The light in the sky was tender this cold morning, the wind had dropped and sunshine spoilt them with a flush of warmth as they climbed up the long path through the many granite outcrops that resisted the twists and turns of the little dirt track. Mina passed the time picking flowers she found growing in the cracks in the rock or chasing the crows that sat and watched their ascent high above the Sea of Gennesaret. They could see the fishing boats and the passenger vessels heaving against the cold breeze, crisscrossing the sea between Bethsaida and Capernaum.

'We must warn the child about reckless behaviour,' said Safa. 'She could have been stabbed this morning. Rajah is not to be messed with.'

'She needs time to adjust.'

'Don't make excuses, Rachel. You are too soft. You must make her understand how important it is she takes the line of least resistance.'

'I know.'

'Well, go on then.' Safa pointed at Mina who was picking another purple flax growing from a crack in the granite.

'Do you see the wonder of how that little plant survives?' whispered Rachel, drawing close to the child.

'It just grows,' said Mina sullenly.

'No, it has found a little refuge. Here in the dirt, in the crack where the rain waters it and the sun shines down on it, it has learned to flourish in the most barren and harsh terrain.'

'So what?'

'So, that is what you have to do… learn to flourish in spite of the great difficulty of all you have suffered.' Rachel began to walk with the child between fallen outcrops of stone. Safa lingered behind. 'It was not good to make a fuss this morning. You must never do that again; you must keep your head down, not look at anybody and learn to live a quiet life. You cannot tell anybody where you have come from.'

'Why not?' Mina snarled suspiciously.

'If they find out you are a Roman citizen, they may panic and…'

'And what?'

'They may want to harm you. And I could not bear that.'

'I am nothing to do with you. I can look after myself. I don't need your help.'

'Don't say that; you will break my heart. Of course you need my help; you are defenceless.'

'Why don't you mind your own business? You seem to me to be a bit of a busybody. When he killed my mother and my father, he killed me too. I don't want any help. I wish I was dead.'

She ran off, causing the crows to leap up into the air.

'That went well,' mused Safa.

'She is so hurt, poor creature; I don't know what is going to happen, Safa.' Rachel fought back tears and walked faster to catch the child, who was shouting and hollering and throwing the flowers she had picked at the worn walls of the gully.

Anger, bewilderment, fear and anguish drove them along the path between towering crags of stone weathered into strange forms as if they were walking in the bowels of a fearful monster slain, gutted and ossified in the heinous body of the mountain. Red, glistening guts, strained through the moss-coloured stone, added to the sense of unease. They were walking through the graveyard of a fearful leviathan split asunder by some mighty blade of death.

After an hour, they drew up on a greener plateau overlooking the lake to the east and the long, dusty trading routes to the west. They stood and looked in awe at the many sails dotting the Great Sea and the many caravans of camels and donkeys trundling along the road to Jerusalem and beyond. Normality had passed them by, its time and measure oblivious to their predicament. Even Mina gasped at the enormity of the scene of civilisation continuing on its way in total disregard of their plight.

The path led through a meadow of lush grass where they disturbed rabbits and caused a small owl to flutter in the straggly trees that clung onto the patch of fertility. Smoke in the sky led them to the small, square cottage where three large, black horses were feeding in a paddock. A boy sat on the paddock fence, stroking one of the horses. He fled into the house when he saw the three girls approaching and brought out of the dark-veined hollow of the house a thin, bedraggled figure dressed in filthy grey robes. Her face was wrinkled and heavily tanned, and a thin silver ring protruded from her large, flat nose.

'Amal?' asked Rachel, gathering Mina, who was looking at the tanned boy and marvelling at how he could be so poorly dressed in such cold. The lad, about the same age as Mina, went back to stroking the horse. Mina pulled herself away from Rachel and went and stood by the boy, watching the horse with wide-eyed interest.

'You have money?' asked the old woman angrily.

'No, this.' Rachel gave the old woman the sealed parchment. With her long, grubby fingers, the nails dark with black stains, the old woman tore open the seal and walked back towards the house reading the contents.

She stopped after a few paces, turned to Safa and Rachel and beckoned them to follow her.

'She will be fine; the boy will guard her,' she said, observing Rachel's anxious looks.

Reluctantly, they followed the old woman into the house, ducking through the low doorway and entering a warm, dark interior. A single candle illuminated the untidy mass of belongings: papers, old pots, horse bridles and saddles, glasses and vials of strange forms suspended in liquid cluttered every surface of the worn shelves and crooked pieces of furniture. A warm fire drew their attention, and Safa and Rachel sat down on a low bench in front of the old woman, who nestled down in a battered chair adorned with faded ribbons.

'Here, drink.' She poured into two wooden beakers an evil-smelling liquor from a blackened pot suspended from a huge iron bar over the fire. To their surprise, it tasted sweet and tempting. Their fingers ached with the cold, and for a moment or two, the pair rested, drinking the strange potion.

'Your horse is the one the boy is stroking. It is reliable, strong and an easy ride; it will carry you all for a good day's ride before it needs feeding,' said the old woman, putting the parchment into a battered leather holdall.

'What are you talking about?' asked Safa.

'The boy will prepare the horse on payment of fifty denarii.'

The old woman began humming and sipping the drink, spitting now and again into the fire.

'We do not know what you mean,' repeated Rachel, to no avail. The old woman ignored them, shutting her eyes and seeming to fall into an impenetrable sleep. They sat for half an hour trying to guess what the old woman's words meant until she opened one eye and stared at them.

'You must come here every day and bring the mistress's nard. You must learn to climb the path in less than an hour. Say nothing of this to her. She will communicate with me only by parchment. If you break this vow of silence, there is no hope of your escaping him.' The old woman wiped her nose with the back of her hand.

'What do you mean, "escaping"?' asked Rachel.

'When the time is right, and you have moved all of the mistress's nard, she will send you to me in the dead of night. You will have to know the path very well. The boy will saddle the horse, and you will be given money to head for Jerusalem where you will find a safe house in which to hide.'

'This is impossible,' whispered Rachel, covering her mouth with her hand.

'Be careful, Rachel. The madam does nothing out of selflessness,' replied Safa, scowling at the old woman, who laughed at her words and slowly clapped.

'You should listen to your friend, she is wise beyond her years, but you are both little mice cornered by the cat, who loves to play with his meat dish.' She laughed aloud and then closed her eyes and fell into a slumber.

The boy was strange; his facial expressions always suggested he was about to say something cheerfully profound and helpful. He pointed to the fence beside him and beckoned her to join him.

'You, pain, feel here,' he whispered, touching his heart. He took her hand, placed it on the horse's head and stroked the soft hair between its ears.

'Tell him your bad things.'

'Don't be stupid – it's a horse,' muttered Mina, who enjoyed the boy's attention. He seemed so full of all that she was lacking; he had a smile that soared from the very midst of him in a wave of calm.

'I tell him,' said the boy, suddenly uttering a low mumble of words into the horse's ear.

'What are you doing?'

'He takes my pain, from my heart. You try.'

'I don't know what you mean. My pain has broken my heart; I am inconsolable.'

'He will help,' said the boy with a little smile.

'You are mad.'

'Try it. Look, I leave you.' He jumped down from the fence, walked across the paddock and sat on the other side, watching her.

'Go on!' he cried.

Mina shook her head but continued stroking the black mare, whose shining, dark eye seemed to stare into her very being.

'You are so lovely, and he is mad.' She watched him gesticulating wildly for her to speak, but she shook her head. He was tall and gaunt, clearly underfed, with a single, ill-fitting, dirty shawl to protect him from the bitter cold.

'Your friend is mad, quite mad, but he seems sincere, and I like him,' she whispered.

The wind pulled at her hairline and eased out a tousled curl from beneath the bonnet of her robe – it fluttered and tickled her face. And by and by, little by little, she began to speak to the horse as if she were speaking to her best friends from home. She spoke of the night when Boataz had broken into her home and terrorised the house, robbing her parents of their finery and jewels before killing first her mother and then her father with a single thrust of his sword.

'He is a monster, a demon, but one day I will kill him,' she said, anger and hatred beginning to fill the great recesses opening up in her soul. She began to cry, and the horse nuzzled her with its soft lips.

'Done well,' mused the boy, who had appeared by her side. He leapt onto the horse's back and then lifted her by the hand to join him.

When Rachel and Safa came out into the cold light, ready to return down the mountain, they were amazed to hear the girl laughing as the boy galloped backwards and forwards up the trail bareback.

'Stop! Stop!' shouted Rachel, feeling terror grip her heart.

The boy controlled the huge mare and cantered over to the two women.

'She is your mother?' he asked, helping Mina onto the fence and off the horse.

'No, she is not my mother. She is nothing to me. Nothing!' she shouted, causing Rachel to bite her lip and look quizzically up at the boy.

'Keep away from her – what were you thinking?'

'You, heart pain, I feel,' he replied, holding his heart.

Rachel shook her head and tried to deter Mina from getting back onto the horse.

'We have to go,' pleaded Rachel.

'I am staying here. Jinan has promised to teach me to ride bareback.'

'You can't stay here! You will freeze to death. Come on, we must get back.'

'Get back where? A whore house? I would rather throw myself from these heights than go back there!' shouted Mina.

'Great,' lamented Safa. 'Look, Mina, trust us. We can come back here every day until we can think of a plan to get out of here, but we must have a plan. Come with us, and I promise tomorrow we will come back and you can play with Jinan.'

'I'm not so sure about that!' murmured Rachel.

'You are not my mother!' growled Mina.

'Rachel is not your mother; we get that Mina. You don't have to be so horrible,' cried Safa. 'Rachel has taken great risks to help you.'

'I can help myself,' Mina said wilfully.

'Come on.' Safa wrapped the scarf around her face. The descent to sea level would be freezing.

'I with you walk for a while,' said the boy, leading the horse over to where Mina sat. She mounted the horse, sitting behind him and putting her arms around his waist. Rachel and Safa followed him through the grass meadow to where the track started its dusty descent.

Rachel and Safa waited to see what Mina would do. The boy, Jinan, lowered her to the ground and told her to follow them. He would see her the next day, he assured her. The three girls were soon descending the mountain under a darkening sky.

'Just let her follow,' said Safa.

'What does this all mean?'

'Be careful, Rachel; wait and see. The madam is not to be trusted – there is no safe house associated with that woman.'

'Why is she helping us?'

She is helping herself; if things get hot, then she wants you to take the child – take the evidence of Boataz's crime away from her – she's cunning as a vixen.'

'Except I will take Mina back to the authorities and tell them everything that has gone on – surely, she must know that?'

The air grew colder and the mist thicker the closer they got to the little village of Theims with its strung-out line of four cottages carved into the mountainside. Rachel felt she had descended into a crypt and longed to return to the sweeter pasture where the old woman and the boy lived. She had a spark of hope warming a tiny part of her heart. The knotted stomach returned as she thought of the revolting work that faced her that night.

CHAPTER 3

✦ ✦ ✦

E ach day, the madam would produce a small jar of nard, sealed with a wooden lid, and silently command the girls to take it up to the old woman with another parchment. They left after breakfast and returned mid-afternoon. After several weeks, the journey became a sacred ritual, in which they would present the fine perfume to the old woman, who would pour the contents of the small jar into a large stone container, sit down and read the messages from the madam.

They were told on every visit the same details: not to say a word to anybody about the arrangement. Little by little, more detail emerged of how Thamina would initiate the escape plan. In the middle of the night, or at moment's notice, she would ask the girls to go to the storehouse to consider the error of their ways and 'repent of their disobedience'. These four words would be the code for when they would flee to the old woman with fifty denarii of silver they would find in the storehouse beneath the bales of hay.

Mina spent time with Jinan, helping him to clean the stables and brush the horses. As a treat, he would take her, on the saddled horse, cantering backwards and forwards along the track, only galloping when Rachel and Safa were safely out of earshot. She loved the animals and adored brushing the manes and the tails, talking incessantly to the creatures of her fears and anxieties. All the time, Jinan would be checking the horses' shoes and washing off any mud splattered on their legs, quietly listening to the girl's conversation.

One day, when the sun was bright and warm, presaging spring, they sat down in the stable, looking out at the terns and gulls wheeling, ducking and diving with the crows and pigeons.

'What is your story?' she asked. 'Where do you come from?'

'I am a nobody,' he laughed, 'or that is what she calls me, the old woman.'

'Is she a witch?'

'Sort of; she has a book of spells, and you can see her shrivelled prey in the jars of fluid she keeps above the fire place.'

'Don't tease me,' said Mina, hitting him on the shoulder.

'I used to live begging on the streets of Tiberias until, one day, the old woman came and purchased me off of the old beggar I used to sit with.'

'Who was he?'

'I think he may have been my grandfather, I do not know, but I have never lived with a mother or father. What is it like?'

'What was it like? Well, in truth, my mother and father were always too busy to spend much time with me. You see, my mother imported textiles from everywhere, and my father was some official. I had a nanny, and she was nice...'

'Where was that?'

'In Capernaum – do you know it?'

'No, but I have heard of it.'

'I need to escape and get back there. My grandfather and grandmother will be looking for me. They are extremely wealthy and important... they can help us both.'

'What help do I need? I am quite content here, talking to the horses.'

'That can't be the sum of your life, just talking to horses?'

'Why not? What else would I want to do? I get fed, and no one harms me or tells me what to do. I serve the old woman as my mistress, and she is fair with me. I have a snug place to sleep in the winter and a wonderful world to explore in the summer.'

'You are such a peasant,' she said, laughing.

'Do not laugh at me. I was greatly afflicted in the city until she came and set me free with her magic, which will protect me. I am bound to her; if I leave her, then I will be captive again.'

'She set you free from what?'

'I do not want to remember, just a great affliction – taunting and disturbing me all the while.'

'Do you mean a demon?'

He looked offended but bit his lip and shook his head. Then he smiled.

'You are sounding a bit like a spoilt brat. I said I didn't want to talk about it.'

'I have heard of the demon-possessed. It is fascinating.'

'Urgh!' He threw his hands up in the air, jumped to his feet, ran, sprang on the back of the mare and galloped off into the distance. She watched the gap growing between them and her heart ached. Why did he bring her such calm, and why could she not control her mouth?

When they travelled back down the mountain, Mina could not stop herself asking a myriad of questions and wanted Rachel and Safa to tell her stories of people who had been afflicted with a demon. Rachel would have none of it, but Safa could not help tell the girl all the stories she had heard growing up around Tiberius.

'Where do they come from?' asked the child.

'Some say they're the ghosts of the dead, others the spirits of animals, others Satan's hordes,' whispered Safa, trying to hang back from Rachel.

'How do they get inside you?'

'Grief, despair, anxiety, sickness, or through great abilities, super talents, but he targets mainly children and the afflicted because...' she looked up at Rachel and held the girl's hand firmly, stopping her, 'he hates the children of Eve. He hates us and will do everything he can to maim us until he finds the one who will crush his head and destroy him.'

'What do you mean?' whispered back Mina.

'The serpent, of course, Satan; he was afflicted by a curse that one of Eve's children would destroy him, so he spends all of his time looking for the Messiah so he can kill him...'

'The Messiah and Satan?'

'Thirty years ago, they say, there were no possessions, but now, throughout the land, we are plagued with them – think about it.'

Mina thought about it and did not stop thinking about it.

'Do you think Boataz may be Satan?'

'I do not want to talk about him; don't mention his name.'

'When I find my grandparents, they will have him hanged for his evil.'

'Where are they?' asked Safa.

'My grandparents? They live in Capernaum. I will find them or they will find me, and then we will see about Boataz.'

'You must stop using his name; it is too dangerous. He would slit your

At eight o'clock, when the first customer appeared at the house, Mina had to go to the storehouse where she was locked away until the house shut at two in the morning. This night was different. After half an hour, the door was unlocked and Rajah and Gamal appeared with a fine-looking dress.

The madam stood in the doorway and told them to dress her. Mina did not struggle. She tried to remember everything Rachel and Safa had told her about dealing with the unexpected.

When she was dressed, they led her back into the house, which had been transformed with layers and layers of hanging rugs, candles and fine-smelling perfume into a den of iniquity. The girls lay with the men, carousing and kissing, feigning laughter and giving the men all the attention they could muster. Rajah and Gamal led the girl through little rooms cordoned off with large veils of silk to a red area with loads of cushions and gold, embroidered pillows. A fat man, in his fifties, lay on his side, eating from a plate of fruit and meats. His face glistened with fat and his balding head sparkled in the candlelight.

'Come, come, my dear, come and eat with me,' he said in a sweet voice.

The two older women sat down with him and stroked his temples and rubbed oil into his naked legs. Mina stayed where she was, looking for signs from the other girls of what to do. Rajah motioned for her to come over and sit with the fat man, who introduced himself as Benjamin. She sat by his chest and hungrily accepted a choice leg of chicken.

'Don't eat like that,' he mused, smilingly childishly. 'Try to eat it nicely or you will upset poor Benjamin, who is much vexed by a hard day's work. Perhaps you would like to dance for me. Is there a musician in the house?' he bellowed.

'Go and get Safa and her harp,' Rajah said, ordering Gamal out of the makeshift tent. Mina looked nervously at Rajah, who shook her head and lifted her finger to her lips. 'It is fine Mina; just dance.'

'Mina? Well, I like that name. You are so pretty!' enthused Benjamin, giggling and puckering his lips.

Safa arrived and looked flustered when she saw Mina dressed as a harlot.

'What is happening?' she asked.

'Benjamin here has been sent by Boataz to enjoy the company of young Mina,' said Rajah stiffly. Gamal came into the room and continued trying to distract Benjamin, who only had eyes for Mina.

'Come, play, and let me see her dance. I have paid a heavy price for this, so no more distractions. You girls can go and leave me with the musician and the dancer.'

He laughed and patted Mina on the head. The two girls left, and Safa started to play her harp, indicating to Mina how she should dance. The child, barefoot, started to move backwards and forwards to the tune, dancing as best she could, avoiding the arms of Benjamin, who tried to grab her legs if she got too close to him. After five minutes, Benjamin raised his hand and ordered Safa to leave them alone. Mina looked terrified, and Safa did not know what to do.

'Go, go!' hissed the fat man, drawing himself up onto his haunches.

'What is going on?' said a voice. Mina looked up and was glad to see Rachel come into the room.

'This sweet child is going to comfort me,' said Benjamin, flicking his tongue and crawling on all fours towards Mina, who shrank into Rachel's dress.

'Good God! No!' Rachel grabbed the harp and struck Benjamin once, twice, three, four and more times over the head until the man rolled over in a heap and started crying and shrieking. Soon the madam was standing in the room with her switch in her hand.

'What has happened?'

'How could you?' growled Rachel, looking fiercely at the madam.

'I had nothing to do with this! This is Rajah's doing.' The woman looked fiercely at the man who was sobbing and rubbing his bruised head.

'I cannot believe it has happened, now, of all times.' She shook her head and through gritted teeth ordered some of the girls to go in and comfort the man while she led Mina out of the house.

'Now, all of you, get in there and think about your actions. Boataz will hear of this, and he will most certainly help you to repent of your disobedience!' Thamina looked exasperated. It began to rain, causing her black eye makeup to run down her cheeks and spoiling the rouge on her lips.

'Go, now! Repent of your disobedience,' she whispered as a peal of thunder shook the heavens.

Safa rushed into the house to grab some cloaks. Rachel retrieved the money found under one of the bales of hay. They could hear the fat man shrieking and calling out for Boataz. The sound terrified them as they ran through the wind up onto the trail for the dark ascent of the mountain. Lightning flashed, lighting up the seething bowels of the Leviathan that seemed to be being resurrected by the hysterical anger of the elements. They made as rapid progress as they could with their pathway acting as a conduit for all the falling water. Mina slipped and fell, and Rachel and Safa battled to keep them pushing ahead. Once or twice, a boulder was dislodged by the force of the water and crashed down past them, cracking and splintering as it went. The water was freezing, the rain pitiless, the wind relentless as they heaved their way up the mountain. The lightning and thunder shouted angrily to Boataz of the escape of the women from his grip.

When they finally arrived at the top of the mountain, they staggered against the howling wind to find the pathway across the flattened meadow to the old woman's house. Rachel hammered on the door, and the boy, Jinan, answered.

'We need the horse. I have the money!' she said. The old woman pulled the three girls into the house and asked them whether Boataz was following.

'No, we have not seen him,' said Safa.

'Here is the money.' Rachel pressed the bag of coins into the old woman's hand.

'Go and get the horse ready,' hissed the old woman to the boy. He left the house, pulling a heavy blanket across his shoulders.

'How do we get onto the main thoroughfare to Jerusalem?' asked Rachel.

'Follow the track for three miles. It will lead you directly to the main road from Lebanon to Jerusalem; head south when you get there.'

'She's ready,' said the boy, standing soaked in the doorway.

'Go, go, fate is against you…' whispered the old woman, who smiled, showing her filthy, gappy teeth.

They went back out into the maelstrom of wind, rain and lightning, following the boy into the stable where a lantern hung.

'Look, I have stolen the old woman's cart. You can sit in there and ride; the weight will calm the mare,' said Jinan. He led the mare out into the fierce conditions. She neighed, fearful of the lightning and thunder.

'Thank you,' said Mina, wondering what would happen to them all. 'Why don't you come with us…?'

Just as she said that, a form pounced out of the darkness and jumped onto Rachel's back.

'You traitor!' shouted Rajah, pulling Rachel's head back, ready to strike her throat with a knife that glinted in the lightning. 'You will ruin us!' she shouted.

Safa screamed and flung herself at Rajah, the two falling into the darkness and rolling in the mud. Rachel was stunned but staggered to her feet. She pulled Mina up into the little wagon and went to help Safa free herself from Rajah. A bolt of lightning lit up the scene as Safa walked slowly towards Rachel, her mouth wide open and blood seeping from her throat. Bewildered and terrified, she fell to her knees and collapsed on the ground. Rachel looked up and saw Rajah advancing towards her with the blade held aloft.

'Boataz will kill us once he finds out what you have done, you traitor!' she howled.

Rachel looked up at Mina, terrified for the child.

'Take me, Rajah, you do not need to hurt the child…'

'Oh, yes, I do…' she howled, lunging at Mina with the knife. No sooner had she moved than the boy was at her, hitting her across the head with the stone lantern. Rajah dropped to her knees, stunned.

'Quick, get in the wagon!' shouted the boy and helped her lie beside Mina. He jumped onto the mare's back and whipped her into action. The mare reared up as Rajah charged the wagon. She was knocked back by the horse's hooves and the wagon careered over her body.

Rachel tried to comfort Mina, who was weeping; she pulled the large goatskin cover over their heads before the girl fainted. The boy drove the mare hard along the trail, gulping in large mouthfuls of air. Water poured over his face, and he glared back at the storm clouds, blaspheming the god of thunder and lightning that had forced him, once again, to face his demons.

CHAPTER 4

✦ ✦ ✦

'Where are we going?' howled the boy, trying to wake Rachel. The thunder had ceased and a light rain fell in the blueish light of a cold winter's day. The woman began to understand that they had reached the main commercial thoroughfare and Jinan wanted to know which direction to take.

'South? To Jerusalem?' he asked.

'No, no, north to Capernaum. We need to find Mina's family,' she said, emerging from beneath the goat skin. Mina poked her head out and marvelled at the sight of the boy sitting astride the mare.

'I will take over from here,' said Rachel, indicating to Jinan he should rest.

'No, not until we are out of danger. If Boataz and his men ride hard after us, we will pass them on the road south. You hide – they will not suspect me if I drive.'

He pulled the mare around to the right and crossed over the rain-sodden main road. The mare trotted past a large convoy of camels and donkeys passing along the road to Lebanon.

'Are you alright?' asked Mina, looking concerned at Rachel's bruised face.

'No, poor Safa – she gave her life to save me. I'll never forget her face, the horror! She was just a child herself, yet she gave her life for us…'

'Us,' winced Mina.

'Don't be so difficult. I just mean we three, in this wagon, going who knows where to find your grandparents in Capernaum. Let's hope they are easily found.'

Mina began to weep.

'What is it, child?'

'Poor Safa! This is all my fault. Now she is dead. What is happening to me?'

'You were abducted by a monster who will do everything he can to kill you and stop you getting to your grandparents.'

The wagon stopped and the boy poked his head under the canvas. 'They are searching the wagons ahead; look, you must crouch in here.' He pulled up two planks of wood, showing a hidden compartment under the rear of the wagon.

'Get in and be quiet. I will get us through the check point the bandits have set up across the road.'

Mina gasped and started to cry. Rachel hugged her. 'Come, be brave. If we can get through here, we stand some chance of making it to Capernaum.'

They lay in the darkened hole beneath the wagon, looking up through the slats at the cold, grey sky. The wagon started and stopped as every package and cart was checked by a band of eight bandits accosting the travellers trying to pass to the north and south.

'Where you going?' asked a rough voice.

'Magdala, to pick up some fish,' said the lad. The wagon rocked as a large body struggled up onto the wagon to search for anything suspicious.

'Who do you buy your fish from in Magdala?' asked another voice.

'Isaac, the belly whale,' laughed the boy, who was clipped around the ear for his impertinence.

'Go on, get on with you,' growled the man, jumping down from the cart.

Jinan kicked out at the mare and the wagon skidded into movement. They continued for about an hour before he halted the wagon and retrieved the two women from their confinement.

'Are we safe?'

'Not until we work out how to get to Capernaum,' muttered Jinan.

Boataz's lieutenant, Gritz the Gaul, had beaten the madam severely and, with the help of the remaining girls, had pieced together the trouble of the night before. Benjamin, the customer, still nursed a sore head and moaned about how much he had paid Boataz for access to the young girl, much to the annoyance of Gritz, who threatened to have him gutted if he continued his bleating.

'The girls attack Benjamin, and then the madam sends them to the storehouse to mind their manners, and they just disappear into the night, three of them. And then a fourth, this Rajah, she goes out with a knife to apprehend them, and she just disappears too.'

'I cannot find any tracks, the rain has washed them all away, but I did find a piece of cloth on the track leading up over the mountain,' said one of the men.

'Let's go up and see what we can find,' growled Gritz.

Rachel and Mina rested the mare in a field so it could eat some of the lush grass. The boy slept in the back of the wagon. A grain merchant, who was on his way to Bethsaida to the north east of the Sea of Gennesaret, was watering his donkeys in the same field and had agreed that they could travel together to Capernaum. By mid-afternoon, they were moving slowly along the road, following the grain-laden donkeys on the road west to Magdala.

Rachel drove the wagon and felt doubly anxious about going back down to the coastline no more than ten miles from Theims. Her determination to free Mina overcame the intense feelings of grief mixed with fear as she remembered poor Safa's sacrifice. She knew she would have to surrender Mina to her family, and a paroxysm of sadness overcame her as she thought of her own daughter somewhere out there. Only Boataz knew where he had taken her, and she desperately hoped Mina's grandparents would force his capture and interrogation to find out what he had done to her and where he had taken her.

Mina sat next to Rachel under a wide sky and gulped in huge mouthfuls of fresh air. Jinan lay under the goatskin cover, holding his ears, trying to fight back the agony of the sound of voices trying to enter his mind.

Gritz did not like the look of the old woman; the tattoos of serpents and strange creatures weaving up her arm, combined with her calm smile, unnerved him. He was convinced she was a witch and did not want her magic plaguing him with misfortune.

'Shall I beat it out of her?' asked one of his men.

'No, no, treat her carefully; we do not want to die,' whispered Gritz. 'Let me speak to her.'

Gritz laid his sword and daggers down at the door, wiped his feet and entered the hovel of the old woman.

'Mother, mother, where are you?' he asked gently.

'Sit!' demanded the old woman, lying back on her chair by the fire.

'Please forgive my men. We mean you no harm; we come with an offer...'

'Offers I like, but threats, no. Those men shall be cursed, their bodies eaten by the dogs on the great heap of rubbish at Gehenna.' She was furious and continued muttering and cursing.

'Please forgive them, mother,' said Gritz, shaking, as the old woman stared wildly at him.

'What is this offer?' she said with a click of her tongue on the back of her teeth.

'One hundred denarii to help us find the party who stole your horse and wagon; then we shall get rid of the bodies of the girls and will bother you no more.'

'Two hundred denarii and I will tell you your fortune.'

'Mother, I do not want to know the misfortune that awaits me – you shall have your money, and the patronage of Boataz.'

'Boataz has nothing to do with me. He has the vilest of demons, more powerful than any of my magic; you must promise me he will stay away from here and afford me peace.'

'It shall be as you wish, but tell us where we will find the woman and the girl.'

The old woman closed her eyes and fell into a slumber, smiling. Gritz sat motionless, looking at all the strange objects the old witch had assembled in her hovel and wishing he was back in Europe, fighting the Romans. He waited impatiently, trying to stop his temper from boiling over, until at last the old woman awoke.

'There you are,' she laughed. 'Show me my money.'

Gritz ordered one of the men to fetch the bags of silver while the old woman put a wooden board on her lap and began to pluck herbs and potions from the darkness around her threadbare, filthy robe. She piled them up and rubbed them before taking a hot coal from the fire and setting the little bundle alight. She took a knife, cut into her thumb and allowed droplets of blood to go into the mix. A thick haze of incense rose up, filling the room with a pungent, acrid smell.

'What do you see, mother?'

'What do you want me to see?'

'Where I can find them!'

But she insisted on telling Gritz his fortune – which he listened to with dread. He longed to return to the forests of Gaul and his tribe, free to trade as a man of means, but this woman's miserable indictment crushed his spirits.

'Enough, gentle mother. I have heard enough. Where are the escapees?'

'They are on the road to Capernaum, heading towards Magdala.'

'Will we catch them?'

'I cannot tell, but they are not alone; they mingle with the crowds.'

'But they still have the boy and the wagon?'

'If you harm the boy, the dogs will eat your entrails – he is to be returned to me. It is not safe for him to linger away from this mountain unless he can find the great light that has broken out in the darkness.'

'Great light?'

The old woman laughed and squealed with delight. 'You have no idea, do you? The sword and dagger will not prevail against him, for his sword is the spirit of God.'

'I need to go, mother. Can I buy an amulet of protection from you?'

'There is only one who can save you; when the time comes, you will see.'

Gritz bowed to the old woman and kissed the back of her hand. He left the hovel, determined to complete his mission and then leave this godforsaken and cursed land.

✦ ✦ ✦

Albinus the merchant rode on a horse and would come back to check on them as they followed his donkeys along the road, weaving in and out of the slower-moving parties of artisans carrying their wares to whatever city or town would have them. The road was often packed but flowed effortlessly with travellers of all shapes and sizes, with a myriad of different trades and supplies, marching between Lebanon to the north and Jordan to the south. Many peddlers and beggars called out to the throng from the side of the road, and the sight of so many people encouraged Rachel to believe they had a chance of escape.

Mina was concerned about Jinan; he had not spoken to them for most of the day. He sat astride the mare, talking incessantly in a low voice that she could not discern, but he sounded anxious and sad. She called to him to sit with her and allow Rachel to drive the wagon, but he ignored her.

She waited until darkness fell and Albinus had his servants walk ahead of the train with lanterns. She stepped down from the wagon and walked next to the mare, pulling at Jinan's cloak.

'What is the matter?' she asked. He looked down at her, and she could see in his eyes a look of terror.

'I should not be here! I need to go back to the old woman; she cared for me...'

'Walk with me.'

He dismounted and they ambled along in the throng, marvelling at the lantern lights glinting off the rich fabrics and the bindings on the donkeys and camels passing them.

'We will spend the night here,' ordered Albinus, directing his train off the road. Servants unpacked large tents and built a huge fire, and Albinus gave Rachel, Mina and Jinan food and shelter from the cold.

'What is the matter?' asked Mina, nestling next to Jinan beside the roaring fire. The boy ate a handful of bread and stared into the dancing flames.

'It is fine now; they have stopped shouting at me,' he said, staring wide-eyed into the fire.

'They?'

'The demons. They have found me and are waiting to consume me again, just like before the old woman rescued me from the streets.'

'You are frightening me! What demons?'

'They used to speak to me when I was very little. I thought they were the ghosts of my mother and father, who abandoned me and left me to be bought up by some old man who said he was my grandfather. I imagined my parents' death was the reason they had left me and entertained these voices as friendly, loving counsel – not knowing the truth that my mother and father were living three streets away and didn't want anything to do with me. The old man lived in a dark place where he drank himself into a stupor and beat me for nothing but easing his boredom. When he told me about my mother and father and how they hated me, it broke my heart, and the voices began to turn on me, to taunt me and belittle me. By the time I was able to work the streets, I had three people talking to me. They called themselves mother, father and grandmother, but I knew they were demons. But what could I do? Their chatter was incessant. And then *he* came along.' The boy looked terrified.

'I don't know if I can carry on with you – I want to see you safe, but if he comes, I don't know if I will be able to control myself.'

'Who do you mean?'

'The ghost of my grandfather. He came to haunt me a week after he had died, blaming me for everything that had gone wrong in his life. He got into my head and made me do bad things, really horrible things, stealing, fighting, maiming people. When he comes back, I do not want to hurt anybody. I must return to the old woman.'

'What can she do for you that I cannot do?'

'She has magic potions and powers to create a safe place for me. She warned me never to descend from the mountain until she had passed away and then to wear the amulet she would prepare for me.'

'You don't have to be frightened. Stay with us and we will care for you.'

'It is not safe to be different in this world. It is far better to blend in, and I just can't do that.'

Jinan pulled his knees up under his chin and shivered. Mina placed the goatskin cover around his shoulders and hugged him as hard as she could.

Rachel asked Albinus for directions to Capernaum.

'You can take the coast road through Magdala towards Tabgha. It takes about a day at our pace, but at a canter, you could do it in less than a day. What is your business there?'

'We are hoping to settle there,' answered Rachel nervously.

'Where have you come from?'

'A little place up in the mountains; it doesn't even have a name.'

He smiled and looked up at her, his cheeks dappled by the orange glow from the fire, his white beard and white hair seeming as soft as lamb's wool.

'You look hard-pressed, my dear. Are you running from someone?'

'We are running from misfortune. I am just worried about making ends meet. Mina's grandparents are wealthy, and we are hoping to find favour with them.'

'I will ask my gods to help you. Tonight, when I pray, I will ask them to favour your cause.'

'Gods? You have gods?'

'Yes, I have five or six, depending on the time of year. They all come in handy. Jupiter, Juno and Minerva uphold the status quo and ensure the utmost balance in everything. I can trust them to counterbalance misfortune with good fortune, so over one's life you can see great justice at work.'

'Justice? I have not had much of that in my life, to date.'

'Then Jupiter it is! He will ensure justice in your situation. And what of your gods?'

'I have one God, the god of the Hebrews. We go to the temple in Jerusalem to placate him with our offerings, but I have never been. Perhaps that is why he has such little regard for me. We have a story about Hannah, the mother of Samuel, the prophet. She was much derided by the women because she could not bear children. She was so vexed and so angry that

42

one day she stood up and said, "Stop! I have had enough!" She went and protested so hard to God that the priest thought she was drunk. She promised God that if he gave her a child, she would give it back to him for service. I feel like Hannah. I long to stand up and say, "Enough! Fate, smile kindly upon me and you can have whatever you wish from me."'

'Then do it. Do it now. Make a stand. Make a difference!' Excitedly, Albinus got to his feet and pulled her up close to the fire. Rachel protested but the elderly gentleman would have none of it; he insisted she shake her fist at God and demand the end of calamity and misfortune. Rachel started to shake her fist at the stars and the great gaps between the lights; she thought of her daughter and vowed to God that if she should find her, he could have her as his own. She cried when she had finished, but they were softer tears, coming from an expression of goodness and humility.

Rachel sat on her own on the other side of the fire from Mina and Jinan. Her head sank between her knees as she continued to weep quietly, remembering her sweet child Anna, whom she had bought up in the hovel, only for her to be snatched away by Boataz on her second birthday. How she missed her smiles and her little tugs and her attempts at speaking.

'What are you thinking?' said a voice. Rachel lifted her tear-stained face and stared at Mina, who knelt beside her, with her arm resting on Rachel's shoulder.

'I'm sorry, I was thinking of Anna. I miss her so much.'

'My grandfather, he will find her. He has soldiers at his disposal and many servants; he is wealthy. Come, have hope.'

'Hope comes at a high price, Mina,'

'Thank you,' said Mina, 'for taking me back to my family. I do appreciate all you have done for me.'

'Thank me when you are under the protection of your grandfather's soldiers for you do not know what we are up against. Boataz is capable of killing everybody in Capernaum – such is his madness. He will not stop searching for us, and I do not trust the old woman or the madam.'

A sudden scream, a hideous high-pitched squeal, emanated from one of the other fires. A commotion broke out as water was thrown on the flames, amidst great cries and shouts of instructions.

'Jinan!' Mina gasped as she saw the boy being rolled in the goatskin cover, his hair alight.

CHAPTER 5
✦ ✦ ✦

'The boy just threw himself into the fire,' said one of Albinus's servants. 'Fortunately, I could grab him before he fell into the heart of the flames. He has some burns, but he got off lightly. Is he alright in the head?'

Albinus looked grimly across at Rachel, who was trying to bathe the burns on Jinan's body. The boy seemed delirious and was tossing backwards and forwards.

'Why did you not tell me the boy was so afflicted?' asked Albinus.

'I don't know what is wrong with him,' protested Rachel.

'You need to go – he is bad luck,' said Albinus, indicating to his servants to load the boy on the wagon, ready to be driven into the night.

'But where shall we go?' asked Mina.

'You need to find the doctor in Magdala. It's the next turn in the road, about a mile along the highway, and then it's all downhill.'

'We have nothing to commend ourselves to a doctor,' said Rachel, wincing.

Albinus shook his head and flicked a finger at one of the servants. 'Give them money for the doctor and food for a day's travel. And then send them on their way.'

Mina poured water on the burns on Jinan's arms and legs, and the back of his head; he was lifted into the wagon and laid beside bags of food and a purse full of silver. Rachel took the reins and got the mare moving across the uneven field back onto the road lit by the moon.

45

A shrine had been built at the junction where the main highway forked into a narrower road. Rachel turned the horse onto it and stared hard at the distant beautiful view of the Sea of Gennesaret, but she steeled her heart and drove the horse down the road where Boataz could be riding to find her. She prayed to Jupiter, Minerva and Juno and every other Roman name she could think of, begging that they would find a doctor in Magdala.

Mina tried to get some sense out of the boy, but he seemed delirious and struggling with a fever that caused him to toss backwards and forwards and then shake uncontrollably.

'What happened to him?' asked Rachel.

'He was just sitting there, and then he said he saw his grandfather in the fire, beckoning him.'

'Is he mad?'

'He said he has demons.'

Rachel shuddered; Jupiter was a useless god. Turning a corner, she had to rein back the mare hard; the road was filled with a party of men, women and children trudging silently down the road towards Magdala. She tried to weave around them, but the throng thickened until she was in the midst of a great crowd of people carrying the old, the infirm, the sick, the lame, beggars and people on stretchers.

'What is this?' she cried out to one of the passers-by, who just shrugged his shoulders and continued carrying a frail old lady in his arms. Rachel pulled the cart over to the side of the road.

'We can't get through,' said Mina.

'I will have to walk the mare,' said Rachel, getting down. She held the bridle of the mare and led her gently through the crowd, wondering why there were so many sick people on the road.

46

'Do you know where we can find a doctor?' she asked a young man carrying a crippled man on his back. His face was worn and ashen, and he looked in such pain that Rachel insisted he place the man up on the cart with Jinan.

'What is your name, good woman?' asked the man, who introduced himself as Thomas, the brother of Mathias, the cripple.

Rachel introduced herself and the man walked with her.

'What are all these people doing?'

'Have you not heard? The great Healer is among us. He is in Bethsaida, healing the sick and driving out demons. Today my brother will be cured.'

Rain began to fall in torrents, the roar of the water stopping any chance of conversation. Rachel spread the goatskin cover over Mathias, Jinan and Mina, then pulled the mare, in a slow descent, into Magdala. Thomas helped her, taking turns to take the bridle as thunder and lightning disturbed the mare. Rachel worried, as they drew closer to the shoreline, that they would run into Boataz's men blockading the road.

Daylight began to glimmer on the horizon of the distant sea, white light folded, in swooning hues, into the fabric of the night, grazing and diluting its opacity. Still the rain poured, soaking the great phalanx of people now flowing down the road into the town of Magdala.

Gritz headed north along the road into Magdala with his men – seven of them on horseback, galloping as fast as they could through the rain, intent on reaching Capernaum by daybreak. His mission was easy: to catch up with the single wagon with the boy, the girl and the woman and capture them all. Then he would slip his men and ride north to

Tyre to catch a boat back to Rome and freedom. The rain thickened and the cold water on his tanned flesh felt like a redemptive bath, washing him of the thick stain of blood crying out for justice wherever he went. He seemed possessed by the cries of the many he had robbed and hurt, and the drumming rain and the peal of thunder deadened their cry for his damnation.

The first wave of people shocked the men as they nearly trampled a party walking down into Magdala from the western road.

'What the hell is this?' gasped Gritz as his men steadied the horses and lightning lit up the great gathering of the sick and the maimed walking along the road.

'Push through, push through,' he shouted, wanting his men to get to the head of the queue of people.

Despite the horses' strength, the crowd was so thick the bandits could not move any faster than the slowest pace, and Gritz cursed his luck. He did not want a price on his head or a sentence in absentia through his association with Boataz – and freedom meant saving Boataz from his own folly. He must do his bidding one last time.

'Look out for the wagon!' he shouted through the pouring rain.

The seven riders set themselves across the road facing into the crowd, at every ten feet of the road, waiting intently for any appearance of a wagon.

Rachel saw the men and stopped the mare on a corner hidden behind an outcrop of rock. She felt sick.

'What is it?' asked Thomas.

'Those men, they must not find us!'

Thomas looked around the rock at the seven horsemen watching the crowds flow past them.

'Take the children on foot, and I will lead the wagon through with my brother,' he said, helping Rachel stir Mina and Jinan.

'We are in grave danger,' shouted Rachel above the roar of the rain.

Rachel held Jinan around the waist and Mina copied her so the two women could support the boy as they stumbled out into the crowd, joining the sick and the maimed on their journey through the gaze of the horsemen.

The sight of Thomas leading the wagon alerted the men, two of whom dismounted and, brandishing swords, accosted him and pulled the wagon to the side of the road. One of the men drew back the sheet and found Mathias the cripple lying there shivering.

Mina hid her head in Jinan's shoulder as she and Rachel lifted him and dragged him through the gap between two of the riders who were temporarily distracted by the sight of the wagon.

'Where are they?' shouted one of the bandits, striking Thomas across the face and forcing him to his knees.

'What are you talking about, you maniac?'

'I'll cut your tongue out...'

Rachel pushed hard passed the riders, mingling with the crowd. The rain was beginning to slow, and the wind had dropped. Daylight was lightening the mood, and a glimmer of sunlight brightened the gloom. But nothing could rid them of the freezing cold. They had no money and no food, and Jinan seemed caught in a stupor. Rachel was at her wits' end when a hand touched her shoulder.

She froze.

'Get him back in the wagon; we will find a doctor for his burns,' said Thomas, sporting a black eye and a cut lip.

'I do not know where to find such a doctor,' moaned Rachel.

'Get up; I have a friend who can help us,' said Thomas, hiding Mina and Jinan under the goatskin cover with his brother Mathias, who was still sleeping.

'Where are you going?' asked Rachel as the mare continued to dawdle, caught up in the great melee of human beings.

'They say he is at Bethsaida, and I must take my brother there to be healed.'

'He being who?'

'The great Healer; Elijah has returned to us.'

'Are you sure it's not just another great hope?' said Rachel rather bluntly, causing the young man to laugh and then smile at her.

'I was blind and now I can see. Blind like you. But I have seen such great miracles.'

'Oh, so you have seen great miracles! That is fine; then I shall just take your word for it.' Rachel couldn't stop her mouth; there was something about the man that irritated her – his naivety and innocence offended the cynic in her.

'He healed me. I haven't just seen; I have witnessed my own body – my hand was withered. He said, "Reach out your hand," in front of the authorities, on the Sabbath, can you believe it? And my hand was healed. Look!' He laughed and pressed his hand on her face, covering her eyes.

'A month ago, it was smashed and half rotting. I did not know what to do, and now look!'

Rachel felt the touch of his healed hand; a wave of light, of sensitivity, of restored innocence, seemed to pulsate through her body, repelling the

pain and the loathing she felt towards him. Never before had she felt this stirring, deep inside, to live again, free as a bird. Hope seemed to well up in her heart and overflow into her mind until she remembered Anna and her great loss and scolded herself for being so weak as to be sensitive again.

'What is the matter? Your face was almost smiling – what are you thinking about?'

'I am not a good person, Thomas. Life has been so hard.' She looked into his face, into his brown eyes, and watched his lips for the sneer once he realised the sort of person she was. But he smiled.

'You need a fresh start, a new beginning, a new life, a new person. He will free you. Come with me. He can heal the boy, and your heart,' he said softly. 'Here, look, my friend lives here.'

Rachel was surprised to see a grand house, off the high road, set back in a large area of land. Several servants were watching from the large arched front door and rushed to help Thomas move the party inside the warm, dry house.

'Thomas, it is good to see you!' shouted the voice of a rich-looking young man, who raced down the hall to greet his friend.

'Barnabas! Please forgive me, but my friends here have a boy who is badly burned and I wondered whether we could send for the physician.'

'Come, bring them into the great hall; it will be warmer,' he ordered the servants, who lifted Mathias and Jinan and carried them back down the corridor into the great hall lit by an enormous fire. Rachel gasped at the splendour of the house, the high ceilings, the wall tapestries, the sideboards covered in trinkets of every shape and size, the ornate candlesticks and wonderfully shaped cast lanterns burning oil that smelt of perfume. The house seemed like a mighty fortress of warmth and light and, compared to the past days of travel, a source of comfort and delight. Perhaps her luck had changed and Jupiter was not so useless after all.

'Look at the state of you!' said Barnabas with a laugh.

'Twice we have been accosted by bandits. The first time, they took our horses and money, and I do not know what I would have done if this fair lady had not rescued us, and then we were beaten by bandits again, not three hundred yards from your house.'

'What is the world coming to?' growled Barnabas, who was looking at Rachel and admiring her beauty.

'And you, fair maiden, you are off to see the Healer?' he asked.

'No, I have a duty to return my charge to her grandparents in Capernaum.'

'Your charge?'

'Yes, Mina; she is attending to the boy Jinan, who was escorting us until he fell into a fire.' Rachel did not like the cross-examination and decided to tell as much of the truth as she dared. She looked at Thomas as he approached the fire and noticed his fine clothes, plastered with muck from the road; he was not the poor man she had thought. A wave of fear dispelled any peace she had gained from coming into the warm house. Who were these people?

'Please, if you can help my friend, then good, but we must be off as soon as we can. We do not want to be any trouble; we have money to pay for the physician.'

'Come, let us eat. The physician has been sent for. Come and sit by the fire; you must be frozen,' said Thomas, somehow sensing her fear.

She followed Barnabas and Thomas over to the fire and sat down on the low loungers that were covered in expensive fabrics and cushions of damask and silk. She lay back next to Mina and stroked her hair.

'They have sent for the physician. He won't be long.'

Mina looked hard into Rachel's face.

'Why don't we just tell them the truth? They could help us with the authorities. We don't need to go from here; they can send riders to fetch my grandparents,' she whispered.

'Don't say anything until I say,' said Rachel, squeezing the girl's hand.

The physician came and tended to Jinan's wounds, soothing them with ointments from small vials he carried in his large shoulder bag. He gave him a drink that would help him to sleep and ease the pain of the burns. Thomas and Rachel asked him what would happen to the boy.

'He wills survive the burns, but I notice they are not the first. How come he has so many scars?'

'I know nothing of his past. We met him along the path; the wagon and the mare are his. He helped us get this far.'

'This far? Are you fugitives?' asked the old doctor suspiciously.

'This far – we are on our way to Capernaum,' answered Rachel carefully.

'Look, the boy seems delirious, to me; he may be a danger to himself and others. I should lock him in a side room or at least watch over him during the night,' suggested the old man, donning his robe and hat.

'Interesting,' said Barnabas, teasing Thomas with a smile. Thomas shook his head and pushed his friend away from him.

'It seems you have run into a spot of bother, and knowing what a pushover you are, perhaps you might let sense prevail for once,' whispered Barnabas.

'Please, we can leave now; we do not want to cause a disturbance,' said Rachel loudly, scowling at Thomas, who protested his innocence.

'Look, let's rest, and when the boy awakes, we can get going again. The sooner we bathe in the light, the sooner we can revel in our freedom.'

'You are a captive, then?' asked Rachel.

'We are all captive to some force or other. As for me, I am captive to my duty to my brother, and you to your charge, and she to this boy. When we leave Capernaum, we are free to join the Healer and true freedom.'

'We?'

'Yes, I will accompany you all to Capernaum, once I can get new horses for me and my brother – so, Barnabas, we will vex you no longer.'

'Come, you mistake my concern,' interjected Barnabas. 'Stay until midday. When the rain ceases, I will get you all you need: a change of clothes for all of you and a covered wagon. You are only hours from Capernaum; you will make it by nightfall.'

'No, we should go,' said Rachel, but when she turned round, she saw Mina and Jinan fast asleep.

'Rest, maiden,' said Thomas, pointing at the low settee by the fire.

'I am no maiden, and I will keep watch over Jinan.'

'My servants will care for him,' said Barnabas quietly.

Rachel lay next to Mina and, despite her best efforts, fell fast asleep by the warm roaring fire.

The old physician cried as they slapped him. His mouth was gagged and his face bleeding. They had taken him when he had left the house and tortured him in the back of a large covered wagon waiting a hundred yards from the house.

'So, who is in the house?' demanded Gritz. One of his men had followed Thomas and the wagon, once they had let him leave, and reported back how he had met up with a woman, a boy and a girl. The doctor had come into the house and then left and been tricked into the back of the wagon.

'Three fugitives and the master's friend, Thomas, and his disabled brother,' groaned the doctor.

'How many servants?'

'He has about twelve servants.'

'They will be no match for us,' said one of Gritz's men. 'We can just go in and get this over and done with.'

'We need to wait,' muttered Gritz angrily.

'Boataz will be here soon. He will not be pleased we have let the child slip away. It may be best, my liege, if we act now,' said another of the men.

'Boataz has told us to wait for him,' bellowed Gritz, annoyed at all the chatter.

'And I am glad I can trust you, Gritz, with an order!' said a gruff voice as Boataz stepped up into the wagon.

'Is this the doctor?' he asked. Gritz nodded. 'Old man, if you want to live, we have a task for you.'

CHAPTER 6

✦ ✦ ✦

The sunlight was warming the puddles in the road, and the number of people travelling along it had turned into an untidy straggle. One of the servants took a call at the door and let the physician in.

'What has happened to you?' asked Barnabas, looking at the old man who stood ashen-faced and bloodied in the hall.

'We need to go somewhere private,' he whispered.

They sat in an anteroom among the musical strains of a fountain playing on the green marble.

'I have fallen over. It is fine, but the fright was enough to fell the strongest man.'

'Here, drink some wine and calm yourself,' said Barnabas.

'It has been bought to my attention that the woman and the two children you have allowed into your home are, in fact, seriously ill patients who need to be returned as soon as possible whence they have come. Outside, a physician is waiting to rid your house of the menace that they represent. Their audacity and stupidity take my breath away. When I think of the harm they could do!' He feigned covering his swollen lips with his hand and wiping his eyes with a silken handkerchief.

'Come, speak it out, physician,' remonstrated Barnabas.

'We must return them immediately to the men waiting to take them back to the leper colony they have escaped from. Imagine, you have entertained three lepers, three unclean, vile creatures in the bosom of your friendship. I knew there was something afoot with this party.'

Barnabas looked aghast and motioned for one of his servants to assemble the household.

'Doctor, I owe you a great debt of gratitude. Please send a message to these people that I will soon send them out. But what precautions should we take?'

'Cover your hands with gloves and then wash them all on their return; they will be safe. But you will have to burn the covers and cushions where they have lingered, gentle sire,' said the bitter old man, terrified by the threats of Boataz to kill all of his family.

'What about Thomas?' asked the head of the household.

'Go and wake him and send him to me. Old man, you can stay or go. My servants here will assist you in any of your instructions.'

'I do have a potion here. If we can get them to drink it, it will render them senseless, and they will be easier to move.'

'Wait here. I shall go and talk with Thomas,' said Barnabas, leaving the room and making for his own bedroom. Thomas appeared, rubbing sleep from his eyes and yawning.

'We have a problem,' said Barnabas, climbing onto his bed and resting back on the many pillows.

'Right,' said Thomas, going over to a bowl of fruit and biting into an apple. He looked out of the wide window at the surprisingly warm day trying to fight its way through the remnants of the clouds.

'Your friends, the woman, the girl and the boy, are big trouble, which I know you will not avoid. Oh, Thomas, Thomas, why does trouble follow you wherever you go?'

'What sort of trouble?'

'The old man, the physician, has just turned up with some cock and bull story about your party being lepers, and they need to be returned to the colony. Outside is a wagon with men waiting to take them back. He looks as if he has been done over a treat, so I'm betting down there in that wagon is the source of your trouble.'

Thomas looked down at the wagon and could see three or four armed men guarding the entrance.

'A damsel in distress! I thought you had changed.'

'I am no longer a boy, Barnabas. She helped me when I needed help. She was not interested in my riches, or my heirdom; she just reached out to help. And I owe her.'

'You owe her nothing, and I suppose the fact that she is beautiful has nothing to do with it – if she were a ninety-year-old spinster, you would still help.'

'Exactly, but I would not want to kiss her so much.'

'Nightmare! Oh, Thomas.' Barnabas got to his feet and hugged Thomas and looked down at the wagon.

Mathias called out from an adjoining bedroom, 'He takes no advice from anybody – don't waste your breath.'

'There may be seven of them, and they look like soldiers to me, or mercenaries. I can't see us taking the wagon,' Barnabas said, looking down from the window.

'Let me talk to her about this,' said Thomas, looking concerned.

A servant woke Rachel, who instantly suspected problems. She gingerly climbed to her feet and then followed the servant out of the great hall, along the corridor and into the side room where the physician sat on the opposite side of a table, waiting for her. Thomas and Barnabas sat in the relative shade of the room, watching.

Rachel scowled at Thomas, who raised his eyebrows and said nothing.

'My dear woman, please sit down. The physician here wants to ask you some questions about where you have come from.'

'Is this wise? It would be better if she drank the cordial,' groaned the physician.

'No, please tell her what you told me,' insisted Barnabas.

'When I left the house, I came by some information indicating that you are a fugitive. You, the girl, the boy, you are running away… See how she blanches… See how uneasy she now looks.

'You are running away from where you will return. There are men outside waiting to take you back, and if you have a grain of concern for the wellbeing of these fair people, you will leave immediately.'

'What he says is true,' said Rachel. 'There are men hunting me, but I have done no wrong. But I beg you, kind sir, please take the child to Capernaum where her grandparents live for she has been abducted by the evilest of men who seeks to stop her confessing she witnessed these men murdering her parents. I will go to them, and you should clear the house, for these men are heinous murderers who will kill you all. Please forgive me for bringing this calamity on you. I just want Mina to find safety.'

The physician began to sweat and dabbed his forehead with his kerchief.

'Cock and bull, cock and bull! These are fine fellows from the leper colony who seek to return these three vagrants to where they belong.'

'So why is it you have the mark of knuckles on your temple and lip, doctor?' asked Barnabas.

The old man closed his eyes and started to weep.

'The brutes beat me and said they would kill me and my family.'

Thomas got to his feet, came over to Rachel and put his arm around her shoulder.

'You must tell us all you know. We have very little time to protect you.'

'What she says is true,' said Mina, standing in the doorway. 'The brute's name is Boataz, and he abducted me on the night he killed my mother and father in Capernaum. My grandfather has great influence, and he will bring this man to justice if only I can get to him.'

'And Rachel?' asked Barnabas.

'I am a harlot, a whore, a prostitute, a woman to be despised – worthless trash,' she said, flashing her eyes angrily at Thomas.

'She was abducted when she was six and forced into working in one of Boataz's houses where he keeps the girls like slaves. She fell pregnant and had a child, Anna, whom Boataz stole,' continued Mina.

'How did you know that?' asked Rachel.

'Safa told me everything about you. How you are the noblest of the noble.'

'This trouble is getting worse by the minute!' groaned Barnabas.

'We stand and fight or flee? What is it to be?' said Thomas.

Gritz was watching the house from the back of the wagon. The old man had been a long time. Boataz was getting on his nerves, berating him for the slowness of his plan.

'Here they come,' he said as the physician and three servants appeared, helping three bodies, hidden under blankets, stagger towards the wagon.

'He has drugged them,' said Boataz with a laugh. 'Go get them, and I will finish the business you should have,' he growled at Gritz, who leapt down onto the ground and went around to the men by the horses. He ordered them to go and fetch the woman, the girl and the boy and dump them in the wagon.

He thought of the old woman's warning not to harm the boy and worried as three crows flew up into the air, one carrying a white feather in its mouth. He could sense misfortune and the reek of bad luck in his nostrils; he carefully climbed up onto the wagon and freed the reins and the horse whip.

Gritz's men waited for the servants to bring the bodies over to the wagon, and they laid them on the ground covered in blankets. Boataz opened the back of the wagon and stood up, looking down on the scene. No sooner had he appeared than Thomas and Barnabas cast off the blankets, drew their swords and assailed Gritz's men. The servants drew their daggers and fought boldly, trying to allow Thomas time to mount the wagon and face Boataz. One of Gritz's men screamed as a sword pierced his heart; another fell to his knees, blood gushing from his throat. The soldiers withdrew in a panic, leaving Boataz alone to face the fray.

Thomas charged at Boataz – but Gritz, hearing the melee, whipped the horses into action and the wagon careered off down the road, almost forcing Boataz to tumble onto the road.

'I'll cut your throat,' growled Boataz as Thomas fell from the moving wagon.

✦ ✦ ✦

Barnabas sent for the Roman envoy in the main town house of the administration. The Centurion Crestas Flavia came to take statements and interviewed Rachel and Thomas in the great hall.

'I need to interview the girl to confirm this Boataz killed her parents. We will then deal with him. He has been a thorn in our flesh for the past ten years. You say he runs this house of ill-repute in Theims? We will send a party of men to free the girls there and wait to see if he shows his face.'

'Please be careful as you question her; she has been greatly traumatised,' requested Rachel.

Mina was sitting with Jinan, who was recovering from his burns and seemed quite lucid when Crestas came and sat beside her.

'I am sorry, but I need to talk about Boataz and the attack on your family…'

'I don't want to talk about it! He is a monster, a fiend. Talk to me when you have captured him.'

'It doesn't work like that. He has been terrorising wealthy families around this area for a decade. We do not know where he hides up, we suspect it is up in the mountains, but whenever we send men, they report back with nothing.'

'That's because you are looking in the wrong place,' said Jinan.

'And you are the boy who rescued these two on the night of your escape?'

'Yes, without Jinan we would not be here,' said Rachel.

'So, what do you know of Boataz?'

'He lives in a palatial house in Tiberias. He goes by the name of Gal Ben Gilgal by day, but at night he scavenges with his horde, preying on the defenceless and innocent. He is a robber, a bandit, and he forces taxes on the shopkeepers and innkeepers in Tiberias and extorts money from them. He runs a number of illicit houses, including the house at Theims.'

'And how do you know all this?'

'I have lived much of my life in the squalor of Tiberias, and you get to know who to fear pretty quickly.'

'Mina,' said Crestas firmly, 'can you tell me how he got into your home?'

'He knocked on the door and just came through, invited; my father seemed to know him. I remember thinking it odd the way he was so rude and demanding of my father, who sounded perturbed. I was in my bedroom, but I could hear them arguing over a business transaction – Boataz said my father owed him monies and he demanded satisfaction. My father refused and demanded he leave the house, never to return. And then –' Mina gulped, 'I came out onto the landing and looked down as he murdered my mother and my father. Then his men poured into the house and killed everybody. He sent a man up to get me, and I feared he would kill me, but he just threw me over his shoulder and took me downstairs where my parents lay in their blood.

'"This is what happens when people double cross me – so don't blame me, blame your father!" he shouted before we left the house. I was tied to him on his horse. It was terrible, to be bound so closely to that horror, and he drove the horse like a man possessed out of Capernaum, along the coast, to the house.'

'He abducts girls to work in his houses,' added Rachel.

'And you were abducted as a girl?'

'I was a mere child. I can remember nothing, only the cruelty, the beatings and the threat that if I were ever to try to escape, he would kill me.'

'I will ride to Capernaum and investigate all of this. In the meantime, I will send an escort for you to follow me.' Crestas left Rachel with Mina and Jinan and walked slowly back into the anteroom with Barnabas and Thomas.

'You two were quite foolish taking this man on. I just hope you do not live to regret it. He is a vindictive and brutal man. But I have gathered very useful information that may well aid us in apprehending him at last. Wait here until the escort arrives.'

63

Crestas left them at midmorning and returned to the small garrison at Magdala.

Gritz swore at Boataz, who had punched him in the face.

'We never run! What is the matter with you?' shouted Boataz.

'Instincts. I followed my instinct.'

'To run like a dog?'

'To wait, gather intelligence and then go again in more favourable conditions.'

'I want the physician and his family destroyed by nightfall.'

'You are losing your touch,' cried a voice from outside the wagon.

'Friend,' smiled Gritz as he leapt down from the wagon and stood looking up at the Roman soldier on his large white horse.

'It didn't take me five minutes to find you,' said Crestas, taking off his helmet. 'This stinking uniform is killing me.'

'Did they buy it?' asked Boataz.

'Completely. We killed every one of the Roman scum in the garrison, and the men had just donned the Roman armour when one of the servants came running in asking for help. Of course, I was pleased to oblige, but there is a boy in there who hails from Tiberias. He knows you by your real name.'

'He is not to be harmed,' blurted Gritz.' He belongs to the old witch. She will curb his tongue.'

'I will decide who survives and who perishes,' shouted Boataz, pushing Gritz hard in the chest.

'Send the men, dressed as Roman soldiers, around to the physician's house and kill everybody in the household, every living creature. I will cut off his ears and tongue – he will witness my wrath,' ordered Boataz.

'Are they all going to get dressed up as stinking filth?' moaned the brigand who had killed Crestas and donned his uniform.

✦ ✦ ✦

Thomas and Rachel walked out into the garden, following Mina and Jinan, who were getting some fresh air and stretching their legs.

'You should never call yourself such bad words,' he said soberly.

'It is what it is,' said Rachel in a matter-of-fact way. She bit her lip, fighting back the wave of panic rising in her heart. She had been corrupted by Boataz, her life ruined, and she had no future – beyond getting Mina to safety and then perhaps trying to find Anna if the authorities forced Boataz to reveal where he had taken her.

'You will feel differently when you have met the Healer. He will give you a new future full of love.'

'I have had my fill of love,' replied Rachel dismissively.

'You have never been loved, not like this.'

'My daughter loved me,' she said, wiping away a tear, angry with herself for showing emotion. 'And then they pulled my heart out and fed it to the crows.'

'You have never lost your dignity, or your bearing.'

'Dignity? You must be out of your head. What dignity is there in a life of enforced slavery?'

'The dignity that comes from a noble character.'

'Noble! Do you know what I am?' She was beginning to get cross with him, which seemed to spur him on to even more heady heights of ridiculousness. 'Can your Healer wash me clean of my filth?' she asked.

'You will have to ask him when you meet him. I will take you and my brother to see him.'

'Will you, indeed.' She sounded exasperated with him, but she knew she was frustrated at never being able to return the love of a man.

CHAPTER 7

✦ ✦ ✦

Jinan felt calmer. His burns had scabbed over, and the wounds had ceased to weep. He sat beneath a gnarled fig tree and watched Rachel talking with Thomas.

'Why did you do it?' Mina asked Jinan.

'The darkness, it consumes me. There are moments when I can do nothing to resist its pressure, its influx, its grip on my mind, and in times like that, I do not seem to be in control of my own decisions – it is as if somebody, or something, else takes me over and I end up doing ridiculous and dangerous things.'

'You said your grandfather told you to do it,' she said, watching him pick at the leaves on the fig tree.

'Yes, I saw him in the fire, standing engulfed by the flames. He was in agony and sought me to come into the fire and relieve his pain. I just could not control myself.'

'Why did the doctor say you have other burns?'

'This was not the first time. Before the old woman purchased me from my grandfather, that is. That is why I did not want to come down from the mountain – there was sanctuary for me up there.'

'Why did you come down?'

'I couldn't stand the thought of that woman hurting you. So I rescued you.'

'Thank you. You are a hero,' she whispered and touched his hand.

'I don't think so. Once you are safe, I will have to return to the old woman. She is the only one who can help me.'

'You think her charms and potions, her cheap magic, mean you have to spend your life wasted away on a mountain cliff top?'

'She said a great light has broken out, drawing to it everything that is dark and evil and malevolent to battle its presence. She said her master would contend with this light and destroy it – it stood no chance against the kingdom of her dark Lord. I was to stay away from the darkness or every creature between here and hell would slither into me and consume me.'

'Do you mean the Healer? Could he be this great light?'

'I know nothing of a Healer,' replied Jinan.

'Thomas said his hand was healed by the Healer, and he is taking his brother to see him. Perhaps we should all go and see this man. Perhaps his magic is stronger than the old woman's.'

Rachel came over to them and smiled.

'I think we may be safe now,' she said.

Boataz cut the physician's ears off with a dagger, and then forced out his tongue, which he cut off with scissors, before slaying the physician's wife and children. His men plundered the house, killing every living thing they encountered. The old man fell to his knees in agony, his life stripped of everything; he wept and gagged and gurgled in his blood.

One of the servants escaped out of the back yard, flung himself onto the back of a horse and rode hard through the soldiers and out onto the main road.

✦ ✦ ✦

Barnabas, standing in the upstairs window looking towards the lake, saw one of the physician's servants riding at breakneck speed along the coastal road, chased by Roman soldiers on horseback. He watched in horror as they pierced him with their spears and then hacked him to death.

✦ ✦ ✦

Gritz, dressed as a Roman soldier, lined up the eight horsemen with javelins outside Barnabas's house. The soldier pretending to be Crestas knocked on the door. They waited for five minutes and knocked again. Gritz dismounted and walked over to Crestas.

'I will check the rear of the house,' he whispered. Wandering around the house and looking through the windows, he could see no sign of life, and the stables were empty of horses.

'Damn!' he shouted, cursing Boataz's thirst for vengeance.

'What is going on?' asked Crestas.

'They have bolted. It seems revenge on the physician has cost us dearly... damn and damn him.' He ran back to his horse and commanded them to get on down the road as fast as they could.

'They have gone! Let's catch them at Capernaum.'

Boataz shouted and screamed, but Gritz ignored him, wishing he could see the day when the dogs would eat the man's entrails. The horsemen galloped as fast as they could along the road to Capernaum, intent on catching their prey.

69

✦ ✦ ✦

'What madness is this?' said Barnabas as they followed Thomas on foot, walking the horses in single file onto a single track of rough stones leading up into the mountains.

'We cannot outride them. We need to go the mountain trail, up and over into Capernaum where we will contact the garrison there.'

'Why not ride south to Tiberias and contact that garrison?' asked Barnabas, looking back at the long line of servants following the party, each riding or walking a pony, donkey or horse.

'We must press on with men guarding the rear and on lookout,' replied Thomas.

'What is our plan?' asked Barnabas.

'Let's find a safe place in the mountains and hide; perhaps we can send out riders to alert the garrison at Capernaum.'

'It will be freezing up there,' said Barnabas.

'We have grabbed everything we could. We can always send people back for more provisions tomorrow,' replied Thomas.

'Someone will be watching the house.'

'Yes, so we need to get provisions from somewhere else,' said Thomas looking grimly at Barnabas.

'This is big trouble, Thomas.'

'Let me check on Mathias.'

Thomas led his horse back down the line to the donkey his brother was riding. His eyes were tired, and his face ached with the pain from his shrivelled legs as the pack animal picked its torturous way across the rough terrain. Mathias smiled at his brother; he grunted a few words and Thomas laughed.

'What did he say?' asked Barnabas.

'He reckons I'll kill him before he ever sees the great Healer.'

'He may not be wrong.'

'How many fighting men do you have amongst your servants?' asked Thomas.

'Not enough – we will have to find some refuge in the caves,' replied Barnabas.

'You don't have to get involved in this,' said Thomas.

'I will go with you, but...'

'That is a long but?' mused Thomas.

'But is this worth it?' said Barnabas, looking at Rachel walking beside Mina, who was riding the black mare.

'Do you mean should we risk our lives for a fallen woman?'

'Well?' asked Barnabas, shrugging his shoulders.

'Well, yes, her destitution is not her fault. She was abducted by this fiend, and I will protect her as much as I can.'

'Be reasonable, Thomas. She is...'

'Corrupt or corrupted, Barnabas?'

'You only have her word for it; you know nothing about her.'

'Do I need your permission to continue? As I said, please, we can part here and now if her condition offends your sensibilities,' said Thomas angrily.

'Don't be difficult. I am just saying what needs to be said. You are putting all our lives at risk for a woman who has had a child out of wedlock, who by her own admission is a destitute...'

'Whore, is that the word you would use?'

'Well, if we are going to be honest, yes; a mess, Thomas, an absolute mess and a liability. I promised your father I would watch over you and your brother, and this situation would have driven him to an early grave. What would he have said, Thomas?'

'Too much, too much, friend.'

'Think of your reputation.'

Thomas reflected on the memory of Rachel's face the first time he had seen her, in the pouring rain, her sorrow marring her loveliness. Her eyes had been so large and so expressive of a tender compassion that lay deep within, which the wretchedness of her circumstances had not taken away. Her lips were broad, yet carefully shaped, beneath a pretty nose, giving her face an effortless beauty. In the howling storm and early morning fragrance of fetid mud sucking at his feet as he had carried his brother, she had stooped down to lift his burden onto her cart and in so doing had won his allegiance and engendered his wish to bring her into the presence of the great Healer.

He kicked the horse on and rode beside her, smiling.

'You do not need to do this. Save yourself, and leave us,' she pleaded, hiding her face beneath a veil and not daring to look up at his handsome face for fear his gaze would unlock the last vial of hope hidden in her heart and pour it out onto the hard, frost-bitten ground.

'You sound like Barnabas,' he said, dismounting and leading his horse beside her. 'We will go up into the mountains and find some place of refuge.'

'No, go! Please go back to your home and protect yourselves. I could not bear to suffer any more loss.' She peeped up at his face as he studied the distant horizon of rising stone; she felt his hand unlocking her heart and winced at the thought of her growing fondness and ease in his presence.

'Please.' She touched his hand, and he stopped and turned to her. 'What have I done? Sorry!' She gasped at the look on his face.

'Your touch, it was just like his,' he said slowly, looking at his hand which had been crushed by falling masonry eighteen months before.

'He healed me with a touch just like that,' he said suddenly, smiling at her.

'I should not have touched you, but Boataz will kill you if he catches you. I have seen him kill a man with a single blow of his axe.'

'He will be no match for the great Healer.'

Rachel felt annoyed that he dismissed her concern for him. It felt like rejection, and her face coloured with anger beneath her veil.

'I do not need a great Healer. I just want justice and the Roman authorities to find out what happened to my daughter, Anna. I do not want to entertain or encourage your strange allegiance to this Healer. It is fine what he did for you and what he may do for your brother, but I do not need healing.'

'He cleansed me of my sins. He said, "Your sins have been forgiven," and then he healed my hand, which was shrivelled and rotten.'

Rachel felt anger flushing not just her face but her words.

'Is that what this is all about – my redemption? You want to make me clean of my filth?'

'No!' But before he could continue, she pulled away from him.

'Thank you, Thomas, for making me feel so hollow,' she whispered through gritted teeth.

'I did not mean that,' said Thomas, aghast at her reaction.

'What did you mean? I have no shrivelled hand – just a shrivelled, rotten reputation that fate has blighted me with.'

'I meant...'

'You meant too much.'

'Calm down. I did not mean to hurt or upset you.'

'Well, you have, so please leave me alone. I want nothing to do with you.'

She let Mina ride the pony by herself and retreated down the line of ponies to find Jinan riding the black mare. Religious freak, she thought. But she knew the truth of her feelings and closed her eyes, wishing for once in her life the road would not be mountainous but a smooth descent, along comfortable perpendicular lines, to a house with livestock, a small vineyard and a garden in which to play with her infant. But she had no idea of how to get to such a place. She, and the people in darkness, lived behind a veil of deceit that hid the rotten truth of enslavement and abuse from the beings who worked, and played, and lived in normal, pretty, little square houses, oblivious to the plight of the many. The few wrestled with their travails like children spinning toys, moaning and groaning about nothing, the plight of the many hidden in the darkness.

Jinan did not seem in a good way. She tried to converse with him, but he did not engage with her. He was agitated, furtively looking over his shoulder and darting glances to far distant scenes where she imagined him seeing strange phantasms and weird apparitions from his over-stretched mind.

She lowered her head and walked by his side, patting the mare and wondering what on earth had happened to her and where she was going. The sky above the mountain was vast, with no boundaries, and something inside her hated the limitlessness of it all. She had spent her young adult life huddled in fear and fighting abuse in the confines of the madam's business. Now, like a caterpillar metamorphosing in a cocoon, she felt undone, emulsified into another substantive form. But she knew, in the depths of her, that she would not make it into a bright sunny future – that Boataz would ruin her. Perhaps she should just go to him and get it out of the way and free the long line of people who had now become entangled in the vileness of the affair.

'He will help you and me,' said Jinan, suddenly breaking into a moment of coherence.

'Who?'

'The Healer – he will set us all free...'

'Have you been talking to Thomas?'

'I am no different to his brother; it's just that I am crippled from the inside by demons that plague me, outside of the influence of the old woman. I do not know if I will make it, but I want to be free, and he is my only chance.'

'You should not listen to Thomas – he has no right to fill your mind with false hope,' muttered Rachel.

'He will set me free; he is my only hope. He will free me from him, over there – he can't stop taunting me.' Jinan shook his fist at the distant sky and shouted, 'Wait until he finds you. Wait and see!' He started crying and dropped his head, his chin on his chest.

Rachel slowed her pace and waited for the long line of men and ponies and provisions to pass her and disappear behind a large outcrop of rock. She paused, leaning back on the rocks, trying to calm herself. Thomas had disrupted her sense of peace. But how dare he assume she needed cleansing as if she were a filthy rag that needed to be disposed of? She had not once chosen the life she had been subjected to – not a single time invited the attentions, the pawing at her flesh, the mind-throttling horror of being abused every day.

Her tears streamed down her cheeks. She wet her palms and rubbed them over her face, smearing the remnants of yesterday's makeup all over her cheeks. She raised her fists to God on high and shouted at him.

'I can wash myself in my horror! I do not need your redemption. It is too late! Too late!' Her shouts caused the crows to leap up from the dry, dead shrubbery and guffaw in the sky.

CHAPTER 8

✦ ✦ ✦

Gritz shook his head. Things were starting to unravel. First Boataz had killed the couple and the whole household in broad daylight in a major town like Capernaum. Now he had slaughtered Roman soldiers just to stop the authorities discovering the child who would condemn him to death on the cross.

Boataz needed to calm down. But there was no reasoning with the devil that lived in that huge hulk of a body. They had met in Rome where Boataz had hired him as a mercenary to help thieve their way back to the accursed lands of Palestine. Along the way, they had formed a band of brigands raiding the rich pickings along the main trade route from Lebanon to Jerusalem. They had amassed enough bounty to live as comfortably as they wanted.

They had been a day away from disbanding, each taking their own share of the bounty, when out of the blue, Boataz had determined to go to Capernaum and complete one remaining piece of business. Gritz knew Boataz should have offered to go by himself, for he was beginning to grow reckless, taking ridiculous risks in the face of the Roman oppressors.

When they had arrived at the house, Phillip, the debtor, had shown no sense. He had argued and insulted Boataz from the outset, and whatever Gritz did to intervene, he could do nothing to avert the debacle that ensued. Boataz had cut the wife's throat and then repeated the act on the man himself. What Phillip was doing owing money to a man like Boataz was beyond Gritz's understanding. His family came from a different world, one of gentility and harmony, where a stubbed toe represented the greatest suffering they had ever had to bear, and they would have had no comprehension of the murderous intent of their intruder. Yet the pair knew each other. They spoke like old acquaintances. How bravely Phillip had spoken! How oblivious he had been to the hell that his abuser would wreak on him and his family!

And the girl, why not kill her? Why take the risk of snatching her for one of his brothels? Boataz was a warped and stunted mind with a talent for mayhem and considerable skill at evading the authorities.

He lived as a wine merchant in the winter months, in a fine property on the outskirts of Tiberias. No one suspected that this dutiful Jew, who sat in a place of highest honour in the synagogue, was the ultimate thief of life and valuables. Gritz, unlike the rest of the men who languished drunk in the great hall of the house over the winter, enjoyed working the land. He learned to fix fences, gather the flocks, drive the cattle, tend the vines and maintain the estate in preparation for his return to Gaul where he would buy a fine property and work the land. Gritz loved the winter calm when the dagger and the sword were put to one side and he picked up the plough. So, when Boataz had ordered the men to raid Capernaum, he had a great feeling of unease.

'What are you doing?' mumbled Boataz, climbing up into the back of the wagon where Gritz was seated.

'Why didn't you just kill this girl? I was just thinking about that night.'

'The grandparents, they now owe me my money plus interest. She is my insurance that I will get paid.'

'Is this all worth it? We have no idea where they are!'

'What ails you, man?' shouted Boataz. 'Let's just get on with recapturing her.'

'We have left a trail of mayhem along the coastline. If the authorities send out the garrisons in Capernaum and Tiberias, we will be caught right in the middle of it all.'

'That's why we will disband.'

'We will?'

'Yes, we shall travel in pairs, some up into the mountain to search for them, others to make their way to the grandparents' house to keep watch, whilst we send outriders out to scout the roads leading into Capernaum from all directions.'

'And I?'

'You will go to the mountains with Chirag.'

'The Moabite?'

'Yes. Any problems?' demanded Boataz.

'Yes, it means you do not trust me if you are going to hamper me with that killer.'

'You read my mind, then. Do you think I am stupid? I know you want to flee back to Gaul, but not until we have retrieved the girl and I have been repaid my debt.'

'You have just killed Roman soldiers. That is insurrection. They will hunt you down until you have nowhere to hide.'

'I will slip back into being the good Jew. Maybe I'll get married and settle down; no one will suspect me. I have seen to that. But you, on the other hand, have nowhere to hide if you attempt to flee!'

Gritz looked fiercely at Boataz, but he knew he was no match for the man in the art of fighting.

'Then I have no choice but to request a more adept fellow than the Moabite.'

'That's more like it. Who do you want?' smirked Boataz.

'Babr is a good tracker. I need to find the trail and follow them until I can snatch back the girl.'

'No, leave that to me. I have a score to settle with the whore who stole her in the first place. Just track them, and when you are half a day's ride from Capernaum, you will find me in the Black Tavern. Where I will set my trap.'

Within the hour, Gritz and Babr were riding hard up the trail beside Barnabas's house, in pursuit.

✦ ✦ ✦

Rachel had stopped weeping. On the outside. But inwardly, she felt a waterfall of pain and tumult overflowing the carefully constructed dams of protection she had set up around her heart. She so wanted to find Anna, so longed to be reunited with the only person who had brought her joy. But what if she were killed before she found out where Boataz had taken her? How could she be sure that, even if she learned where she now was, the child would be returned to her? What if he had just moved her to another brothel?

Perhaps it would be better to retreat down the track and turn herself in to Boataz and let him end the pain once and for all.

To her surprise, a small hand pushed itself into her own. She looked up and found Mina standing beside her.

'Come on, you cannot give up now,' she whispered.

'How? Why?'

'I just had an instinct you were struggling and came back to find you. Come on, I owe you my life. So let's find my grandfather, and he will help you in return for your help to me. He is a powerful man.'

They walked a while back up the trail of muddy, broken stones, between huge outcrops of rock, finding Mina's pony eating grass by a nook in the cliff face. Mina insisted Rachel ride the animal and walked along beside her.

'I am worried about Jinan; he just does not seem right to me. Why is he so afflicted?' asked Mina. 'He is sometimes delirious, and he sees strange creatures, like huge black beetles, scurrying along the walls around us, hissing and spitting curses down on our heads. He says we are in the midst of a titanic struggle between good and evil.'

'Please don't tell me you believe all this stuff about the Healer,' moaned Rachel.

'What if he is the Messiah, and Jinan is right: the forces of darkness are emerging from the depths of hell to contend with him? Every evil spirit, every demonic power let loose upon the earth to oppose him?'

'The Messiah is a king, and all kings sit on their backsides in palaces doing nothing – he will have nothing to do with the likes of you and me. You will be greatly disappointed in him, of that I am sure,' said Rachel, surprised at the hurt tone of her voice.

'He will drive out the Romans and set up a kingdom more splendid than David's; he will rule for ever.'

'Mina, these are delusions. We have more pressing issues than can be solved by any Messiah.'

'You are not a believer?' The question faltered as Mina looked up at Rachel and remembered the woman's life of pain. 'Forgive me, I do not know what I am talking about; you have suffered greatly, and I see that my enthusiasm causes you offence.'

'No, please, child, tell me whatever you want. I am just too cynical. The world has betrayed me at every turn, but that should not blight your youthful zeal for your Messiah... Tell me, why you are so excited?'

'Thomas says...'

'Oh, Thomas has a head full of fairy stories...'

'But what if he is right, that the Healer has come to set us all free? He healed his withered hand and then told him his sins were forgiven! Imagine, who has the authority to forgive people's sins and to heal so wonderfully?'

'I'm sure Thomas is exaggerating.'

'You don't believe him? He says many saw the event; he was in a packed room.'

'What do you and I have to do with this Healer? We just need to get you to safety and see if your grandfather can force the authorities to get out of Boataz what he did with my daughter... That would be the greatest healing, to have Anna back, but I am sure your Healer means well.'

The sky was darkening as the party wended its way higher and higher up into the mountains, snaking between huge cataracts and fractures in the grizzled rock. They seemed to follow a fault line, a fissure weaving through the impenetrable crags, until, as the light began to fail, they drew up on the summit and the trail widened into a road. Blasted by a freezing wind, they pressed on towards an outcrop of ancient stones which provided some protection from the wayward gusts.

They set up camp in a gulley, lighting fires hidden in the deep depression, fearful of the light attracting the attention of any of Boataz's men who may have pursued them. Thomas and Barnabas set guards over the entrance and sent men back down the trail as lookouts; other men went further along the mountain peaks to scout out the next day's journey.

The servants prepared a meal of salted beef and pickled fish, and Rachel, Jinan and Mina sat closest to the fire, eating hungrily. Mina was nervous that Jinan would fling himself into the fire again and continued, as much as she could, to talk to him. But the boy was incoherent and jabbered incessantly. He dare not step out of the light of the fire until the morning came. Demons were hunting for them. Large, loathsome creatures clung to the walls of the ravine towering above them, crying out to the darkness to unleash hell upon their heads. Darkness was rising up to find the one, to extinguish the light, to obliterate the Son of Man who had come to overcome Satan and all of his hordes. The demonic filled every quarter of this agitated, defiled and molested land. The cacophony of mutterings went on into the night until Rachel and Mina finally fell into a slumber.

The narrowness of the trail had slowed Gritz and the tracker, Babr, to a walking pace, but they were certain they were on the trail of a large party whom they would catch before nightfall. Gritz had nothing more to do than to think as he allowed his horse to follow that of the tracker's.

For some reason, he could not get out of his mind the old woman of the mountain and the future she had foretold. It had not gone well. As he pressed ahead on the ascent into the mountains, he could not but hide his resentment of the journey. What had he done but thieve to deserve so horrific an ending? He rued ever meeting Boataz and listening to his stories of a good winter life with rich summer pickings. The more time he spent in this land, the more accursed he felt. Trapped, he was now powerless to avoid the old woman's prediction, which he knew lay over the top of the mountain range, down in the town of Capernaum. But instinct, the mechanism of survival, kicked in, and he determined to find a way out of it all. Why did he not just flee back to Gaul, to the soft country, where the summers were green and pleasant? To his homestead, to walk amongst the great trees of the forest, hunting bear, boar and deer.

Sure, these lands around the great lake were verdant, fertile and overflowing with wine, grain and good pasture, but the sun was merciless in the harsh sky, undappled by the forest canopy of temperate climes.

His treasure, the labour of three long years of brigandry, lay buried on Boataz's land in a location only the fiend knew. He could not leave all that work behind; there was an ache within him to collect his treasure and flee. But what could he do? Unlike Boataz, he had been careful not to kill anybody, just coercing, brutalising, yes, but never slaying those poor unfortunates who had fallen into their traps along the many trade routes that crisscrossed this peculiar land. Yet the old woman had said they would die together, he and this hulk of misery – the one bound to doom and the other to destiny. What had she meant?

If he returned the boy to her, would he find favour with the old woman and find a different route from doom or destiny? He would have to square this all with Boataz, who was as superstitious as the next man. But how could he find his treasure and get back to Gaul, avoiding the painful death that awaited him over the top of the mountain?

His thoughts plagued him and corrupted his mood. As the wind picked up and a light drizzle dampened his beard, he cursed and shouted at his misfortune.

CHAPTER 9

✦ ✦ ✦

'Asri, remember that your name means lion of God,' whispered the rabbi, holding the old man's arms as he sobbed.

'She is beside herself! I am so frightened. What will become of her?'

'Remember your roar, Asri. You must hold firm to your calling.'

'I can barely meow,' said the old man ironically. 'My son's death, and the slaughter of his wife, are bad enough, but they have taken Mina, and I cannot but hold myself to blame.'

'Why so?'

'My son, he had a problem that I helped him solve, and the solution was not entirely honourable.'

'You reaped what you have sown. Now is the time to turn to the Lord and seek His help. You have washed yourself; I saw you bathe in the waters. Surely this is enough for you to be ceremonially clean?'

Ceremonially clean. The old man spat and swore inside. He had been unwise, a fool, in indulging his son, and now his life was in ruins. Why had he been so weak?

He bade the rabbi farewell and decided his mourning would end that morning. He returned to his office, avoiding another row with Elizabeth, his wife, who had taken to her bed a month ago and lay, unclean, unkempt, barely eating, in a sodden mass of clothes. His secretary seemed surprised to see him and stood up and bowed as he entered the room.

'Sir, I did not think you would return so soon.'

'Ezra, sit down; we need to talk.'

The lion of God could speak with Ezra, the man of peace, without causing offence. Elizabeth had not stopped shouting at him for a month, and his ears resounded with her constant laments.

'We used to buy our wine from a merchant in Tiberias, many, many years ago. I am talking twelve years ago. I sent Phillip off to see him, to see if we could negotiate a better contract. I need you to find his name and his address as a matter of urgency… You have all my resources available to you to find that man. I cannot remember his name, but I want you to find it as if my very life depended on it.'

Ezra looked back, concerned for his master. 'Can you remember why we bought wines from Tiberias? What was the type of wine, and the value? How did we get to meet this man?'

'I have searched my mind a thousand times but cannot remember. Ask the storekeeper – he may remember more than I. I just remember the fellow was extremely tall and well built; he had a long scar down his cheek and was…'

'Was?'

'Peculiar. He was peculiar in his manner. As if he was frightened of nothing. He showed no cowering deference to anybody. And laughed as if he had somehow tricked the whole world with his wonderful joke.'

'That is not a lot to go on, but I will try as hard as I can.'

'With all your might?'

'With all my might.'

Asri sent Ezra off with his blessing, slightly cheered by the thought that he would be free for at least part of the day from the wailing and mourning that had filled his house, his head and his heart, spilling out and ruining the once-perfect repose of his soul. Phillip, he suspected, had been even more foolish than he had thought possible and had poured fury and malevolence on all of their heads. He felt aggrieved at his son's stupidity, which had ruined everything he had striven to achieve for the family over so many years of want and hardship.

He looked at the pile of papers on his desk and enjoyed the pleasant tedium of checking bills and notices from the many agents of his business now spread across the empire. He thought again of the hundreds of thousands of denarii he drew in from all his business interests and bemoaned the fact that money, his great love, had cost him so dearly in the end. But there was always the chance of restoring Mina to the family at a price he could afford.

He remained in the office for as long as he dared before reluctantly returning to the house of mourning.

The wailers were wailing and the singers singing a low, mournful chant that seemed to go on for ever. He tried to hide in his bedroom but was caught by his wife's maid, who entreated him to go and see her.

'She needs a wash – she stinks,' he replied crossly. 'I will not go in until she has bathed and you have changed the beds. Enough is enough of all this misery.' The maid curtsied and looked angrily at him.

'She needs you, sir.'

'And I need her to be more presentable. So go, and less of your attitude, girl. Get those wailing women out of the house before I sling them out myself.'

He closed his door and sat at his desk in the window, looking down at the people going about their business, oblivious to his broken heart. But his mind was whole, and where emotion sought to overpower him again, he decided to roar.

Ezra entered the room to inform him that Portius, the centurion, was waiting for an audience. Asri shook his head and gazed up at the midday sun, cursing his misfortune. The last person he wanted to see today, of all days, was Portius. The Romans had been nothing but thorough in their investigations into the murder of his son's family and the abduction of their daughter. But there were twists in the tale that only he, the grandfather, could unravel, and he could well do without the attention of the synagogue or the Roman authorities.

Asri followed Ezra downstairs, now dead to the grandeur of the palace he, once a poor boy, had built in the town.

'Portius, how good to see you!' lied the old man, addressing the short, balding centurion who sat beside a fountain enjoying the tinkling sound of the water.

'Sir, just a curtesy call,' the centurion replied, gazing up at the old man's face. His nose was like a beak, and his eyes, dark and deep-set, peered out like an eagle's studying its prey.

Asri did not trust this man and approached him cautiously.

'We have made enquiries but have, alas, come to nothing. So, I wonder if we might look again at some of the details of that night,' said Portius.

'It really would not bless me to dwell anymore on that tragedy. I was not there, so I have nothing more to add. Please excuse me as I return to my grief.'

'Certainly, sir, but I just have one or two questions that need answering before I can go.' Portius stared resolutely at the old man until he sat down in a chair opposite him.

'You see, there are some peculiarities in this case that I need to discuss. Some things that make no sense...'

'It makes no sense that brigands should descend upon my son's house, slaughter the household, ruin my life and snatch my granddaughter.'

'Exactly so, sir. Do you have any idea why they would do such a thing? Did your son have any enemies?'

Only one, thought the old man, who felt unnerved by the question.

'He had no enemies, none that I know of. It was probably an opportune assault on a rich family.'

'This does not have the traits of an opportune attack. It seems pretty premeditated to me. None of the neighbours reported any disturbance when these brigands entered the house. It almost seems that your son knew the assailants. Could that be true?'

'Why do you say such a ghastly thing?' asked Asri, feigning horror.

'We have reports of four men fleeing the house on horseback but no reports or eye witness account of these men forcing their way into the house. That seems odd to me.'

'Perhaps they just knocked on the door.'

'Hmm.' Portius raised a hand to his chin and stroked it. His grey eyes shone, and his thin lips arced gently into a hint of a smile of derision.

'Could your son have known his assailants? Was there bad business between them?'

'Why do you make such outlandish claims?' protested the old man, hating the force of nature peering at him.

'They seem to have punished the family, leaving all for dead, but taking the girl. That is odd to me.'

'Odd. Is that how you describe it? I would tend to use longer words to describe my worst nightmare.'

'Have you had any ransom demands?'

'What are you talking about?'

'Have you had any ransom demands? Maybe they took the child to demand a ransom. They took no jewels or treasure from the house, just the girl.'

'Let me assure you she is the greatest treasure and the brightest jewel in our eyes.'

'No doubt, but perhaps they knew that. Perhaps they came demanding money, and when your son declined, they took the greater worth.'

'What worth would she be to them?'

'Surely, they would look to you to turn the child into gold. Hence my interest in whether you have received any contact from this gang?'

'No, there has been no contact.'

Portius stood up and collected his helmet from the settee.

'Did your son owe anybody any money?'

'No, none that I am aware,' said the old man through gritted teeth, deploring the arrogant intent of the man in front of him. Ezra helped Asri to his feet, but the Roman officer merely left the room as silently as he had entered it.

The old man sat in his room fretting. He must find the purveyor of wine from Tiberias before Portius did. It had been a simple enough transaction. Phillip received that which was promised for the payment of 5,000 denarii. What could have gone wrong? The payment terms were discussed and agreed upon, and Phillip had plenty of money to keep his side of the bargain. But his son was avaricious and deceitful, and Asri rued the lack of discipline he had instilled in the boy, giving in to his every whim.

The door pushed open and Ezra entered, looking uncomfortable.

'The mistress is causing a scene unless you go to her,' he said.

'Has she bathed?'

'I believe she has, sir.'

'And the wailers, they have gone?'

Ezra nodded, and reluctantly the old man followed him out of one wing of the house, through the hallways into the other, entering the quarters of his wife.

She was reclining on a low sofa, freshly washed and dressed in clean day clothes. Her beauty had long faded with age, but her face seemed handsome enough for the old man's satisfaction.

'So, you have decided mourning is over,' she said bitterly.

Asri walked past her and stood at the window, wishing he was free to fly. He looked down at the people walking back and forth on the street below and wished he could change places with the least of them.

'I cannot focus with all of this distress, all of this noise; it has gone on long enough.'

'I have lost my son.'

'But not your sanity. It is time to get on with life – we must find Mina.'

She began to sob and wail, and the old man rolled his eyes and fought back his anger.

'That does not help!' he bellowed. 'Enough of this self-pity!'

'Self-pity! Self-pity!' She raised her hands and pulled hard on her maidservant, who nearly fell over.

'Do you hear his cruelty?'

CHAPTER 10

✦ ✦ ✦

Rachel woke early. The sun had barely broken the hold of darkness, and a grey mist filled the gullies and ravines below them where the mountain fell down into the lap of the great lake. The crows were squawking, and higher up the gulls were shrieking as if to warn the party of some dire consequence that awaited them. She moved away from the smouldering fire, through the sleeping figures, past the two guards and down a small track that led to the edge of a vast precipice. She stood letting the breeze lift her skirts and gown in the undulating pattern of the wind gusting up from below.

The broken slabs of grey stone glistened in the drizzle washing away the stains of the night. She looked down into the depths of the great hollow before her and fancied seeing strange forms congealing in the retreating shadows – creatures slinking, skulking and hovering in monstrous motions of ill will and contempt towards the light. She felt like letting go, falling head-first into the abyss of unholy convocation – freed at last of the pain that burned inside her. If Anna was safe, why would she wrench her away from the soft reality of normal people, of a predictable, orderly life? No, Rachel would be better dead than alive. But if Anna were in trouble, abused in one of Boataz's brothels, then she could not rest until she had saved her. Neither outcome would bless her.

She chided herself. Why had her constant attempts at escaping been foiled when the child had first been taken? Why had the fates conspired to imprison her over and over again? She shuddered at the thought of

Boataz murdering her – it had been an ever-present threat throughout her life. She had seen him kill before, and it terrified her. Even now, she shook with terror of the man who had ruined her – trying to suppress a side of her that wanted to go and beg his forgiveness and slink back into the care of the madam.

'What are you doing?' asked a voice.

She looked behind her and found Barnabas staring at her.

'Just thinking, deeply,' she replied, looking at the short, stocky man with the well-cut beard and oiled hair. He was a picture of rude health and gentility, his clothes carefully cut and cleverly stitched with golden thread around the edges. His face looked troubled, his eyes unstinting in what Rachel discerned as contempt for her.

'What do you want to say to me, Barnabas? Just spit it out.'

'Am I that easily read?'

'Unfortunately, I have grown adept at reading a man's intentions.'

'What are your intentions?' he asked.

'My intentions?'

'Towards Thomas. You know, he comes from a very noble and well-to-do family, and...'

'And what, exactly?'

'And quite frankly, his association with you will come as quite a shock.'

'That association would be no more shocking than to me as I do not have any intention or inclination to spend my time with such a dreamer – so your fears are quite unfounded.'

'But he likes you, and I know what Thomas is like.'

'Are you suggesting he has a penchant for fallen women?'

'No, he has a penchant for you, and nothing will stop him pursuing you for as long as you are here.' His words trailed into an awkward silence. She looked away from him, back at the contorted mass of rock, and wanted to dash herself against the rocks in protest at this little man's effrontery.

'What do you suggest I do, kind sir?'

'We can take the child to her grandparents in Capernaum. You need not fear our resolve and sense of duty, madam. Why not leave these hills now? Slip out of the camp and save yourself. Flee to Lebanon, Egypt or Jerusalem. You would love Jerusalem – it is so vibrant and happy. Why remain here, being pursued by this monster, Boataz, and his brigands?'

'I have a bastard daughter whom Boataz took from me as a child. Mina's grandparents could help me locate her. Why would I depart from this, my only hope of finding peace?'

'Good God, I am sorry, but Thomas…'

'Thomas can look after himself,' said a voice behind Barnabas.

'Thomas, please see reason. You cannot bring dishonour on your family name like this.'

Thomas walked over to Rachel and offered her his hand. For some reason, she reached out her own and gripped his as hard as she could as he pulled her from the edge of the precipice and led her along the trail, away from Barnabas. His face was ashen and his eyes blazing with indignation.

'Rachel, I am so sorry,' he said when at last they were behind huge rocks out of sight.

'It is I who am sorry, sorry that I embroiled you in this mess,' she wanted to cry but dabbed her eyes with the back of her hand. 'Your friend seems to believe strange and fanciful notions of the likelihood of your affections towards me that I cannot fathom or countenance.'

'They are not unfathomable, Rachel. I want to help you…'

'I am a pitiful project who needs the cleansing waters of your master's messianic powers – when all I want is the return of my child born out of wedlock and in the depths of my own horror. You can tell him I want nothing to do with you, Thomas. You are a child, and I, inside, am an old hag of a woman aged by the sorrow of a thousand memories of ruin. I am corrupt, toxic, blasted and poisonous to your very happiness, so please leave me alone and put your poor friend's fretting mind at peace.'

'Do not speak like that, Rachel. I know this not to be true.'

'Then you are a naïve fool – you are playing with fire. I suggest Mina, Jinan and I cast ourselves on our own fortune and ask you to leave us as we travel the last part of the journey into Capernaum.'

'No,' he said, crossing his arms and looking crestfallen and deflated. 'I will not let that monster harm you.'

'Nor will I let this monster who stands before me cleanse me with his offer of holy redemption.'

'Is that what I am to you – a monster?'

'Most decidedly; the worst kind – a moralising bigot.'

'Then I will escort you to Capernaum and leave you in peace, woman. It is time the camp stirred. I must speak to the scouts.'

Rachel crossed her arms and watched him retreat from the scene and rejoin Barnabas. The two men argued as they returned to the camp.

Inside Rachel, a tender, innocent maiden, caught in a cage of iron, shook with violent despair, banging her fists and shouting out at her captor in rage. But what could she do, the ruined woman, but keep herself under lock and key until she found her daughter?

It had not taken long for Gritz and Babr to catch up with the party. They watched from a safe distance as the camp stirred into life. The long line of ponies, provisions and people stretched out as it began moving along for the day. The ponies moved slowly, inching along the tiny track that snaked along the top of the mountain.

'What do you think they will do? Find shelter or press on towards Capernaum?' asked Babr.

'It is hard to say; we can follow at a distance and see what happens.'

'We will freeze if they stay too long on this damned mountain,' muttered Babr.

'If they settle, you can go ahead and warn Boataz about where they will rejoin the road to Capernaum, and I will stay in pursuit of them.'

Babr seemed uninterested and returned to the horses hidden out of sight and grazing on what scrub they could find.

Gritz thought of the old woman of the mountain and her boy Jinan, who was somewhere in the distant party. If he could capture him and return the boy to his mistress, perhaps she could, through divination or other strange means, discern where his treasure was buried. He could escape back to Tiberias, load a wagon and flee back to his homeland. The thoughts had disturbed his night, and he had slept poorly. He tried to wipe the tiredness from his eyes, pressing his knuckles into his eye sockets, but nothing could rid him of his headache and fatigue.

Once the party ahead had started moving, they mounted their horses and followed the trail, careful to keep out of sight. They travelled all day and well into the night until they came across the party setting up camp at the entrance of a cave system. A roaring bonfire had been lit, and the two men shuddered in the increasing cold of night.

The fire had been lit in the mouth of a huge cave that accommodated all of the party. Mina sat with Jinan, warmed by its furious flames.

'What do you see in the flames, Mina?' asked the boy, who had been deeply agitated all day.

'I see nothing,' replied Mina.

'I can see Shadrach, Meshach and Abednego, bound but not consumed by the flames. They are protected by he who stands in dignity and majesty beside them. How funny that he should appear now, of all times, this man of fire, this saviour, in our time.'

'You mean the Messiah? You can see him in the fire?'

'He has always been there, in all of our history, but we will not recognise him; we will cast him into the fire like discarded wood.'

'Thomas says the Healer is the Messiah and he will heal you and set you free. He teaches along the shores of the lake. Once I am reunited with my grandfather, we can all go and receive the healing we need. He will take this pain from my heart and this horror from my mind – he will heal Mathias – he will set you free of your malady and heal my grandfather and grandmother of their great loss – imagine!'

'Not all will be saved as not all will believe this truth,' muttered the boy.

'But the Messiah will reign for a thousand years. He will beat back the Romans and set up a new kingdom that will last for ever. Who will not believe?'

'She won't let me go,' he said mournfully.

'What do you mean? Who?'

'The old woman. She has sent a man to capture me and bring me back to her. I can hear her talking to him, sense her intentions to have me returned to her lair where I will pander to her every whim and fancy.'

'You can't possibly know that!' cried Mina.

97

'He doesn't know what fate awaits him. He is fearful of her and will do everything he can to grasp his treasure,' whispered the boy.

'Jinan, please rest. Thomas will protect us. He will get us to safety – no one will capture you.'

The boy laid his head on her lap, and she stroked his scabbed face until he slept. She leant back on the bundles of clothes that were her bed and shut her eyes, waiting for slumber to come.

✦ ✦ ✦

The snap of a twig or branch awakened Babr, who grasped his knife and awakened Gritz, who sprang up, ready to strike at the figure standing before them.

'Spare my life or she will be angry with you,' said the boy, holding a lantern that lit up his face.

Babr raised his fist to strike the boy, but Gritz intervened.

'Leave him; he may have much to tell us.'

'What is he doing here? How did he know we were here?'

'We live in strange times, Babr, strange times. This is the witch's boy; who knows what power she wields?'

'You have to take me back, or she will kill me!' cried the boy.

Babr looked confused.

'You continue following the party. I must take this boy back.'

'Back where? To steal our gold? No, you don't!' Babr lunged at Gritz and pushed him onto the ground. He picked up a short sword and lifted it over his head to plunge it into the fallen Gaul, then suddenly cried out in pain and fell to his knees.

'She is at work – flee!' cried the boy as Babr rolled on the floor, convulsing.

'Get the horses,' commanded Gritz, watching in horror as Babr writhed in agony on the rocky ground.

Jinan and Gritz mounted the horses and rode back down the trail towards Magdala, leaving Babr in silent paroxysms of pain.

'What happened back there?' shouted Gritz.

'Demons! They have entered him – they are everywhere,' Jinan told him, with a shrill laugh. 'The Lord of darkness has entered the land with his cohort!'

Gritz shuddered. How had the boy known where they were hiding? How did his presence line up with his thoughts unless the witch had put them there in the first place? What if he were being tricked? Boataz would wreak savage punishment for his disobedience if he could not escape the land with his gold intact.

They rode south through the darkness, allowing the horses to pick the safest course over the rocky terrain. Gritz waited until sunrise to interrogate the boy but found him maddeningly vague and wayward in his thoughts.

✦ ✦ ✦

Mina was beside herself. Jinan had disappeared, and despite all their searches, they found no clue to his departure, except a stolen lamp. Scouts were sent north and south along the track to find him. Thomas and Barnabas were the first to find Babr.

He was sitting on the rock face above them as they rode south, his clothes ripped from his body and his skin scratched and bleeding; clearly insane, he bellowed and barked and shouted at the sky.

'Who is this madman?' exclaimed Barnabas as Thomas skirted around the rocks trying to find a way to climb up to the poor fellow. After a number of tries, he managed to find a route to the top and approached the man, who was naked in the cold sunlight.

'Get away from me,' hissed the man when he saw Thomas.

'We are looking for a boy; he went missing last night – did you see him?' asked Thomas, nervous about the answer.

'The boy came to us demanding he be taken off to be with mother… where he belongs…' said one voice from the man.

'Bewitched, she has bewitched me…' cried another.

'Speak not to the vileness…' he suddenly cried with a grimace.

'Get away, get away…' He leapt from one rock to another, edging closer to the precipice. 'The boy will soon be back with mother,' he said with exaggerated calm.

As Thomas stepped forward, Babr threw himself off the rock and fell, with a cry, beyond Barnabas' grasp, dashed to death on the rocks.

Barnabas joined Thomas, and they inspected the area around the rocks. They found Babr's clothes ripped and shredded by his own hands, his sword, his sandals and a burned-out fire. Barnabas made out the tracks of two horses.

'It looks like we were being followed by two riders. The boy disturbed them and has been abducted.'

'There is much evil here,' whispered Thomas fearfully.

'What did that creature mean by the boy came to them to be with mother?'

CHAPTER II

✦ ✦ ✦

'Jinan decided to go back to whatever he knew as home,' Rachel said softly to Mina, who had stopped crying.

'But she is an evil hag if what you say is true.'

'Look, let us get you to safety, allow the authorities to apprehend Boataz, and then we can go and find Jinan; we know where he will be.'

'This is your fault,' muttered Mina.

'My fault?' replied Rachel with surprise.

'If you had more trust in the Healer, Jinan would have trusted that he could save him.'

'That is grossly unfair – how can I believe in someone I have not met?'

Mina stormed off, shouting abuse at Rachel. Thomas came over to her and tried to support her.

'Please, leave me alone,' protested Rachel, pushing past Thomas and following Mina down the trail.

✦ ✦ ✦

Gritz followed Jinan, who seemed to know a way through the mountains that avoided the need to descend into Magdala and take the coast road to Theims. He kept his distance, not wanting to invoke any anger from the boy or the old woman whom he called mother. Jinan did not stop talking to himself or his horse; Gritz concentrated on carefully guiding his horse behind the boy.

They stopped for lunch, and Gritz unfolded food and presented a flask of water to the boy, whose face and arms were badly scarred and scabbed by the fire.

He seemed calmer when he ate but still spoke nonsense to himself in a low set of whispers.

'I will beg your mistress, mother, to help me find my treasure that is buried in Boataz's grounds. Do you think she will help me?'

Jinan, he decided, was no longer present in the moment; he appeared to be somewhere quite different in his soul. Gritz shook with fear. He had faced death a hundred times, with a smile, and found his way back to life, but this power, this present evil, unnerved him.

'Can you tell your dear mother that I will do everything I can to get you safely back to her? In exchange for information.'

The boy looked at him with darkened eyes and a sullen expression. His cheeks seemed to draw in, and his lips tighten, and for a moment, Gritz saw the reflection of the old woman in his mien.

'Bring the boy to me... and you shall have your treasure...' Jinan mumbled in a grave voice, far beyond his years.

'What did you say, boy?' Gritz asked. But Jinan returned to mouthing silent incantations.

The visit of the centurion, Portius, had unnerved Asri, who sat in the darkened room, wishing he could share his burden with another fellow human. Not that he had ever spoken much about it, even when he and Phillip had spent time alone. It was an unspoken rule not to mention anything about the secret transaction with the wine merchant from Tiberias. But at least the pair knew; they understood each other. They had a mutual understanding. All Phillip had to do was pay the merchant what he was due. How could his son have screwed up with a man like that?

He sat waiting in Ezra's room. The day was breaking down, desecrated by the oncoming shadows of night dirtying the sky. Could he take the servant into his confidence? He dared not share anything that would incriminate him in front of the synagogue or the Roman authorities and fretted over what he would lose if the truth were to come out.

Elizabeth had calmed down since he had disbanded the mourning party. She had slumped from hysteria into a general malaise of depressed silence. Not that he had chosen to spend much time with her – he was determined not to be distracted from the main task of the rest of his life – to find Mina and restore her to the family fortune.

Ezra entered the room and bowed.

'Sir, I did not see you there; forgive me – I would have knocked.'

The man was tall and slender and had purpose written through every particle of his being. He was dependable and resilient, obedient and resourceful, everything his son Phillip was not. How Asri had longed for a son like Ezra.

'Any news, Ezra?' asked Asri, surprised at his own tone of annoyance and impatience.

'This was a long time ago, master. Our records are scant, but I checked with the store master and he remembered doing business with a tall, unruly wine merchant from Tiberias. Although he did not recall his name, he remembered that the man had an agent here in Capernaum, Tobias the vintner, who lives in the square. I visited the man, who remembered the fellow well – he goes by the name of Gan Ben Gilad. He's a very wealthy merchant in Tiberias.'

'We must ride south and meet this man.'

'Master, this is the surprising thing. Tobias the vintner said not a day ago he saw this Gan Ben Gilad in this very town. He was sojourning at the Black Tavern. I asked Tobias to arrange a meeting with the fellow, but the old man was so gripped with fear that he refused to have anything to do with him.

'I took the liberty, master, of making enquires at the Black Tavern, and true enough, this Gan Ben Gilad took rooms yesterday for four nights. I left a message with the tavern owner to arrange an urgent meeting with his guest and have just returned with news that we will meet one of the fellow's intermediaries down by the shore at eight o'clock tonight.'

'This is good news. Perhaps this fellow can lead us to the men who have abducted Mina.'

'Master, you need not take me into your confidence, but why would this man know anything about that terrible night?'

'You are right, Ezra; I need not take you into my confidence,' said the old man with a sigh.

'You need to go unattended, and if the intermediary suspects you have been followed or have alerted the authorities, this Gan Ben Gilad will have nothing to do with you. Master, it is not wise that you should go alone. Why do we not send a party ahead of you just to hide and be on hand in case there is any trouble?'

'No, Ezra. I will go unattended. My life could not get any worse; it has no value anymore, so I no longer fear even death.' Asri stared out into the growing darkness that had entered the room. Sin was crouching at his door and he had no way of mastering it, not since his heart had been ripped from his chest. He regretted being so wound up, so brutal with his servant, and mused over how much he should say.

'Phillip owed this fellow a lot of money; I mean a lot of money. You do not need to know for what reason. I have checked his affairs, and it seemed this merchant from Tiberias had rendered diverse services to Philip, at an exorbitant cost. I just assumed Phillip had paid him all of the money that he owed. For this Gan Gilad is not a person that one trifles with. I always knew he was a violent and dangerous man masquerading as a respectable merchant because of the nature of the tasks that he performed for us.

'If Phillip had double-crossed such a man, I would not be surprised if revenge was the motive for killing my son and his household for the man was quite clear on his terms and the consequence of any failure of my son to repay his debt.'

'Master, why not send for the procurator? They will apprehend this man.'

'A man who would not think twice about murdering my granddaughter? No, I seek to repay the debt that is owed plus the interest he will no doubt charge in exchange for my granddaughter. You have done well, Ezra.'

The old man decided to visit Elizabeth just to reduce the nagging guilt he felt about neglecting her. His grief found outlet only in tears before the rabbi, who provided some solace in his indomitable trust in God. Elizabeth had been a nightmare of loud moaning, wailing and gnashing of teeth, which he could not bear to witness.

Now she was quiet, lying in her bed, the clean covers pulled up and almost covering her face. Her maidservant left the room as Asri entered.

'So you have decided to show up,' she said sarcastically.

'I am meeting certain representatives who I am hopeful will bargain for the return of the child.'

'Please do not mock me with such a thought too precious to bear.'

'Hold your nerve, Elizabeth, and we may have her back.'

'And that will make everything right, will it? What about the blood-soaked walls and floors of their house? Who will scrub them clean?'

'If you raise your voice, I will leave you.'

'Raise my voice? You are the ruin of us all with your stupid ideas and contrivances!'

It did not take long for the vitriol to fuel abuse, and the old man left her shouting and ranting. He headed for the counting house where he could while away the time tending to his business affairs.

When night fell, he dressed in warm clothes, wrapped a thick ermine cloak around himself and left on horseback for the lake. The streets were almost empty, and a cold wind hurtled around every corner. The sky was starless and dull when he arrived at the shoreline and allowed the horse to graze on the dried-out grass heads dotting the beach of stones.

Eight o'clock came and went. An hour later, cold and somewhat annoyed, Asri turned the horse to return home when he noticed another rider, watching beside a boathouse along the shore. The rider motioned for him to join him, and nervously Asri rode over. The two started to ride slowly along a track pulling away from the town towards a bluff pushing out into the lake. The rider was silent until, hidden in total darkness, they came to a standstill by a small jetty.

A lantern was suddenly lit, and Asri could see men in a boat beckoning him to dismount and join them. He walked down the jetty and got into the boat, which was soon heaved out onto the surface of the lake. The moon breaking through the clouds showed them far from shore, floating on dark mauve and green waters. The lantern was extinguished and at last someone spoke.

'What is your business, old man?'

'I come to undo the wrongs of my son,' said Asri bitterly.

'Some wrongs have terrible consequences,' said Boataz, gripping the old man by the throat. 'Your lousy son was a thorn in the side, so, if he was like his father, we can end this now by throwing you weighted into the lake!'

'Gan Ben Gilad, if you had come to me, there would have been no trouble. The deal was struck between you and me; my son was merely to pay the price.'

'Your son paid the ultimate price in crossing me – so heed my warning, old man. If you cross me, I will destroy you and your whole household. My men have very specific orders. Even if I were taken by the authorities, nothing could protect you from my wrath.'

'The authorities need not know anything of this. I just want my granddaughter back – please tell me she is still alive.'

'She is alive, and well, but I need to see some intent before we even discuss her further.'

'Intent?'

'Yes,' said Boataz and laughed. 'Do you take me for a fool? Your son owed me a thousand denarii. Pay me that and we can talk. Then, if you are found to be trustworthy, you can pay me two thousand denarii more for the return of your granddaughter.'

'Three thousand denarii? How am I meant to find that sort of money?'

'I do not care. I just want my money!' growled Boataz.

After a day's ride, the weather turned for the worse. Rain deluged down upon the mountain, and thunder bellowed in the heavens riven by streaks of lightning. Gritz was almost grateful to see, at last, the small light illumining the old witch's hut. Jinan brought the horses into the stable, wiped them down and prepared their feed.

Gritz followed Jinan through a side door into the evil-smelling house encased in a darkness that was alive and malignant. The old woman was nowhere to be seen. The pair sat by the fire and began to eat the contents of a large pan of boiled rabbit that had been prepared for them. After eating, the boy lay on the floor, imperceptibly shaking. Gritz looked at the strange contents of the many jars around the fireplace.

When the boy was asleep, the old woman, stooped and decrepit, appeared in the doorway. She came over to the fireplace, stroked the boy's head and muttered some incantations, causing the boy to shake and then rest in a deep slumber.

'Mother, I have bought him back at your bidding,' said Gritz, frightened by the ugliness of the old woman.

'A great light has broken forth in the darkness,' she said, sitting down opposite Gritz. 'And the darkness reviles it. The boy is now free of demons… He should never have gone beyond my authority.'

'Demons?' Gritz shuddered at the memory of childhood tales of ghouls and demons haunting the forest and falling upon poor souls who had lost their way.

'They are pouring into this land from the north, the south, the east and the west – the great and the least, mighty ones whose dominion spans aeons, all focused on the wrath that is to come when they shall smite his heel and he shall crush their heads.'

'What of me, mistress?' asked Gritz, nervously fingering his beard.

'You have a place in it all, oh thief. But first, we must repay you with the location of your gold.' She cackled, throwing powder into the fire that caused a great splash of colour and sparks.

To Gritz's relief, she closed her eyes and began to describe Boataz's outbuildings and land. She mentioned a disused well beside an old block of abandoned stables. There he would find his gold and more. But he needed to fly through the night and ride hard the next day to avoid the authorities who were now investigating the murders of the Roman soldiers in Magdala. Soon all routes in and out of Tiberias would be guarded by soldiers who would apprehend any alien.

'Can I escape the curse?' asked Gritz, fighting against the foreboding rising in his heart.

'You cannot escape your destiny, thief,' said the old woman, chuckling, 'but in your case, it is worth trying. Now go.'

CHAPTER 12

✦ ✦ ✦

The disappearance of Jinan and the death of Babr had intensified the gloom hanging over the camp. Rachel spent the morning tending to Thomas's brother Mathias, who had developed running sores on his legs where he had been tied onto the pony. The youth was tall and handsome but disabled by a crippling disease he had suffered since a child, leaving his limbs weak and spindly.

They had retrieved the body of Babr and buried him some distance from the camp, leaving Rachel alone with Mathias.

'What madness is this, that a man should throw himself onto the rocks like that?' whispered Rachel, cleaning the wounds running right down the inside of the youth's legs.

'It is demonic. He was clearly possessed; that is what they are saying, at least.'

'And that is what you believe – in demons?' asked Rachel diffidently.

'Why are you so angry with the Healer?' asked Mathias softly, with some difficulty in breathing.

Rachel was surprised at both the question and her antipathy towards this unknown source of disquiet in her heart.

'I do not want to talk about it – let's change the subject.'

'No, Rachel, it is important. Why are you so angry with the very notion of a Healer?'

'I have no problem with healers. It's just the kind that want to wash away your sins that I have a problem with – kind of makes you feel filthy, don't you think?'

'I am sorry that you have suffered so much, Rachel. But we have all sinned… our whole nation contends with sin. He heals us and washes us of the filth of life. He just puts us right before God, whom he calls Father. Imagine that. David, whom he knew as a friend, could only call him Lord: Lord of refuge, Lord of stronghold, Lord of shield, of might, of power, who stooped down to make him great, yet we can know him as Father. Abba, Father. If we let him in.'

'You are religious, that is clear to me, and I am happy for you. But what would you prefer: your healing or your sins forgiven?'

'Sister, I long to be made right before God so that I can remain in His presence for as long as I live. If he chose to heal me, that would make my remaining years on earth most pleasant, but I would prefer to spend eternity in the presence of God my Holy Father first and foremost.'

'I see religious mania runs in your family,' scoffed Rachel, choosing to suppress the anger she felt whenever the word sin was mentioned. 'Do you come from a large family?' she asked, tidying away the swabs and bandages she had made from her dress.

'It is Thomas, me and our mother. Our father died last year, and the family business was passed on to Thomas. Believe it or not, we are fishermen who have never fished. My father owned a fleet of boats that went out from almost every port and village around the lake, but Thomas was too busy with his studies ever to learn how to fish.'

'What did he study?' asked Rachel tentatively.

'He followed the scribes in Jerusalem and trained to be a rabbi, much to my father's delight. All was going well, according to my father, until he met the Healer, and then everything changed. Thomas had an accident – his right hand was crushed when a tower fell through scaffolding on our estate. The wound festered and ate away at the rest of his arm, and for many months we feared for his life. But he pulled through, maimed and disabled by a rotting hand.

'He heard about the Healer from the fishermen, many of whom gave up their nets and followed him. My father was livid with the man and sent Thomas to investigate.

'Thomas came back a changed man, his hand healed but his life turned upside down. He avowed to follow this Healer, and even though my father could see with his own eyes the miracle of his healing, he would have nothing to do with Thomas. He threatened to disown him unless he returned to his studies as a scribe and denounced this Galilean trouble-maker.

'Nevertheless, Thomas followed the Healer, listening to his every word, only returning to fetch me so I, too, could join the Healer and his family. But a week ago, when we set out to join him, we were set upon by brigands who stole our possessions and our horses. Then, when we were desperate, in the darkness and the rain, we met you... the most beautiful creature he has ever set eyes on.'

Rachel laughed and playfully hit Mathias on the back of the head.

'Don't be hard on him, Rachel. He is a good judge of character and very loyal. He may say the wrong things, but he has a good heart.'

'I am a whore Mathias...' Rachel said bleakly, resisting the young woman's cries deep within her.

'Don't say that.'

'Well, it is true. What has a harlot to do with a scribe, whose very studies state that he should stone me at the city gates? That is a dangerous alliance, do you not think?'

'You have not met the Healer. He will give you a new identity.'

'Healer, Healer, I cannot bear the sound of it! I just need to be left alone to find my daughter, even if it is just to know that she is safe, and then perhaps I can flee this land and find some sanctuary from scribes and their stones.'

'It is a shame.'

'What?'

'My brother does not stand a chance. You are even more beautiful when you are angry.' He laughed, earning himself another playful hit across the back of the head.

He had to lead the horse down the mountain track into Theims, from where he could gallop through the night, southwards along the shoreline to Tiberias. Gritz, the thief, relished the chance to outwit both Boataz and destiny and flee back to Gaul with a wagon filled with gold. The thought obsessed him and ate at him and he drove the mare hard into the night until at last, by sunrise, he was in sight of Tiberias, the mighty city built on a graveyard. The city was said to be cursed, but to Gritz it looked beautiful, its new white sandstone buildings warming in the sunlight and the rooftops, wet with the night's storm, glistening.

The house was empty, and Gritz found it easy to enter and walk through its palatial rooms, wondering why Boataz, or Gan Ben Gilad as he was known locally, would ever risk all of this by continuing a life of robbery. But Boataz would never be suppressed; he needed mayhem, cruelty and crime to keep him interested in life.

Gritz tethered four horses to a cart with the assistance of the stable hands and drove them to the well. On removing the battered hatch, Gritz found, after careful inspection, a set of steps carved in the walls of the well. Gingerly, he descended into the darkness with a lantern. At the bottom, he found casket upon casket. With a rope drawn between the handles of each box, he pulled them out one at a time, climbing and descending until each treasure chest was packed in the cart. The work was painful, hard and dangerous, but Gritz could not help taking the whole stash, robbing Boataz of years of hard work.

He wasted no time, once the treasure was loaded, in covering the caskets with barrels of wine and sacks of wheat. He drove the cart out of the estate and onto the high road that led to the trading routes to the ports of the Great Sea. He would sail to Rome and then travel on through Italy, across the Alps and into his native land.

His heart beat fast. He was anxious to get out of the city and as far north as he could in the coming day. The threat of brigands, ironically, worried him most, but he had packed swords and daggers aplenty to help him ward off any attackers.

The city gates were not manned by soldiers, and Gritz slipped out of the city unnoticed. He wondered why the old woman had said he had a place to play in the great battle between darkness and light in this most strange land. She had prophesied that he would be caught, tried and condemned by the Romans, but she had not alluded to when. He hoped that, back in Gaul, he could at least settle into the life of a farmer, marry one of the local girls and bring up a family before he was apprehended by death. The hag had said he could not escape destiny, but something inside him swore that he, Gritz the thief, would cheat death itself.

'They are all crazy in this godforsaken land…' he thought as he whipped the horses into a gallop along the main road leading through the mountain passes onto the main road to Antioch.

✦ ✦ ✦

'She is right,' said Barnabas, looking at Mathias, who was lying on a blanket by the fire.

'I am not a scribe,' protested Thomas.

'But she is who she says she is. Wherever she goes, she is in danger of being stoned.'

'The Healer can protect her, and I can take her to him.'

'What can he do?' asked Barnabas.

'He can do all things,' whispered Thomas. 'I need to get her and Mathias into his presence – he will know what to do.'

'You should not keep going on about your Healer – it makes her feel unclean and more detestable than she already feels,' said Barnabas.

'My brother will not listen; he is truly smitten,' teased Mathias.

'I am smitten by the unjustness of her circumstances. She is a woman of natural integrity and nobility – is it her fault she was snatched as a child into such a heinous life of horror? It is too much for me to think what she has been through.'

'Smitten by the unjustness of her circumstances,' scoffed Mathias. 'It's just coincidental that she is so beautiful.'

'That is purely coincidental,' said Thomas, shaking his head and suppressing a smile.

'I think it is time to move towards Capernaum – we are but a day's ride away. I see no point in waiting here now they know where we are,' said Barnabas.

'I agree. We need to push on and see what fate awaits us,' added Thomas.

The camp was broken up and all the supplies and provisions loaded back on the ponies and donkeys ready for a final descent into Capernaum.

Rachel packed her and Mina's things into a simple bundle and loaded Jinan's black mare. Mina sat sullenly in its saddle and allowed Rachel to lead her into the midst of the group beginning to leave under a pale but warm sky.

'Once you are reunited with your family, I will go and find Jinan and rescue him. Please do not fret. He feels safe with the old woman.'

'He needs deliverance from the spirits that afflict him – all she does is bind him with the darkness of her magic.'

'Please, I have done with magic. Let's just get you to your family.'

'And then what? I have no family. My grandfather and grandmother are nothing to me – not without my father and mother. We hardly saw them. You are not the only one who has suffered great loss, Rachel.'

'We do not have to weigh up the horror of it all. Grief is grief. You are still mourning, and it will take time for you to recover.'

'Recover what?'

'A sense of future, of hope,' said Rachel as vehemently as she dared.

'Apart from the Messiah, there is no hope.'

'It is dangerous to put your hope in a person or persons that you do not really know – they tend to be unreliable in the extreme.'

'He will usher in the kingdom,' said Mina loudly.

'Stop. Messiah, Healer, demons, magic – it is all rubbish. Why do you fill your head with such trifles? Face reality. We are both being pursued by a callous murderer who will stop at nothing to see us both annihilated – well, at least me. You, maybe, he will see as having some worth, but me – I am worthless.

'Will your Healer, Messiah and deliverer stop a man like that? No, he would probably faint if Boataz got hold of him.'

'So you are frightened,' said Mina quietly.

'Of course I am frightened! Your and Thomas's naivety appals me. I have had to face harsh, cruel reality, pawing and slobbering over my whole body every day of my life, only to find out that the fairies could have saved me if I'd just had sufficient faith.

'I cannot be saved, Mina. I can never be rescued. It has all been too much to bear. I am ruined. Your Messiah will have nothing to do with the likes of me. I am scum. Fallen. Corrupted and moribund. Do you think I will be invited to his palace when he is crowned King? He will have nothing to do with the likes of you and me.'

'I am sorry, you are so...'

'So what? Horrible?'

'So lovely I forget what you have been through. Forgive me. I owe you my life.'

The young woman in the cage deep inside her was weeping at the meaning of the girl's words, but she blocked her ears and allowed scales to fall over her eyes.

'Let's just get you to safety,' she said, returning to lead the mare along the path.

✦ ✦ ✦

'Three thousand denarii! That will take weeks to raise.'

'Ezra, you have a day to find a thousand and two days to find the rest. Do whatever you have to, sell anything, pledge all our lands if you need to. I need this money urgently.'

Ezra sat down at the table and rubbed the back of his head. He looked steadily at his master.

'Is this what it will cost to have Mina back?' he dared to say.

'That is none of your business.'

'I am sorry, master, but I think I know more than you would understand.'

'Meaning what?'

'You sent me to sort out the affairs of your son last year when he got into financial trouble. I helped him steady the ship and save his own failing business, and we worked many nights and long days together. Day by day, Philipp took me into his confidence.'

'What did he tell you?'

'He owed someone a thousand denarii for a debt of two hundred denarii that had grown through extortion into a small fortune. He was frightened by this person and said he feared for his life.'

'And you didn't think that that was worthy of my notice?' bellowed Asri.

'I promised Phillip I would not tell you; he bound me by an oath. He said he wanted to pay the debt himself but it was leaching the life out of him. But if he did not pay, he feared the debtor would take Mina back.'

'Back?'

'Yes, master, he used that word. I am sorry, but I do not know what is going on. You need to tell me so I can help you as best as I can.'

Asri slumped down onto a low settee and laid his head back on the pillows. He swung his legs around and rested, closing his eyes. For the first time in a very long time, he prayed that God would give him the strength to prevail.

'Secrecy has done us no good,' he whispered, vowing to tell the servant all he knew and at last unburden his soul.

CHAPTER 13

✦ ✦ ✦

'I say we split the party – if you two take Mina down onto Mount Eremos, I will travel north onto the main road to Capernaum and the rest of the party can return to Magdala,' said Barnabas.

Thomas winced and shuffled. 'I would prefer that we stay together or I go with Rachel.'

'She will not have it, Thomas; she thinks this is the best plan. You must get Mina to her grandparents. Get her into the city and to safety, and I will protect Rachel.'

'What is Boataz doing now?' asked Mathias, who was back on his donkey, his feet tied underneath the animal.

'He knows we are taking the mountain route. I suspect he will post lookouts around the grandparent's house and the main trails from the mountain. But if we can slip through unnoticed in twos, we may stand a chance. I have given you the address of a friend; we can regroup there.'

'But what of our own scouts? Perhaps they have alerted the authority and we will meet a company of soldiers – we may get lucky,' added Thomas.

'I think we will need more than luck,' said Mathias, spurring his donkey on along the road.

✦ ✦ ✦

The report was quite alarming. A small company of Roman soldiers had been murdered in Magdala and the procurator had demanded that Portius investigate it. Despite the immense pressure to discover who had murdered the Roman citizens in Capernaum, he now had to suppress some uprising in some godforsaken fishing village, which was closer to Tiberias than Capernaum. The city authorities there were indolent, and Portius was not surprised they had sent for him.

Someone was out of control in the district, and Portius had a mind to put the two events together. Another family had been murdered in Magdala by men disguised as the Roman soldiers they had butchered.

A soldier came into his room and saluted him.

'Sir, there is a man downstairs claiming to need your help – he is in quite a state.'

'I don't have time for this, Servus!' exclaimed Portius.

'He comes from Magdala and says he is escaping a fiend dressed as a Roman soldier who is threatening his master's life.'

Portius raised his eyebrows and commanded the soldier to go and fetch the man. Barnabas's servant entered the room with some urgency and begged the centurion to hear him out.

'My master's life is in danger! Please, you must hear me.'

'What is your name?'

'Eli. I am the gamekeeper for my master, Barnabas, who has taken the mountain trail pursued by a monster called Boataz who, dressed as a Roman soldier, has sought to kill us all. He is pursuing a young girl who has been rescued from his grasp by my master, who is heading here to reunite the girl with her grandparents.'

'What is the girl's name?'

'I cannot remember – she is fifteen, dark-haired; she was abducted from a family here in Capernaum by this Boataz, who is a madman. He sent Roman officers to our house offering to escort us safely to Capernaum, only for us to find out that he was masquerading as a Roman soldier – my master saw them killing one of the physician's servants on the road that runs along our estate.'

'Servus, have we heard of this Boataz?'

'He is the ringleader of a band of brigands that raids the trade routes in the spring and summer months. He has been a pain in our side for years.'

'Do we know where he can be located?'

'No, he is like a ghost – he comes and then just disappears.'

'What road has your master taken, and what can we do to help him?'

'He is asking you to mobilise your men and try to meet him on the road coming in from Capernaum – if you are visible, he will try to make contact with you.'

'How big is the party?'

'We are twenty strong, but he plans to split into smaller groups before coming into the city for fear of being captured by Boataz and his men.'

Portius began to write, asking the servant a host of questions about the party, the girl, Rachel and everyone else the servant could name. After an hour, the man was allowed to leave.

'Shall I mobilise the men, sir?' asked Servus.

'Boataz is in this city, somewhere. I want you to find him. We will not mobilise anybody until we can arrest him. If he sees us galloping out on our horses, he will just disappear.'

'We use the girl as bait?'

'Exactly.'

✦ ✦ ✦

Thomas, Mathias and Mina took an age to get off the main ridge of the mountain and navigate the trail of rocks leading down towards Mount Eremos. The path was windy and narrow, and the threat of a fall real and frightening. They pressed on through the morning and into the afternoon, stopping only for a small meal.

'Who are those?' asked Mathias, pointing down the path towards Mount Eremos.

Thomas leapt to his feet and climbed up on a rock to see whether Boataz's men were approaching. To his surprise, he could see a long trail of people walking on a parallel path across the valley up onto the softer plains of Mount Eremos.

'There is a sea of people!' said Thomas.

'Who are they?' asked Mina.

'I think they are followers!' cried Thomas. 'Come, let us push on and join them – if they are here, then the Healer is not far away.'

'Crowds are good, crowds are good,' cried Mathias as they helped him up onto his donkey.

✦ ✦ ✦

'Why do you fight against it?' asked Barnabas.

'Boataz is my destination – only he knows what he did with my daughter. Mina's grandparents may be able to exert some influence on the authorities to capture him and interrogate him.'

'I just can't see that happening. Mina's family will not want anything to do with you – regardless of your plight or your sacrifice in helping their granddaughter.'

123

'Why do you say such a heartless thing?'

'Look, leave them to me. Go, flee, lie low for a couple of months. You know where I live, but give me time to pursue the truth and then come to me and I will tell you all that I have found. Capernaum is a dangerous place for you.'

'Every place is dangerous to me.'

'Not in the way Capernaum is – it is very religious.'

'And, of course, I have no place amongst the holy men of Capernaum.'

'Flee, Rachel, and trust me,' begged Barnabas.

She laughed. 'How many times have I heard that – you would not believe the number of men that have pledged their love for me and their undying antipathy to my plight. No man can resist a damsel in distress, but it is all meaningless.'

'Why won't you trust me?'

'Because you are a man.'

She kicked on the mare and left him worrying about her safety and the inevitable outcome that awaited her in Capernaum.

Portius was in no mood to be messed about by the old man who feigned ignorance of anything he said.

'So, you say you do not know who this Boataz is; you have never heard of him. Yet it is he who attacked your family and is in pursuit of your granddaughter, who has escaped him in the mountains.'

'I know nothing of the man,' pleaded Asri nervously.

'What is going on here, Asri? Something is not right in all of this. Why would this brigand attack your family and take your granddaughter at random? He is known to attack highways – not rob houses. I believe you are not telling me the truth.'

'I can assure you, if I knew who had abducted my granddaughter, I would let you know.'

'Would you? I somehow doubt that.'

'Has he demanded a ransom? And have you paid anything?' asked Servus, getting to the point.

'I have had no contact with anyone.'

'Old man, if you are lying to me, I will have you scourged… You are a fool if you negotiate with this man, especially as we know he doesn't even have the child. She is being escorted by complete strangers through the mountain passes. If anybody makes contact with you, I must be the first to know. Do I make myself clear?'

Portius and Servus left the house.

'Do you think he is lying?' asked the soldier.

'Most certainly. I believe he has paid money – I want him followed but not by anybody in uniform – use one of the agents.'

Ezra watched the two men walking away down the street. Asri peered over his shoulder.

'What a mess,' whispered Ezra.

'Even if the merchant doesn't have the child, I must pay the ransom or he will never leave me in peace,' said Asri.

'But if we deliver him to the authorities, you get the child back without payment.'

'I must pay him off or he will harm the child one way or another – even if he is locked up, he has ruthless influence.'

'But who is this Boataz?' asked Ezra.

'Maybe he has other names.'

✦ ✦ ✦

Twenty miles along the road to Antioch, Gritz was recognised by a party of Boataz's men who were returning from looking for the girl along the roads to Capernaum.

'Gritz, what are you up to?' asked one of the men riding close by him.

'Boataz has asked me to collect the girl. She has been found,' lied Gritz.

'Thank God for that – we can get back to normal winter life!' said another with a laugh.

'We can ride with you,' said the first rider.

'No, you are to return to Tiberias, telling any of the men you see the same thing. We believe the Roman authorities may be alerted to the madness in Magdala, so get off the road as quickly as you can.'

'Have you got any food? We are starving,' said the first rider, looking in the back of the wagon.

'Just wine and wheat to hide the girl!' said Gritz, laughing, although his heart was pounding.

'It's unusual to see you on your own, Gritz. You and the boss are inseparable,' said one of the men.

'Where did you get the wagon from?'

'Back in the yard. He sent me back to get it.'

'Back in Tiberias?'

'Yes. I need to make haste…'

'That's odd. The lads in Magdala had a wagon – why would you have to go back to Tiberias?'

'The axle broke. I don't know; I just do as I am told, especially when he is in this foul mood – so you can either ride with me and witness his fury or get back to your winter work,' said Gritz bravely as a couple of the men rode around the back of the cart and started poking about in the contents.

'Look, I must get on,' said Gritz, whipping the horses into action. 'Either come or go, but I must keep moving.' To his relief, the men shouted and guffawed and then rode off back down the road to Tiberias.

✦ ✦ ✦

Asri received a note late morning explaining how he was to pay the denarii. There was a consignment of wool in a merchant yard to the south of the city, and he was to contact the owning merchant and purchase the warehouse contents for the thousand shekels.

'We should play for time,' proffered Ezra.

'No, go and make the payment and then gather the remaining money as quickly as you can.'

'But the only way I can do that is by selling large swathes of land at a ridiculous discount. It will cost four thousand to raise three thousand, master. Are you sure?'

'Yes, get on and gather the funds. We will recover without those lands.'

'What if we are being watched by the Romans?' added Ezra.

'This will all be arm's length transactions, I am sure.'

'Any interference from the Romans and our man will bolt, and who knows what he will do,' said Ezra.

'One step at a time. Let's make the first payment and see what transpires.'

CHAPTER 14

✦ ✦ ✦

It took an hour of slow descent before Thomas, Mina and Mathias could cross over the gulley and get to the path that led back up to Mount Eremos. They joined a throng of people who were brightly dressed, fresh-faced and enthusiastic about bringing the sick and the disabled in their hundreds up the torturous path onto the plains leading to the summit of the tall hill at the base of the mountains. Far below, they could see the ships and boats sailing on Lake Gennesaret and a long trail of people still climbing towards them.

Thomas spoke to many people in the long line and asked them whether the Healer was there on the mountain. Many just nodded and expressed their assurance that this was indeed where he planned to teach and minister to them.

Mina felt an inexpressible relief that they could hide in the midst of the crowds.

'Is the Healer here?'

'I do not know, but we will soon find out,' replied Mathias.

They left the horse and ponies grazing, tied to a walnut tree, and went and sat with the crowds gathering around the brow of the hill. Several men and women were standing in a circle praying; the crowds gathered silently around this circle, sitting down on the grass, waiting. A palpable silence, a reverence, a portentous storm of expectation hung over the whole assembly as the exuberant chatter of the journey subsided.

Mina helped Thomas to lift Mathias off the mule and carry him deep into the throng of the sick and the curious. They were surrounded by the baffled and the blighted, but the silence held them in its thrall. Maniacs sat silently and still; those in pain gasped at a new sense of peace and vitality running through their bodies.

'Can you feel him?' whispered Thomas to Mina and Mathias, who shook his head, his face filled with a smile of peace.

The circle of praying men and women sat down as they waited for the Healer to appear. Mina stretched up on her haunches to catch sight of a man who walked around the circle, placing his hands on their heads and blessing them. He was slender, of medium build, tanned and dressed in humble attire. There was nothing in his appearance that marked him out as a prince, a king in waiting, and Mina felt disappointed that he did not seem any grander. She had imagined the Messiah to be more noteworthy, more triumphant, a tall warrior King shining with light. This Healer perspired and wiped his brow continually with a dirty rag. His hair was unkempt and his beard unclipped. His hands looked crooked with overuse and he stood with a slight stoop. There was nothing handsome in his features, and his face did not shine like burnished bronze or his eyes blaze with fire. He seemed so ordinary.

And then he spoke.

His voice was low, slow and penetrating. It demanded attention, not because of the excellence of its message but predominantly through its tone of all-encompassing love. A love so ambitious that it encompassed everything that a master demanded of a loving servant. Or a perfect father of a dutiful son or daughter. He expected so much of love, of loyalty to his revolutionary concepts, that Mina could barely understand.

His was a kingdom of love, of obedience to his example. He spoke of lessons, of warnings, of the bond between himself and his followers.

Then he spoke of God as his Father, and Mina gasped at such blasphemy. Her mind revolted against such notions, knotted up at the thought that this mere man who masqueraded as Messiah was out of his mind.

And then he spoke of the poor, the broken, the distressed, the abandoned and entreated his followers to tend to them like a shepherd tends the flock. He revealed his ambition for change. His expectation of deep commitment to the emerging kingdom of God was validated by an overwhelming sense of love that bathed Mina's heart and seemed to replace her doubt with a seed pearl of hope.

But her heart could not override a sense of confusion over how different this man was from what she had been taught about the nature of messiahship. Perhaps he was just a rabbi, a teacher, after all.

Those closest to him, whom Thomas described as the family of brothers and sisters, pleaded with the man to explain his sayings, eager to plumb the depths of their meaning. Mina found it all hard to follow – it was such revolutionary thinking to understand.

And then his people went into the crowd and brought to him the sick and the broken and he laid hands on them. Mina felt giddy, as if all of the elements in her body were being drawn towards the Healer. The passing day seemed to pause, the sun standing still in the dull sky, slow motion gripping the scene as he prayed, and one by one, everyone he touched experienced his healing and his vitality.

A poor fellow who had been dragged along on a stretcher stood holding his arms up to the sky, praising God. Mina went over to him and looked at his face flushed with joy.

'Can you walk?' she asked softly, suspicious that this man's malady was overstated. He looked at her in a most peculiar way, his body shaking.

'I can walk and I can see!' he replied, lifting his hands towards the Healer hidden in the crowd.

'You can see!' Mina was incredulous. 'You were blind and now you can see.' The man was weeping, holding his face with shaking hands. One by one, people entered the circle and then reappeared rejoicing, crying out to the Son of David. The lame were carried in but walked out. The deaf could hear, the blind see, and the crippled walk.

But not everybody got to enter the strange centre of power emerging in their midst. After half an hour, the followers disbanded, leaving the Healer praying in the centre of a wide circle of the restored.

'What is he doing? Why doesn't he continue?' asked Mina.

'He will be exhausted. They can come again tomorrow,' replied Thomas.

'What of Mathias?' asked Mina, pressing Thomas's arm.

'His time will come, when the family are ready.' He smiled. Mathias nodded, his face beaming with joy.

After an hour or more, his followers, the family, began to break up the crowds with polite requests for them to meet the following day on the shores of Capernaum.

Mina watched the Healer sit on the grass beneath a tree. He was alone whilst his followers dispersed the crowd. She could not help but walk closer to him as he rested his eyes, his head leaning against the tree. He seemed tired, and his face suggested he was struggling, pained. She walked closer and closer, in slow motion, as if a pathway had opened up, mysteriously and preternaturally, through the throng of people, for her to stand at his feet and gaze upon him.

He did not open his eyes. But she knew he could see her.

'Why do you struggle?' she asked softly.

He smiled and opened his eyes.

'It is you, child,' he said gently.

'Master, why do you seem to be in pain?'

'There are many who are sick and infirm who have to wait until tomorrow to be healed in the name of my Father, and it pains me to see them leave here in their malady.'

'Why so?'

'I only do what my Father says... and yes, you are right. There are consequences of my calling him Father. They are quite unavoidable.'

Mina blushed; he seemed to have read her mind.

'Are you the Messiah, then?' she asked.

'No, not your Messiah, that is for sure...' he said with a smile.

She felt compelled to silence. Her heart warmed, and her lungs felt a fresh impetus to breathe in great gulps of air. Each inhalation calmed her mind, softening the iron grip of grief.

'Will you follow me, child? That is the real question,' he said, closing his eyes. She did not feel dismissed or trivialised; she felt invited to sit with him or lie at his feet. She had nowhere else to go where she could find such an overarching sense of safety and well-being.

'I just need to understand it all,' she said slowly and respectfully.

'"It" has a name,' he said and laughed.

Mina was gently pulled from his presence by a petite woman who introduced herself as Ruth.

'Come, child, we are eating with Thomas and Mathias. Leave him to rest; he is tired.'

Ruth's face shone with love and happiness, and Mina smiled at her and followed her back to the brow of the hill where Thomas and Mathias were talking with a group of followers.

She ate the fish and the bread on offer and listened to the men and women discussing the morning's teaching. Thomas was laughing and smiling, and Mathias was being made comfortable by three of the women in the party who sat next to him, propping him up into a seated position so he could eat.

'So, Thomas, you need to bring Mathias to Capernaum tomorrow. He is teaching there, and we can ask him to see your brother,' said one of the followers called Andrew.

'I can wait; there are many worse off than I,' said Mathias with a smile.

'The master has work for you, Mathias. We need you up and about!' retorted Andrew.

'This morning he taught us to pray, as if we never knew how,' said Mina to Thomas.

'We never knew how,' he replied. 'We start every prayer with Lord, with provider, with deliverer, with healer, but he taught us to start every prayer with Father. Our Father. The family of God revealed through the master,' added Thomas.

Mina remembered the conversation she had with the Healer when he had been aware of her doubts and read her mind. But surely this was a form of madness for the Healer to claim he was the son of God? He had used the word 'Abba', the gentlest term of respect and mutual love, to describe the God who had crushed and cleansed the lands for her forebears to claim. The great God Almighty, who would judge the world for the Messiah, was now called daddy. She could not rest with this. She had hidden from this terrible God and cursed him when calamity had befallen her. Now she was invited to let him be her loving Father – it was almost too much to bear, yet she did not doubt it.

'He says he is not the Messiah, so who is he?' she asked, perplexed by the array of new notions flowing through her mind.

'He said he was not your Messiah,' said Ruth.

'You were there?'

'Yes, I followed you as he beckoned you,' she replied.

'What did he mean, my Messiah?'

'He was merely saying that you do not understand who the Messiah is. But we heard him in the synagogue say that this very day the scrolls have been fulfilled in him. The spirit of the sovereign Lord is upon him to preach good news to the poor,' continued Ruth.

'To proclaim freedom to the captives,' added Thomas.

'And heal the broken-hearted,' mused Mina. 'So, you are saying the Messiah is the king of the poor, the captive, the down-trodden and the broken-hearted?'

'Did you not hear him say blessed are the poor, the meek, the humble? He is indeed the Messiah of the maimed – and he has come to set us free, to see the kingdom of God breaking out in this land,' said Ruth.

'But the Messiah will come and drive out the Romans – he will lead us to freedom.'

'So he will,' replied Thomas.

'Does he come from a royal line?' asked Mina.

'He is a carpenter from Nazareth,' laughed Mathias.

'But nothing good can come out of Galilee – the Messiah is of the line of David, king of kings, not a carpenter from the lowest region of Galilee,' protested Mina.

'We are all learning a new way, Mina. Do not fret; you have been called to follow him. So go and think and pray about this – surrender your life and come and join the family as our sister,' invited Ruth.

'I will think on these things...' said Mina.

CHAPTER 15

✦ ✦ ✦

Rachel and Barnabas made good progress down the mountain onto the road to Capernaum. A constant stream of wagons, pedestrians, riders and sometimes heavily laden camel caravans hid their entry onto the thoroughfare in the gloom of late afternoon. The sky was pressed now into a band of pale yellow on the horizon, tinged with red ochre hues. In the west gathered voluminous clouds of grey and mauve shimmering in the lateral rays of the receding sun. Beneath the largest storm cloud lay Capernaum, its intricate architecture gleaming.

Fear and trepidation hammered a relentless beat in her head. She felt sick at being so close to freedom yet so vulnerable. She had not been out of Theims, out of the cloying despair of the house carved in the stone mountain, for so long that the immensity of the sky confounded her. It was almost too much to bear. She imagined the mountains rising up, like an immense stone monster, to suddenly clutch and strangle her, pulling her back into their hideous, craggy prison.

They rode slowly, trying not to draw attention to themselves, down into Capernaum, entering the outskirts of the city at nightfall. Wending their way through narrow streets and muddy roads, Barnabas led them via a circuitous route to the main square where they waited in the centre to see whether they had been followed before heading down one of the side alleys to the house of Barnabas's friend, Ethan the priest.

The man was as young as Barnabas and dressed in all the finery of a priest of a well-to-do synagogue. His house was almost as palatial as

Barnabas's. Rachel could not wait to get off the street and into the safety of a house, but when it came to exchanging greetings and entering the house, Barnabas was awkward and ill at ease.

'I'm sorry, Rachel, but you will have to stay in the stable. I know you may not think this fair, but Ethan cannot have you stay in his house,' said Barnabas, who seemed to have upset his friend with something he had said.

Rachel was shocked and didn't understand until she saw the look of horror on the face of the priest and recognised the look of abhorrence she had seen a thousand times before.

'It is fine,' she said, shaking her head. 'The priest would not want a whore living in his house, would he?' she said angrily.

'Don't speak like that; it is not prudent or safe. One of the servants will tend to you,' said Barnabas stiffly.

A maid carrying a straw mat and bed covers led Rachel to the stables where, piling up bales of straw, she made a bed for her. She was tired and cold and hungry but bid the girl good night, laid her head down on the straw and covered herself with the warm bed clothes.

She thought of Anna and wondered what she was doing right at that moment. She closed her eyes and wondered whether Mina, Thomas and Mathias were safely up at the house. She could not believe that she had made it thus far, that tomorrow they could be speaking to the authorities and she could at last force Boataz to reveal the truth about her daughter.

She slumbered until one of the horses whinnied and made a disturbance. She opened her eyes to see a figure towering over her. She gasped, and a hand grasped her by the throat and lifted her to her feet.

'Whore !' he said through gritted teeth. Boataz's face was riven with hatred and the same anger she had seen before when he killed a girl. She tried to fight him off, but her blows amounted to nothing. He dropped her to the floor where she banged her head and lay defenceless. He kicked her and punched her, then sat on her, pinning her arms to the floor.

'Bring me the girl, at the Black Tavern, or I will kill your Anna – by nightfall tomorrow!' He slapped her hard across the face and left her.

She wept and shook with fear. She gulped in air but felt she couldn't exhale. She felt violated again, her body ravaged and brutalised by a man whom she hated. Alone, in the darkness, she could not stop crying – what was she to do? Could she never escape the brutality of the man? How could she save Anna and Mina? What about her slight hope that Mina and Anna were the same person? She felt exhausted, wasted, blown over and corrupted by fear and self-loathing.

She could not move her body and seemed wedded to the mucky floor of the stable. Outside, the storm clouds poured tears on the city, the weeping sky trying to wash away the filth of the day.

'What the hell were you thinking of?' shouted Thomas, pushing Barnabas in the chest.

He, Mathias and Mina had stayed out on Mount Eremos with the followers of the Healer all night and had followed the family and many others into the city. They enjoyed a sense of well-being and raised spirits hidden in the crowd of people who poured into the streets, ready to follow the Healer down onto the shoreline for that morning's teaching and healing.

'She could not stay in the house; she would defile it,' explained Ethan, the priest resolute in keeping to his beliefs and well prepared to repel the criticism of his friend Barnabas.

'She has been beaten black and blue and is unconscious! What sort of friendship is this?' protested Thomas.

'She is not allowed in this house, and if that is too much for you, then I beg you, consider finding some other place,' said the priest angrily.

'This is a nightmare. What must she think of us?' exclaimed Thomas.

Mina came back into the room, wiping tears from her face.

'She is awake, but she will not speak to me. Perhaps you should go to her.'

'You can have nothing to do with this woman, Thomas,' declared the priest.

'And why, exactly, not?'

'She is unclean, ritually, spiritually, physically, in every respect. It is cruelty to keep her here. She has no place here, and she knows this well enough,' shouted the priest.

'Cruelty to expose her to a beating, if not worse!' Thomas shook his head and left the house, pushing Barnabas away when he tried to hold him back. He went through the house, descended from the kitchen and entered the stable where the maid was dabbing an apron on Rachel's bruised face and cracked lip.

'I am so sorry,' said Thomas softly, hating himself for leaving her with Barnabas.

She said nothing and did not look at him. He dismissed the maid and sat next to her, looking at her black eye and the dry blood crusted around her nose.

'Stop it!' she shouted as he tried to wipe her face with the wet flannel.

'What happened?'

'I fell over in the night,' she said frostily.

'Was it him?'

She ignored him and wiped her face hard with the flannel.

'What did he do to you?'

She dropped the flannel and shook her head.

'What is it to you what he did? Whatever your imagination tells you is what he did.'

'Don't say that!' remonstrated Thomas, appalled at her condition.

'He beat me and would have killed me if it were not for lights up at the house that disturbed him. He fled before he could finish his work on me.'

'Dear God,' groaned Thomas.

'Is that your Healer – the priest – who left me lying in the muck?' she asked angrily.

'Of course not; the man is a bigoted fool.'

'And you are different, of course, because you want to lie with me with completely different motives from all of the rest of them,' she said bitterly, trying to stop listening to the force within her that wanted to be held.

'How can you say that?' said Thomas, hurt by her words.

Her young inner self was screaming at her to relent, but she set her face like flint towards Thomas and rebuffed him. She would have nothing to do with impossible pipe-dreams. She had a massive dilemma to face and she had to face it alone.

Thomas returned to the house and sat with Barnabas out of earshot of the priest.

'She is refusing to move or say anything except Boataz attacked her last night,' said Thomas.

'We were not followed; I did everything I could to evade notice. We need to move to another quarter. But if it was this fiend, why did he not kill her?'

'She said lights in the house disturbed him.'

'I have checked with Ethan, and there was no disturbance in the night. No one heard a thing and no one lit a light. I am afraid she is lying and possibly hiding something he may have said to her. We have to move fast and move Mina to a safe place; her security is compromised. I will go to her grandfather's house and raise the alarm this very morning. In the meantime, you must take her to another location. We can hide her in a covered wagon and send one of the servants to take her to my cousin's house.'

'And what of Rachel? She is depending upon the capture of Boataz. Should we not just go to the Roman authorities?'

'The grandfather is the only one who can bring that influence to bear on the case; they will not heed enquiries from Rachel.'

'She has done nothing wrong, yet the world treats her with such contempt.'

'Do not be naive, Thomas. She is damaged goods… and there is nothing you can do about it.'

'Stop talking about her as if she is some object!' cried Thomas, at his wits' end about how to protect Rachel from herself.

Mina was not happy with the recommendation to move and refused to leave Rachel, whom she had washed and dressed as best she could. Nothing Barnabas or Thomas could say would change her mind until Rachel intervened and insisted she went.

'All will be lost if you do not go. They know we are here, and at any moment they could invade the house and kill you all.'

'I cannot leave you here in these conditions…' protested Mina.

'You must,' whispered Rachel, touching the girl's head. 'Our very lives depend upon it.'

'When will I see you again?'

'Soon we will all be reunited,' said Thomas.

Thomas and Mina lay in the back of an open-top wagon, hidden by sacks. They followed Barnabas out onto the narrow streets into the square from where he sent the carriage on a fast and furious tour of the city's alleyways and side streets, he following at a distance to see whether anybody was following. As on the previous day, he could find no evidence of being tracked. He left the wagon after half an hour and set off for the house of Asri the merchant.

✦ ✦ ✦

Thomas was beside himself with worry about Rachel, but Ethan had promised to ensure two male servants would guard her from further harm. Mathias had agreed to sit with Rachel and comfort her. Peering through a gap in the wagon's tail gate, Thomas could catch glimpses of the city, and he looked out for anybody who might have been following them. After an hour of travelling around, he noticed a rider on a dark horse, his face wrapped in a linen scarf, had appeared from the crowd of passers-by, and whatever direction the wagon took, he remained a hundred paces behind them. He managed to shout to the wagon driver to take them down to the coast road and loop back on himself.

The dark rider continued following them at a distance. Once down by the coast, the wagon slowed, caught up in an eddy of people streaming down onto the beach in search of the Healer.

'Stop!' cried Thomas, and the wagon came to a standstill. He could see the outrider confused and caught up in the great influx of people.

'Quick, turn the wagon around!' Thomas cried. 'Mina, we have to get out through the tail gate and get into the crowd.'

The wagon turned, Thomas drew the bolt on the tail gate and he and Mina slipped into the crowd. He closed the wagon and ordered the driver to ride straight past the confused outrider, who had not seen them get out of the wagon and disappear in the crowd.

Mina held Thomas's hand and they fled into the crowd milling around the edge of the beach. The Healer was standing in a boat ten feet from the shore, and they went as close as they could to sit and listen to him, their hearts beating fast and their minds far from any sense of peaceful insight into the kingdom of God.

Portius had set up agents around the grand house of Asri, pretending to be buying wares or sitting drinking wine and eating outside the many traders' stalls in the square. They were to track anybody exiting or entering the house, regardless of the person's status.

Barnabas arrived at ten o'clock in the brief sunshine of a changeable day with huge clouds skidding across the sky, borne by a stiff, cold breeze from the north.

'There is someone to see you, sir,' said Ezra. 'Apologies, but I thought it was important, so I have summoned the man here immediately.'

Asri looked up from his papers and stared as Ezra led Barnabas into the room. The men introduced themselves.

'What is your business, sir?' asked Asri.

'Mina. We seek to reunite her with you but fear interference from fiendish influences – namely, that of a brigand called Boataz, who has been assailing us since Magdala.'

'Where is she?'

'She is in safe hands, but I dare not bring her lest the brigands attack the house. It is prudent that we talk with the authorities and get a company of soldiers to protect her.'

'That will not be necessary – all you need to do is to bring her here. She will be unmolested – this I can assure you,' said Asri with a hint of irritation.

'You can't assure me that this maniac won't kill us all. With respect, you know what he is capable of – he needs to be apprehended.'

'He has been dealt with, rest assured. As I say, we shall have no further dealings with him.'

'Please tell me you haven't paid him off,' said Barnabas.

'That is none of your business,' interjected Ezra.

'Look, there is a woman who rescued your daughter, putting her own life at risk for her sake, and we have promised her that she will have your support to command the authorities to capture Boataz and find out what happened to her own daughter.'

'What do you mean, her own daughter?' asked Ezra.

'Anna, her child, was abducted by this fiend sixteen years ago. She just wants to see her daughter.'

'We know nothing of this Boataz, but let me assure you that if I can be of help to this woman, she will have all my resources at her disposal. What is her name and where can I find her?'

'Her name is Rachel, and she is housed with my friend, Ethan the priest.'

144

'I know Ethan; he is a good man.'

'But there is something you need to know about Rachel.'

'Please let me write to Ethan. My servant here, Ezra, can take the message himself.'

'That may be dangerous.'

'Look, I must ensure that she is treated correctly.'

'Unfortunately, you may not be able to supply her needs as she is... unclean,' whispered Barnabas.

'She is a leper?' asked Ezra.

'No, unfortunately, she is a woman who has been cruelly abused by Boataz and forced at an early age into a life of wanton ruin,' said Barnabas.

The significance of the words created a long silence until Asri picked up a pen and insisted on writing a short note. He sealed it and commanded it to be delivered immediately by hand.

Ezra left the room, and Asri stood up and walked around the room, his hands shaking and his breathing laboured.

'Look, I know you mean well, but we have been through so much. I had to secure a stable future for my wife and my granddaughter, and the cost is irrelevant to me. I cannot report this Boataz or get the authorities involved, so please return my granddaughter to me this very day or the consequences will not be favourable for either you or this Rachel.'

'Are you threatening me? I have placed my whole household at great risk to protect and return this child and this is how you repay me – by threatening me?'

'If you go to the authorities, I will accuse you and this Rachel of abducting her and forcing me to pay you a ransom.'

'Are you mad?'

'No, merely expedient. I have paid over one thousand denarii for her return, with the promise of more, and I shall claim that this very day you demanded the remainder of the monies from me.'

CHAPTER 16

✦ ✦ ✦

'What are you thinking?' asked Mathias, trying, with some difficulty, to prop himself against a bale of hay. The cold was causing his legs to ache, and they shook uncontrollably until he calmed them by rubbing them.

'Oh, nothing really,' replied Rachel, dabbing the flannel onto her lip.

'Do you hurt like mad?'

'All over,' she groaned.

'They think that Boataz forced you into some agreement; that is why they have moved Mina.'

'They are right,' she said, looking round and staring at the crippled young man who was struggling with his own traumas. She felt selfish and hard and leant over to him to help him rub his legs and calm the shaking in his limbs.

'He told me that unless I deliver the child to him tonight, he will go and harm my daughter Anna. And I do not know what to do.' She sat back, drew her knees up and rested her chin on her arms, her hands stroking her temples.

'Why didn't you tell Thomas?'

'I can have nothing to do with your brother.'

'That is harsh; do you mean that?' asked Mathias slowly and deliberately.

'I cannot have anything to do with the unbroken. I would bring ruin down upon his head, and I could not face that.'

'Oh, you are a model of caution and sobriety, aren't you?' Mathias smiled.

'What about you? Why haven't you found a wife?'

He laughed and raised his hands, looking at his legs.

'Who would marry a cripple?'

'And who a whore?'

They laughed and Rachel looked at his face, recognising the brokenness and frustration in him.

'What are we to do?' he asked.

'We? There has never been a we in my life, not since they took Anna from me.'

'That must have been agony?'

'I was allowed to spend as much time as I liked with the child until she slept, and then I would have to work. So I loved lying with her and letting her wake me in the morning, little fingers playing with my hair, her smile so infectious and her little chatter so wonderful. How happy I was...

'Then he came in with his men and beat the women, and beat me. They took us down to the beach where they flogged us. I hoped they would leave, but as I lay on the sea shore, he went into the house and took the little crib I had made and put it on his horse's back. He climbed up on his horse, held the child to himself and rode off.

'I fought the pain and the dizziness and climbed to my feet. I ran screaming to stop them, but I was kicked to the floor, and that was the last time I saw her.'

'And Boataz – did you find out where he had taken her?'

'Whenever I asked, the madam would have me flogged. All she told me was that she was in a better place.'

She began weeping when Mathias pulled her onto his chest and hugged her.

'I am so sorry,' he whispered.

Neither of them noticed the rider coming into the courtyard with his message secreted in his pouch. The stable hand took the horse into the stable, rubbed it down and fed it hay while Ezra greeted Ethan the priest, who had been expecting him.

'Why can't we just stay here with the Healer and the family?' asked Mina, watching the Healer teach from the boat. His voice seemed to be so clear. She felt that he spoke directly to her alone, his themes, his entreaties, his parables and stories directly challenging and calling her to a place of decision-making. She wanted so much to rest her weary, broken heart in the peace that flowed in from around the Healer's boat like a calming mist.

Her head ached slightly with the sound and tone of his voice. It was a luminous sound lighting the darkness in her mind, evoking a strong yet strange yearning to belong to this man and his family.

She thought of his words – the greatest question being whether to follow him or not. She dug her hands into the cold pebbles on the shore and listened to the soft, wheezing breathing of the sea as it sucked on rocks and stones. His voice was towering higher than the mast head, wider than the sails, reaching higher than the flight of the gulls – and she felt compelled to follow him.

'What does it mean to follow him?' she asked Thomas.

'It means you surrender all of your sense of self to a new way, child.'

'Would he become my teacher, and my rabbi?'

'He becomes your Lord.'

'What does that mean?'

'Only time will tell – how far and how deeply you desire to be like him.'

'To emulate him?'

'He sends them out in twos and they go and preach the good news of the kingdom – once they understand – but it takes time.'

'Have you been sent?'

'No, but once my brother is healed, I am hoping the pair of us will be equipped with the wisdom and power to follow him and be sent out to the poor, the maimed and the hurting.'

'And what of the rich, the wealthy like my grandfather? Can he be sent?'

'Anything is possible, but it is easier for a camel to go through the eye of a needle than the rich to inherit the kingdom of God. They have their fill here on earth, but the broken and the rejected and the meek shall be blessed by the full knowledge of the coming kingdom.'

'Can I be sent out? I am a mere woman.'

'The women are sent just as much as the men, in pairs, to seek the lost amongst the poor and the sick.'

'But what of the temple, the priests and the law?'

'He has established a new covenant that supersedes that of Abraham, Moses and David – we are all priests, because he is in us, and he is higher than Melchizedek.'

'This is all too much to understand, yet he awakens such a yearning in my heart. I feel undone before him.'

Thomas laughed and comforted her.

'We all feel like that – he says that it is the Holy Spirit coming and bringing revelation to our bodies about the coming shekinah.'

'The presence of God, tangible and living?'

'Yes, that when we are born again, the shekinah presence, the Holy Spirit, comes and dwells in us and makes us new again. Then we have a choice whether to live in the flesh or in the spirit, which will be made possible when he has completed his earthly mission.'

'But I thought he would create a great kingdom on earth – through military might.'

'It seems the kingdom will come first in the poor and defenceless – the last will be first; the harvest is plentiful but the workers few.'

Mina watched the Healer being pulled ashore in the fishing vessel. He leapt into the waters and strode out onto the beach where he stood and surveyed the gathered throng. He seemed to cast his eye the length, breadth and depth of the great congregation of people with a look of love and pity. His followers began to form a circle around him and brought a poor crippled woman on a stretcher to his feet. He crouched down and held her hand, and Mina could hear him speak to the Father. A hush fell upon the people as everybody waited, awestruck, for the moment when the old woman stood up and praised God for her healing.

Unable to do anything but grab the feet of one of the priests, Mathias cried out for mercy and justice as Ethan commanded the party of neatly dressed men to take Rachel to the square.

'She shall have justice, Mathias, and release from her plight...'

'What the hell are you doing, Ethan?'

'Setting her free of her wretchedness and atoning for her sins.'

'You are going to stone her!' Mathias gasped.

'She is an adulterer many, many times over, and the law demands retribution,' said one of the other priests.

Ezra came back into the stable to inform Ethan that everything was ready and in place. Mathias looked in horror as he saw a large rock in the stranger's hand. He shrieked and begged Ethan for mercy but was left crawling in the dirt on the floor.

All had gone well with Gritz. He had at last left the road to Capernaum behind and was making good progress along the coastal road to Akko where he needed to negotiate the exchange of gold for shekels so he could fund his voyage to Rome.

As he drove the horses and wagon on through the morning and into the afternoon, his thoughts were tinged with a sense of guilt that he had stolen all of the gold from the other men. Every man was due his apportioned lot in life, and Gritz deplored the fact that he had taken everything. But another side of him laughed and marvelled at his good fortune in stealing the hoard and outwitting Boataz and his tribe of brigands. He the clever, resourceful Gaul had plundered the plunderers.

Sense prevailed and Gritz thought more soberly that he had one more hurdle to overcome in the form of Ode, the bookkeeper. The man was more treacherous than any other, a snake in the grass, who would do anything he could to press his advantage. But Gritz knew no other way of turning some of the gold into cash to get him back to Gaul.

The port was laid out in a horseshoe shape – two arms protruding into the sea packed with ships of every shape and size. The sight of the unfurled sails of the vessels sailing in and out of the harbour excited Gritz's heart.

How he longed to be standing on the deck of an outbound masted vessel, watching the seagulls hovering high in the air, free at last to return home.

Ode was his lugubrious, bad-tempered, pugnacious, fat, loathsome self. The man was immense, draped in layers of flamboyant patterned silks that seemed at odds with the simplicity of his humble shop front.

'Do not expect a fair bargain today, friend. I have lost much this winter – the storms have cost me dear: seven vessels, seven vessels filled with fine linen, porcelain and treasure beyond your wildest dreams all sunken to the bottom of the sea. I am ruined, friend, so none of your tricks. I will pay under the odds or pay nothing at all,' he ranted as if admonishing the sky.

And on and on Ode went, bemoaning his misfortune, all the time lying through his teeth.

'Brother, I have a fortune in gold bullion and many fine trinkets that I need to sell to fund my voyage to Rome. If you can help me plan and safeguard my passage, I will make it well worth your while,' interjected Gritz, growing tired of the man's charade.

'Gold, you say, and fine trinkets? But I have nothing to offer; my coffers have been emptied. But pray, show me the value you speak of for I may be able to raise some funds to help you.'

Gritz felt like cutting the man's tongue out of his head – it was such an active instrument of trickery and deceit.

Ode instructed his servants to help Gritz manoeuvre the wagon into his yard. He salivated when the nine trunks were uncovered and Gritz opened one to reveal a hoard of stolen gold and silver treasure.

'Oh, that I could help you... You have amassed a splendid and delicious fortune, my fine fellow. Please do me the honour of eating with me and perhaps we can discuss sensible terms. Gone are the days when I could pay what you willed, friend, but I want to help you as you seem to possess a fine character.'

Gritz pulled a dagger and pressed it against Ode's throat.

'Cross me and I will gut you like a fish... understood?'

'Perfectly...' gulped the keeper of books.

The meal was sumptuous and Gritz ate hungrily all that was set before him. He drank fine wine, too much wine, and began to relax into a lifestyle that he deemed worthy of his newfound status as a wealthy man.

'One casket and I can get you to Rome... two caskets and I can get you home...' said Ode, ripping a chicken leg in two.

'One half of a box for each leg of the journey.'

'You can't just take cargo like that in the back of a wagon – there are shipping costs, insurances, bribery of port officials, my reputation, and then getting you out of Rome, a den of thieves, and I am talking about the authorities, and across bandit-ridden countryside... that's five armed men and a secure wagon... the costs are enormous. And I am taking a great risk...'

'Risk?'

'You would not be here if you hadn't purloined or stolen your good fortune – whoever the injured party is, they will one day turn up at my door and ask certain questions, which two caskets will silence.'

'Two caskets are too heavy a price to pay.'

'Take it or leave it. I seem to remember you from somewhere – you are part of a group of brigands whom I dealt with before, and I cannot quite put my finger on it, but I should have good reason to fear.'

'My master is a wine merchant; you need not fear him,' lied Gritz, who could not imagine the fury that Boataz would pour out on this land once he knew his treasure had been stolen.

'Sleep here tonight, and tomorrow I will make all the arrangements. I have a ketch leaving for Rome tomorrow evening, so all the better we strike our deal and get on with it. I will send you with money and letters of introduction to my whole network of agents, who are highly trained in matters like this.'

'Two of the smaller caskets…'

'Two of my choice…'

'One of your choice plus a smaller casket.'

'I shall accept that offer, friend.' Ode laughed, shaking Gritz's hand with his fat, greasy paw.

CHAPTER 17

✦ ✦ ✦

The men gathered in a circle, their heads bowed, praying. Rachel tried to fight her way through them but was rebuffed at every turn and pushed back into the centre of the ring.

She shivered, aching with the beating she had received from Boataz. The end had come, finally, and she sat down on the floor and waited for the first rock to crush her head. She thought of Anna and felt such a torrent of love for her that she rose up on her haunches, charged at Ethan and hit him below the kneecaps, causing him to hurtle over her, flat on his face on the hard square. She leapt up and ran for her life through the gap in the ring, only to be caught by her hair by one of the crowd which had started to gather around the stoning scene. Strangers grabbed her and manhandled her and pushed her back to Ethan, who tied her hands behind her back whilst another priest tied her legs together. She stood in the circle, bound, listening to the shrill tones of Ethan's voice rising through the square.

'Let this be a warning to all who trespass against the Law!' cried Ethan.

'The Lord is holy and righteous,' murmured the other ringleaders.

'She or he who transgresses even the slightest of ordinances in our most holy scriptures will suffer the wrath of judgement.'

'The Lord is holy and righteous.'

'This woman is a whore who has had relations with many men. She has escaped her filthy abode in Theims, near Magdala, but it is our duty here in Capernaum, where the law is still a mighty boon, to charge her and find her guilty and then rain down upon her head the judgement of stoning.'

'The Lord is holy and righteous.'

'Thereby cleansing this land of this most pernicious evil.'

Rachel did not weep or whimper; she closed her eyes and tried to remember her last days with Anna. They were about to throw the rocks that she hoped would end her life quickly for she had heard of stonings that had gone badly and had taken an age to kill the poor women.

There was some clamour in the crowd. Rachel opened her eyes and saw him, a plain, tough, rugged man, walking as if he were a king through the crowd, which parted out of a natural respect for his bearing. Thomas was by his side, and so were Mathias and Mina. Rachel trembled. Mathias was walking, and this man was looking at her as if she were the only person alive.

Ethan turned and faced him. And he could not speak. The man pushed past him, came over to Rachel and smiled.

'Who charges this woman with adultery?' he asked, softly but with such power that it temporarily deafened Rachel. She sank to her knees and watched as the man shook his finger at the complete circle of priests.

'Who brings charges against this woman?' he asked again, standing in front of Rachel.

Ethan seemed to stumble under a heavy weight and tried to stand tall before the waterfall of power that fell upon him.

'I do,' he said in a confused tone.

'And is your testimony supported by two witnesses?'

Ethan shook his head and let the rock fall from his hand. He stumbled and staggered as if he were about to vomit. The remaining priests threw their rocks at the feet of the man and fled into the crowd.

He untied the ropes from Rachel, held her hands and gazed into her eyes. She saw herself as a child sitting on a swing in her childhood garden, being pushed by her father, the motion gentle and relaxing. She remembered being fathered, the sense of belonging, of protection, security and love, and felt instinctively that this man was offering her the same sanctuary. She fought against his touch, his kindness, his knowing truth, reviling any man's touch, but his was so different, so light, so freeing she did not know what to say.

'Rachel, follow me,' he said. 'Go where I go and love my sheep.'

His eyes were dark and brooding, his lips pulled into a look of childlike delight, his nose crooked and his beard straggly and as unkempt as his hair. There was nothing to boast of in the outward appearance of the man – yet nothing on the outside could match the peerless beauty of what lay within.

She pulled her hands from his and gasped. Her body was flushed with a wave of sensation, of a power that eased her aches and pains, that mended her lip and removed the bruising around her eye. The pain in her back went; the throbbing in her head abated. But it was deeper, the work; it consumed her bitterness; it battered down the labyrinthine measures in her mind that fought for survival, releasing the pain of being her. But an anger fought back as the Healer sought to free the child within her – she struggled with him, contended with the depth of his concern for her and fell to her knees on the ground.

'I did not ask you to do this,' she growled.

'When you are ready, I will be there for you,' he whispered, helping her to her feet.

Mathias was the first to hug her.

'You can walk… What is this madness…?' she said, bewildered at seeing Mathias standing in front of her.

'The Healer!' he beamed.

Thomas and Mina came over to her, and Mina hugged her. She had been crying and Rachel tried to comfort her.

'What is the matter?'

'I cannot believe they were about to stone you. Why are they treating you like this – haven't you suffered enough?'

'Hush,' she said, cuddling the girl and pressing her face onto hers.

'If it had not been for Thomas asking the Healer to return with us, I do not know what would have happened,' said Mina.

'Why did you ask him to come here?' Rachel asked Thomas, who was standing away from them.

'Only to come and see my brother. When we arrived, we found him abandoned, and he told us what Ethan planned to do. Mathias was healed, and we came as fast as we could to the square to rescue you.'

'There was a man who came with a note. It was he who caused this to happen,' said Mathias.

Barnabas appeared, troubled and angry, as the Healer left the square with his followers walking obediently behind him. Ruth looked at Mina and smiled. Mina wanted to go, to end all this contumely and walk in the shadow of this man they called the Healer.

'What was Ethan thinking of?' cried Barnabas.

'Ask him; he bought the note,' said Mathias, pointing at Ezra, who was hovering in the shadows of the square.

'That is my grandfather's manservant, Ezra. What do you mean, he bought a note?' asked Mina, looking confused.

Mina helped Rachel walk across the square and along the narrow street to Ethan's house.

'She is not going to be put out in the stable,' avowed Thomas.

'Fine, fine,' replied Barnabas as they all pushed past Ethan's maid and entered the house, finding rest in the large anteroom where they waited, listening to fountains tinkling in the next room.

Barnabas excused himself and entered the main room, closing the doors behind him. The rest of the party waited. Soon they could hear loud voices as Barnabas and Ethan shouted at each other. They tried to make out what was being said and strained their ears to hear, not noticing the banging on the front doors.

Two men entered, followed by a party of five men bearing swords. Thomas and Mathias flung themselves across the room to protect Rachel and Mina. Ethan opened the doors and shouted at them to desist.

'These are Roman officers – stop!' he cried, and Thomas and Mathias reluctantly sat back down.

'It is time for us to talk at last,' said Portius, then ordered Servus to secure all the entrances to the building.

'Come into the main hall…' said Ethan, and Portius and Servus ordered the whole party to go ahead of them and sit at the large table in the main hall of the house. None of the Romans wore uniforms, and Thomas voiced his concern that they only had Ethan's word to trust and he had turned out to be completely untrustworthy.

'So, you are Mina?' asked Portius, sitting at the head of the table.

'How did you find us?' asked Thomas.

'Interrupt me again and I will have you thrown into a cell,' barked Portius. 'You are all implicated in serious crimes of murder and civil unrest, and it is my duty to ensure that the full weight of the empire is borne down upon the heads of the perpetrators.

'Now, Mina, starting from the beginning, tell me everything that has happened to you.'

160

✦ ✦ ✦

'You say Portius entered the house?' asked Asri with concern in his voice.

'Yes, master, I followed Mina to Ethan the priest's house where they all entered, and then shortly afterwards, a company of Romans appeared at the door. I recognised Portius and that soldier, but none of them wore uniforms.'

'And what of the whore?'

'I cannot explain it, but there was a man who contested the validity of the stoning, and the priests just dropped their rocks and disappeared into the crowd.'

'This woman, Rachel, is a great problem to me – I gave very specific instructions. What right did Ethan have to listen to some passing do-gooder? And Barnabas, I suppose, is with them.

'Trouble on trouble. The last thing I need is the authorities to get involved. They will only be concerned with catching Boataz – the rest of us can all die in the process. Mark my words, the Romans think only of preserving the order.'

'Shall I continue raising the money for the ransom? Now Mina will be back in our midst soon enough.'

'Continue selling the lands. This fiend needs to be bought off, or we will all be murdered in our beds.'

Ezra left Asri sitting in his bedroom. The old man pulled back the curtains and allowed the sunlight to flood over his face. He looked down at the people going about their daily business and wondered whether any were as heavy-hearted as himself. Matters were beginning to get out of control, and he rued sending a note to Ethan. It would have been better to give a verbal instruction that could not have been traced back to him.

He prided himself on being able to manipulate every situation to his own advantage, but the death of his son and daughter-in-law was too much to bear and he felt that he needed a rest, a very long rest.

Elizabeth appeared in the doorway. She looked hopeless, dressed in all her finery, with her hair unkempt and her makeup smeared through weeping.

'They have found her,' Asri said without any pity.

'Mina, they have found Mina?' The old woman gasped, leaning on a walking stick.

'Yes, but she may not be the same granddaughter that we lost; she must have been through a great ordeal, so we need to give her time.'

'Where is she? I must see her.'

'She will be returned in time enough.'

'So the last time anybody saw this villain was when he attacked you, Rachel?'

Rachel nodded and felt sick in her stomach. How was she to save Anna, and find out where she was, if she confessed to Boataz's demands?

'She was forced into a bargain with the fiend,' said Mathias, causing Rachel to cry out to silence him.

'Continue,' said Portius.

'It's alright, Mathias, I can tell him,' said Rachel trembling. 'Boataz said that unless I return Mina to him tonight, he will harm my daughter

Anna. I just cannot do that, and it breaks my heart to think what harm will befall my daughter.'

'And Anna is the daughter he took from you sixteen years ago?'

'Yes.'

'Where did he say that you had to deliver her?'

'I had to go and sit in the Black Tavern and wait for instruction by nine o'clock tonight.'

'Then I see that that is what you will have to do. If we are to catch this villain, then, unfortunately, you and Mina are our best hope. I will flood the area with my men and guard all of the main city gates. When you have met him, you will raise the alarm and we will have him.'

'That is preposterous! You cannot put these women in such danger,' protested Thomas.

'This man has evaded capture for twenty years, but now he has overstepped the mark and the full force of the empire will prevail against him. You will do as you are told or I will put the lot of you in prison for perverting the course of justice. Do I make myself clear?'

Thomas shook his head and put his hand over his mouth to suppress his disquiet.

'Rachel will take Mina to this tavern, and we will let the plot unfold. But one thing bothers me.'

'Being?' asked Servus.

'Why did the grandfather order Ethan to stone the girl?'

Mina blanched.

'My grandfather did what?'

'He wrote me a note telling me to stone her because of her many crimes,' said Ethan sheepishly.

'And you just said yes, of course, I'll murder a woman on an old man's whim,' growled Thomas.

'It is the law,' shouted Ethan.

'Why would he want Rachel out of the way?' asked Portius.

'Because she is a taint to this town and any town that she frequents...' Before Ethan had finished speaking, Thomas was at his throat, and they had to be separated by two of the soldiers.

Portius ordered Mina and Rachel to retire to a bedroom to get some rest and be ready to leave under cover of darkness.

Mina started crying and Rachel hugged her.

'Hey, don't cry. You do not have to go through with this.'

'It's not that. Of course I want to help you find Anna. It's just my grandfather – we wanted him to help you, but he arranged your stoning... I just don't understand.'

'Life is full of such things, child. We women are but chattels to men, but you are not to accept that.'

CHAPTER 18

✦ ✦ ✦

The couch was comfortable, the room sumptuous, and Gritz lay down and slumbered, hoping that at last his luck had changed and from this day forth, he would live the life of a man of means. Ode had left him to rest while he made arrangements for the safe passage of Gritz and his cargo.

He still felt pensive and would find it hard to rest completely until he was a hundred miles from this land that had held a pall of misfortune over his head. He had allied himself with a maniac in Boataz, and deep down, he knew that this would cost him dearly all the time he remained in this most unholy of lands. His thoughts turned to his own gods, gods of the forest, the deer, the bear and the boar, and he longed to offer them the grateful sacrifice of a penitent heart. Why had he left the lands of his birth to end up so desperate for peace? What contumely had he unleashed on the lives of the many people he had robbed along the highways and byways of the Roman Empire? But he was born a thief – it was the only skill he had ever possessed – stealing even from his own tribal chiefs so many years ago when his crimes had driven him from his land.

But he had never meant to harm anybody – not physically; financially and emotionally, perhaps. Yes, he had robbed the rich to meet his own poor needs. The deaths had been tragic mistakes, accidents of intent, failures of compliance, soul-damning damages. No, he had threatened and bullied and beaten people, but he had never willingly slit their throats as Boataz had.

The thought of the man still unnerved him, but he was drawing some peculiar and unique sentiment from having outwitted him and stolen his treasure. He wanted to crow, to boast and to beat his chest that he, Gritz the Gaul, had outplayed the great Boataz in all his strength, guile and madness. But not until he was far away, setting sail for Rome, could he let these feelings have free rein.

Ode returned late afternoon and advised Gritz that he had a number of people who wanted to converse with him.

'You mean a number of people who want a little more gain?' said Gritz.

'They each offer optional services that you may find are to your advantage; they may cost a little more than you are paying me, but it may be worth your while listening to them.'

Gritz washed and prepared himself for his final night in Palestine, setting his eyes on the stars that were emerging in the pale green sky.

'You have been lying to me, and if it were not for your Roman citizenship, I would take you from this house and have you flogged for your insolence,' barked Portius.

Asri slumped in his chair and tried to remain calm. He had been thinking all afternoon of what to say when his turn for interrogation finally came.

'Barnabas is lying. I have paid no ransom to this Boataz. I have never heard of him until today.'

'But you are selling lands everywhere – raising a small fortune for what purpose, then?'

'I wish to help the synagogue build a school for the disadvantaged.'

'Rubbish. If you continue with this pretence, I will charge you with the most serious charges with which none of your money will help you.'

'I know nothing of this Boataz.'

'So, you deny that you threatened this Barnabas when he wanted to go to the authorities?'

'The man came here demanding money; he is a fraud. And you should deal with him.'

'Like you tried to deal with the harlot?'

'This town has higher standards than Magdala and Theims, that is for sure.'

'And how did you know she came from Theims?'

'This Barnabas told me so.'

'Why would you have her killed… a woman who sixteen years ago lost her own daughter to this villain? None of this adds up unless…'

'Unless what?'

'Perhaps I need to speak to your wife about this. Is she available?'

'My wife is out of her mind with grief. It will not serve you to interview her, nor will it help with her recovery.'

'Nonetheless, I will speak with her in private, and then your servant,' said Portius and ordered Servus to go and fetch the woman.

Asri trembled with indignation and protested vehemently, but Portius would have none of it.

It took an age for Elizabeth to be washed, dressed and presented to Portius. The light was failing and the room was lit by a myriad of candles of every shape and size.

'I want you to tell me of your late daughter-in-law – she had only one child?'

'Yes,' said Elizabeth, shaking and trying not to cry. 'Mina. We have only one son and one granddaughter.'

'Did they not try for more children?'

'I am not sure what this has to do with anything. Mina – you have rescued her. Where is she?'

'It is not safe to return her here until I have answers to my questions,' continued Portius.

'Not safe, but we are her grandparents, and her mother and father were taken from us.'

'Did your son and daughter-in-law try for more children?'

'Yes, but Mina was a difficult birth and there were no more children.'

'Were you at the birth of your granddaughter?'

'No, Phillip and Elisa went abroad when they learned Elisa was pregnant; it was for Elisa's well-being. They went to Rome to stay with relatives, and when they returned, four years later, that was the first time we saw our granddaughter.'

Portius sat and thought, and something just did not add up. It annoyed him that these people trifled with his authority and remit to maintain the order of the empire. He dismissed the woman, who could not stop begging him to see her granddaughter, and then Servus summoned Ezra.

'You and your master will lie to me, no doubt, but how much is the ransom?'

'I do not know about a ransom,' lied Ezra, looking frightened. The fear touched a nerve and Portius ordered Servus to take the servant and have him flogged.

'For what reason?' protested Ezra, trembling.

'Tonight, we have set a trap for Boataz, and when we capture him and torture the truth out of him, I suspect your master will be facing trial in Rome before the emperor for perverting the course of justice, which has the death penalty. You are aiding and abetting a felon who has murdered Roman citizens and Roman soldiers and terrorised the highways of Galilee for twenty years. He has escaped custody by disappearing each winter, and I believe you have information that will help us condemn him. But alas, it is a truth that will also convict your master unless it is freely given without the coercion of over-zealous soldiers.'

'My master is confused; he is out of his mind with grief. Surely there are mitigating circumstances?'

'Tell me what you know or you will be taken from here and flogged,' demanded Servus.

'We know nothing of this Boataz. My master was approached by a wine merchant from Tiberias called Gan Ben Gilad, who said that he had the child and demanded a ransom of three thousand denarii.'

'Good grief, that is a fortune! And he was willing to pay this?'

'I do not understand. My master is out of his mind. Even though he has learned that the child is safe, he persists in paying this fiend this vast fortune as if his very life depended upon it.'

'Find out everything you can in Tiberias about this Ben Gilad. This may be where Boataz hides in the winter, under the pseudonym and guise of a wine merchant. It would be the best way to funnel all of his stolen wealth.'

'Yes, sir,' said Servus and left the room.

'Now, let us confront your master.'

✦ ✦ ✦

A complete change of outfit lay on the bed. Gritz could not believe his childish sense of excitement in changing out of his filthy clothes, bathing, having his hair oiled, his beard trimmed and nails scrubbed by a manservant and then dressing as a well-to-do merchant. He loved the quality of the material, the delicacy of the stitching, the gold sleeve trims and the ornate neckline. His body was anointed with oil and his head scented with a beautiful, earthy fragrance. He looked in the shiny plate mirror and could not believe the handsome man staring back at him.

His new self followed the servant downstairs and allowed him to ritually wash his feet, cleansing them of the slightest dust, putting on fine leather sandals and leading him into the room where Ode sat waiting for him.

'Welcome to the top table, fine sir!' Ode laughed, clapping his hands and filling the air with kind words of admiration, which was much to Gritz's new self's liking.

'Your wealth has transformed you! You are a new man, a savage born into luxury. How proud your family would be if they could see you now, bedecked in such finery.'

Gritz sat down at the table amidst fine wine, fruit and a sumptuous spread of meats and sweet desserts.

'Allow me to introduce you to the next step in your journey to a new life…' gloated Ode, pointing at the double doors that slowly opened. Gritz turned around, happy with the way things were going.

A company of Roman soldiers entered the room in their steel helmets and chestplates, bare knuckles gripping short, broad swords. Gritz was no match for them in all his weaponless finery.

Ode was pretending to be frightened, and Gritz watched his mouth move, unable to comprehend his words.

'This felon came, master, with two trunks stuffed with contraband. He threatened my life, insisting that I buy it, but I knew it was all ill-gotten gains. I remember him, kind sir; he is one of Boataz the brigand's men. They have threatened me before, but as an upstanding member of society, ever keen to be granted Roman citizenship, it is my duty to resist such evil men.'

They tied Gritz's hands behind his back and around his neck put a steel ring attached to a chain pulled by two burly soldiers.

'Enough, Ode! It is too much to bear,' said the officer leading the arrest.

'There were twelve caskets of gold, not two,' moaned Gritz. Ode and the officer laughed.

'Is that right? Well, if you want to keep your tongue in your head, you need to tell us everything you know about this Boataz.'

It took four men to press the Gaul to leave the house. Their collective brutality was too much for him to bear. They ripped off all his clothes and beat him with a metal bar until, falling on his knees, he submitted to their yoke.

They took him in an open wagon down to the small garrison in the harbour and locked him, battered and bruised, in a cell. Gritz could not believe his misfortune. He stood on the low bed and looked out of the prison window at the boats now in harbour for the night, their great white sails being furled up onto the masts. His escape had been a delusion. The old hag was right: he could not escape his fate.

'You have lied to me from the outset,' said Portius angrily.

'My servant does not know what he is talking about. He must have a vendetta against me,' replied Asri, who clung to his version of events.

'So, you have never met this Gan Ben Gilad or this Boataz, who, we suspect, are one and the same person?'

'I once traded with the gentleman, many years ago.'

'Sixteen years ago, to be precise.'

'You have greatly disturbed this household. Now, unless you have specific charges, I would ask you to leave this house,' retorted the old man angrily.

'Once we have captured this villain and interrogated him – by very effective means – we will know the truth, and you will be charged with perverting the course of justice. I will see to it personally that you rot in jail for the rest of your life.'

Asri sat back on a couch and looked at Portius in the light of the candles. The officer was trained in order and competence but had never met the likes of Gan Ben Gilad, or Boataz, who, Asri knew, would not say a word about his transgressions, even under pain of death.

'Then we shall both wait for the truth,' said Asri smugly, causing Portius's face to flicker with anger.

'So, the course is set, old man. So be it,' said Portius and left the room in anger.

✦ ✦ ✦

'What happened to you? You can walk!' said Rachel, sitting on a sofa in the priest's house.

'Thomas and Mina asked the Healer to come and help me. I was lying in the muck and dirt on the floor, filled with despair and fear for what they would do to you, when he appeared at my feet. He just bent down, held out his hand and said, 'Brother, come, stand.' I held his hand, and there was such belief in his eyes that I could, indeed, stand. What happened was a miracle: the Healer asked the Father to bless me – and he did. The power entered my body; it searched me, found me, flowed in every part of my body until my legs grew warm and tingled, and I felt a pressure for the first time to move them. To my amazement, I could feel my legs, feel my feet, and though my legs were once so thin and so wasted, they were nourished with flesh and muscle, and I could stand, and then I could walk.

'I bowed down first, at his feet, and I worshipped. Truly, I want to follow this man all the days of my life.'

He started to weep and Rachel comforted him.

'Why do you cry?'

'He asked you to follow him, yet you rejected him.'

'Mathias, rejoice over your healing. I am not sick and do not need his healing,' retorted Rachel.

'You are sick, Rachel; you are very sick.'

'Please, Mathias, leave it, or I shall become angry with you.'

'And push me away as you did to the Healer and my brother, who just want to show you love?'

'Love? What is love between a man and a woman if it is not just the one controlling the other like a chattel?'

'He reached out to you, the Healer, as he did to me, yet you did not respond,' wept Mathias.

'Where are my withered legs, my blindness, my deafness, my rotting hand, my madness or my possession that I should want a Healer?'

'Look at the state of your heart – it is mangled.'

'I have suffered too much for such self-reflection,' she continued, turning her back on him.

'You are stubborn and foolish, Rachel. And what of my brother Thomas, whom you spurn at every turn? You know he has feelings for you.'

'Feelings that can never be reciprocated.'

'Why? Because you condemn yourself and write yourself off. It is your own heart that is the problem.'

'What is going on?' asked a voice. They turned around to find Thomas standing in the candle-lit room.

'I will leave you,' said Mathias, leaving the room.

'Rachel, how are you?' he asked softly, with a hint of real concern.

'I am fine, apart from all the people who think grief is an illness.'

'Please, let's not argue. I am at my wits' end worrying about you. Tonight is so dangerous.'

'I do not know why I stopped to help you and your brother; it was the worst thing.' She heard the pain in her voice and stopped, feeling confused.

'I am so glad we found favour with you,' said Thomas sarcastically.

'What do you want of me?' demanded Rachel.

'Salvation, Rachel, that is all.'

'Salvation!' scoffed Rachel. 'Salvation! Pray, from what? My sin?'

'From the pain and the hurt and being so alone… There is a whole new family waiting to embrace you.'

'The only family I have has been taken off me!'

'Why won't you consider a different way?' said Thomas, his voice trembling.

'I cannot face the union with a man ever again, not spiritually, emotionally or physically. You and your Healer need to run a mile from me. I am beyond healing. Beyond salvation.'

'Then can I not at least walk with you?'

'Walk with me?'

'After this is over, I want to go where you go. I can protect you and we can search for your daughter together. We can keep our distance, mind; we do not need to be close.'

Rachel collapsed. The sound of the young woman screaming in her head. The memory of the Healer's touch. Of Mathias being able to walk. Of miracles. And this man's offer of dutiful love. She wanted to weep and hold him but could not.

'Please, leave me. I need to compose myself,' she said meekly.

CHAPTER 19

✦ ✦ ✦

They covered the half mile from the square to the Black Tavern, on their own, in complete darkness. The sky was moonless and they held hands, gingerly pushing open the tavern doors and finding a seat at one of the rough tables. Rachel ordered a drink of water and some bread and the pair waited in silence for something to happen. The tavern was busy and lit by large candles burning brightly from every surface.

After an hour and a half, Rachel wondered whether anyone would come. And then one of the servant girls came over and pointed at a table hidden in the shadows where a single figure sat.

Mina sat down first, followed by Rachel. They both stared up at the face hidden in the darkness.

'You can go now and leave the girl with me,' said a voice Rachel did not recognise.

'No, I hand her over to Boataz or no one at all,' she said.

'That will not be possible,' said the voice.

'Then we shall leave,' said Rachel standing.

'We need some answers from Boataz about Rachel's child, Anna,' said Mina.

There was silence, and then the figure leant forward to show his face in the light. Rachel recognised him as one of Boataz's spiteful men, and her heart sank.

'She goes with me now or I will slit your throat.'

'We both go or she will return with me.' Rachel glared at him.

He paused, and Rachel could read the unease in his mind.

'Follow me,' he said, and he led them to the rear of the building where they stepped out into the cold evening air. Two horses waited and the man lifted Mina and then Rachel onto one, whilst he mounted the other.

They galloped fearfully and dangerously through the streets on a crazy trajectory, the rider going forwards and backwards, jolting suddenly to the left or the right, returning in a canter, then speeding up to a gallop so no one could possibly follow them.

They were eventually led down by the coast, riding in pitch blackness at breakneck speed, out towards a distant jetty light. Rachel was terrified for Mina. She could not see how Portius's men could keep track of them and feared for their lives. Her fears were intensified when they finally came to a standstill on a jetty where a large vessel waited, lit by numerous lanterns in its rigging.

Boataz was standing in the light of a lantern, and Rachel gave the signal that he was present by putting a white handkerchief in her waist belt. But this felt so far away from civilization as to be a joke.

The rider joined Boataz, and five men leapt down from the boat to approach Rachel and Mina.

'What have we done?' whispered Rachel, clenching Mina's hand.

'Do not fear,' said one of the men. In an instant, an arrow flew through the air and pierced the heart of the rider. The five men ran and jumped on Boataz and pulled him to the floor. Roman soldiers ran from the darkness and piled onto the fallen man, who was beginning to beat his way free of the first five men.

Portius appeared in the darkness, holding a lantern.

'How did you know?'

'We had a report of a boat being hired to sail to Tiberias. We filled the boat with our men and flooded the area with archers. Fortunately, we got our man.'

'Please, I beg you, let me talk to him. He stole my child. I need to know what he did with her,' cried Rachel.

Boataz appeared at the end of the jetty, manacled and with his neck in a metal brace held by chains.

'Trust me, I will get to the bottom of that matter, but right now you two will be escorted home.'

'Home?' said Mina.

'Your grandfather and grandmother are waiting for you.'

'I have no home,' said Mina.

'What have you done with Anna?' screamed Rachel as Boataz was led past her. Portius restrained her and lifted a light into Boataz's face.

'Is this the man who killed your parents, Mina?' he asked.

'Yes, but why did he kill them? And what has he done with Anna?'

Boataz laughed and spat at them.

'What a fine little whore you would have made – Rachel could have taught you all the tricks of the trade,' he cried in derision.

The men led Boataz away, and Portius entreated the girls to join a waiting troop of soldiers to return to the house of Ethan the priest.

'I need to know what he did with my daughter...' pleaded Rachel.

'And why did he kill my parents?' added Mina, weeping at the fearful memories Boataz evoked.

'These will all be part of his trial, the murders and the abductions. But until we have rounded up all of his men, you must remain vigilant.'

'Where will he be taken for interrogation?' asked Rachel.

'We will interrogate him and compile a case against him. We shall then present in court where he and his men will be charged, and then the investigations will proceed until there is sufficient evidence to bring them to trial.'

The darkness was cloying, palpable, as the coastline was battered by a change in the wind and rain began to fall. A troop of soldiers on horseback escorted the two women back to the house where they found a fire burning.

Thomas and Mathias were relieved to see the girls, who soon explained about the evening's events.

'Portius says he can be trusted to look into these things,' said Mina.

'But what happens next?' asked Mathias.

'No stone will be left unturned until they find out why Boataz has acted as he has,' said Barnabas.

'But how long will this all take?' asked Mina forlornly.

'It will take as long as it takes… and no less,' replied Barnabas.

The old man had kept to himself since his run-in with Portius. He sat in his bedroom on his own, warmed by the heavily fuelled fire. He had not slept and longed to find some peace. Dawn was breaking on a blustery winter's day with rain pounding the windows.

Elizabeth had sent for him a hundred times, but he could not face her. Her pain was too much to bear. His heart sank when his door opened and she entered, limping and leaning on her stick.

'Asri, what are you doing sitting there in the dark? You are frightening me.'

'Go back to bed,' he said, but she came over and sat opposite him.

'What is going on? Why hasn't Mina been returned to us?'

'You do not need to know.'

'I need to know what the hell is going on!' she snapped.

'I made a mistake, and now she probably hates me.'

'Mistake?'

'She escaped captivity with the help of a harlot called Rachel, whom I do not trust. This woman is corrupt and beyond help. She is a whore, and our granddaughter may not understand why I sent instruction for this woman to be dealt with sternly by the priests.'

'What do you mean, sternly?'

'I requested Ethan deal with her, separate the two, but he took the stupid action of seeking to stone her.'

'She is dead!' exclaimed Elizabeth.

'No, for some strange reason, she most certainly is not dead, but Mina blames me for attempting to take her life.'

'Why did you do such a terrible thing – if this poor woman rescued her, why would you repay her with such cruelty?'

'Mina is hurting; she has been abducted. Who knows what feelings could have been stirred during this trauma? She could have bonded with this woman, who would lead her astray and possibly take her away from us. I had to do something.'

'There is something you are not telling me. Please, Asri, I beg you, tell me what it is.'

'You are to go back to your room and wait until I can get Mina back.'

'I shall do no such thing!' declared Elizabeth vehemently. 'Not until you tell me what is going on.'

'One of Boataz's men has been captured in Akko with a wagon full of gold and stolen goods. We believe he is one of the villain's right-hand men,' said Servus.

'Send orders for him to be transported here,' said Portius.

'I already have, sir. He should be with us shortly.'

'And what of Boataz?'

'Boataz is not answering any questions. He refuses to acknowledge that he has another identity. What shall we do, sir?'

'Send for Sextus and his men; they will loosen his tongue. I want a full confession before we send him up to Pilate.'

'That may not be easy; he is quite mad,' added Servus.

'I want a full statement on why he killed these people and abducted the child. What happened to this Anna? And a way of indicting Asri for his arrogance.'

'This may take much longer than you think, sir. The man is a monster.'

'Sextus has his means of breaking even a hulk like Boataz. But we shall also have access to this Gaul, whom we can use to play the one against the other.'

'I have the note here the old man sent to the priest.'

'Is it explicit?'

'It quite clearly orders the priest to stone the woman, sir.'

'So what is he doing trying to kill her? It makes no sense.'

'Maybe he is a religious fanatic, sir. This woman transgresses his law.'

'Not as much as he transgresses our law. And he shall pay a heavy price for his insubordination and deceitfulness.'

✦ ✦ ✦

He was frozen and covered in filth. The fleeting glimpse of prosperity he had enjoyed was now a taunt as he grovelled under the burden of his manacles in the back of a prison cart.

Gritz swore an oath that he would do everything in his power to get revenge on Ode the bookkeeper and prayed to every god he could muster to this end. But he knew deep down that his days were coming to an end and the old hag's prophecy was being fulfilled. He could not escape this land that held its fingers around his throat. His nose was bleeding and it was hard to open his eyes, such had been his beating, but he tried to think of his favourite forest walk back home and imagined running free.

They could kill his body, but his spirit would be free to return to the way of the bear and the wolf. He prayed to the god of thunder that he would be allowed to come back as a savage beast of the forest to live as a wild animal, free from the cares of mankind.

The cart stopped and he was dragged out by two soldiers, who hit him with long poles until he got to his feet and walked into a long, low set of buildings making up the garrison at Capernaum.

He was pushed into an interrogation room and bound by his feet and hands to a wooden chair where his head was supported in a machine-like grip. A senior Roman officer sat with a lieutenant on the opposite side of the table.

'Do you want to escape death, Gaul?' asked Portius.

'That depends upon the cost of it,' replied Gritz.

'What were you doing with so much treasure?' asked Servus.

'I was stealing it from Boataz so I could go home a rich man.' Gritz laughed.

'So, you admit that you are an associate of Boataz – a brigand, a thief and a murderer?' asked Portius.

'I have not murdered anybody; I am a thief, and a thief alone. The murders you can pin on Boataz, who is a madman.'

'Were you there when he killed the whole household in Capernaum, or the guards in Magdala, or the whole household of the physician?' asked Servus.

'I had nothing to do with those excesses. I merely thieve, and Boataz has grown more and more reckless with every passing year.'

'How long have you been his associate?' asked Portius.

'For twenty years.'

'Why did Boataz slaughter Phillip and his wife and abduct the child? What did the father do to so enrage him?' asked Portius.

'The idiot reneged on paying a debt he owed Boataz. A large sum of money that had been unpaid for years. For some reason, Boataz snapped and wrought vengeance, taking the child to extort money out of the grandparents. This is all I know.'

'And what was the nature of the debt that Phillip owed Boataz?'

'I do not know, but it irked Boataz.'

'This was not the first time he had abducted a child, was it?' asked Servus.

'What do you mean?'

'Sixteen years earlier, he had taken a child from its mother, a whore in a brothel in Theims.'

'Boataz has many brothels, and when the women have children, he takes them from their mothers and puts them in nursery houses so they can be grown into slaves or whores – he is an unscrupulous abuser of girls and boys.'

'Sixteen years ago, where would the child he took from Theims have been taken?'

183

'He has a school for orphans in Tiberias; well, it masquerades as a school. He takes the children there and trains or beats them into submission as they grow old enough to be placed into service.'

'What if Boataz sold a child to a rich family who could not have children?' continued Portius. 'Is that possible?'

'Boataz sold the children to the highest bidder, so yes, that was possible via the orphanage.'

'Do you think he could have sold Mina to the couple he murdered because they refused to pay what they owed for her?'

'Yes, but poor fools they were to enter into such a transaction with Boataz. He would have added an exorbitant interest rate that would have inflated what they owed into a hefty burden. If they had bought a child and reneged on payment, then yes, that could have been the reason he slaughtered them.'

CHAPTER 20

✦ ✦ ✦

'Child, thank heaven you are alive!' cried Elizabeth, hugging Mina. 'Please, Grandmother, I have come to tell you I am not coming back here to live. I have found friends who can better care for me.'

'What nonsense is this?' cried Asri. 'We are your family!'

'Not any more,' said Mina. 'Not since you tried to kill my very best friend and protector, Rachel, by stoning.'

'That was a misunderstanding. I merely meant you to be separated from the woman, who is a bad influence on you.'

'So, you accidentally got her stoned?'

'Less of your damn cheek, child. I can tell already by your insolence that she has had a negative influence on you. You will go upstairs with your grandmother, who has already prepared a room for you.'

'No, I am going my own way.'

'Own way! Did you hear that, mother? She is going her own way. What disgusting insolence. Now, I am prepared to forgive and forget, but any more of this and I shall have you flogged like a dog. Now get to your room.'

He motioned to get hold of Mina, but Thomas intervened, standing in the way of the old man.

'She is free to make her own choice.'

'No woman is free to make her own choice! What foolishness is this? Get out of my way.'

185

'She is now a follower of the Healer, the great rabbi, and we will accompany him as he returns to Jerusalem. You need not fear – your granddaughter will be well cared for.'

'Mina, get to your room this instant.'

'Please, child, please, you will break my heart,' begged Elizabeth, but Mina, escorted by Thomas, Mathias and Barnabas, walked out of the house and down into the yard.

'Are you alright?' asked Thomas.

'Yes,' said Mina with tears in her eyes.

They were travelling back to the priest's house when one of Ethan's servants ran towards them looking greatly agitated.

'Barnabas, my master wishes to inform you that some soldiers have just arrived and arrested Rachel.'

Thomas's heart sank. Mathias put his arm around his brother's shoulders to comfort him. Mina looked up at Barnabas in horror.

'What madness is this now?' she exclaimed.

'I am arresting you for your own protection,' said Portius.

'Protection?'

'Certain allegations have been made against you.'

'What allegations?'

'That you were in conspiracy with Boataz to kidnap the child and demand a ransom from her grandparents.'

'That is preposterous! Where do these allegations come from?'

'From Theims.'

'Theims?'

'Yes, we raided the brothel yesterday, and our investigations led us to the old woman who lives in the mountains. She had a pile of letters that she says you gave her. Would that be true?'

'Yes, the letters I told you the madam gave me to give to her.'

'The letters all purport to be written by yourself and outline your plan to elicit the help of the old woman to get you to a safe house in Jerusalem in exchange for the nard, ready to receive your lover, Boataz, and the ransom.'

'That is ridiculous! That was all the idea of the madam, who is just trying to cover her tracks. Why did I bring her here then?'

'To force me to help you find your daughter – that is what they say.'

'They?'

'Boataz is incriminating you as well. He says you were always an accomplice and came up with the whole idea.'

'When will this stop?' exclaimed Rachel.

'It would seem many people are out to harm you, Rachel,' said Portius, 'and as you seem to be in endless trouble, it is for your own protection that I will keep you under house arrest. You will find your room comfortable and you can have visitors. Servus will take you there.'

Rachel's head was spinning. Why would the madam cause her so much trouble when all this time she had thought that she had been helping her get rid of Mina from the house? Why was Boataz now trying to implicate her in the whole mess of events that had occurred since the night of Mina's abduction?

Mina was allowed to visit her and sat on a couch in the room, nervously chewing her fingernails.

'They believe I have planned all of this just to force them into finding Anna,' blurted out Rachel. Then she saw Mina's malaise. 'What is it? What is wrong?'

'Safa said you thought Anna may have been taken and sold to a rich, childless couple. Why did you not tell me?'

'I am sorry. I didn't mean not to tell you.'

'I don't believe you. I think you thought I could be your daughter, and you never shared this with me.'

'I am sorry. I just did not want to confuse you or hurt you or for you to think that of your parents.'

'I do not know what to think anymore, but that would explain so much. If they owed Boataz money for my purchase, and they reneged, he would wreak havoc on them and then use me to blackmail my grandparents.'

'That could all be true, but that doesn't mean you are Anna. You could be some other poor woman's child, not necessarily mine.'

'But why would my grandfather try to have you killed? Come on, Rachel, there must be something that you know that connects you to me or my grandfather.'

Rachel searched her memory but could find nothing that could tie Anna to Mina or her grandparents.

'I will have this out with my grandfather,' declared Mina.

'You say Rachel had nothing to do with this crime?' asked Portius.

Gritz nodded. 'He said nothing to me of this whore. This is all nonsense. Boataz despises women; he would not have anything to do with such a lowly creature, let alone listen to her instructions.'

Servus interrupted the interview, and Portius stepped out of the room.

'Pilate wants to try these brigands in a showpiece execution to beat down the growing unrest, so he has ordered us to send all who are charged to Jerusalem immediately. What shall we do about Rachel?'

'Has he asked that we accompany them?'

'No, sir, he just wants the accused, and his people will take over the interrogation and the trial.'

'This is most unhelpful. With Pilate involved, they will be crucified, and Rachel with them if we do not find evidence to help her.'

'Sir, we have done all we can.'

'Despite her past, she is innocent, and if she were a Roman citizen, we would move heaven and earth to vindicate her. But just because she is an alien and a woman pressed into harlotry, we just let her die?' protested Portius.

'Seven Roman citizens have been killed, two households and a garrison attacked. Pilate will crucify however many he can to beat down any hint of insurrection on his watch.'

The rain and the wind had abated, and a winter sun shone down onto the square as Mina entered her grandparents' house. She made her own way to her grandfathers' quarters and pushed open the door to find him writing at his desk. He looked up and shook his head in annoyance.

'I have been far too lenient, fool that I am. Is there no woman in this building who can show me due respect? What do you want, child?'

'Boataz has been captured, so there is no need to pay your ransom. I am free.'

189

'Free, indeed, to indulge your newfound licence to be insolent. How dare you come marching in here unannounced? Does your grandmother know you are here?'

'No... I want to know the truth.'

'What exactly is truth?' he asked angrily.

'How much did you pay Boataz to buy me as a babe?'

'Between you and me, it was a fair price, if your father had kept to the agreement, but by defaulting on the payment, he allowed the fiend to charge an extortionate amount of interest to the point where the debt was ten times what had been agreed. If you tell this to your grandmother, then I will deny it. But yes, we bought you from an orphanage, not knowing, of course, it was a front to this man's empire of ruin.'

'Why didn't you tell me?'

'That was down to your mother and father, who went through the great pretence of being pregnant. They had to be sent away and then came back with you, pretending to the whole family that you had been born abroad. A pretty penny that masquerade cost me, as well.'

'Why did you try to have Rachel stoned? What threat did she pose?'

'I told you: once I heard of your association, and knowing what you are like, I tried to break up the relationship. I did not intend for Ethan to be so legalistic.'

'Grandfather, I have read the note. It is quite clear what you intended.'

Asri shook with rage. 'Get out of my sight! How dare you stand there and accuse me of lying to my very face? You should be horsewhipped for your insolence.'

Mina stood her ground.

'How come you knew about Rachel, when you say you bought me from an orphanage?'

190

'Get out.'

They were disturbed by a noise at the door. Elizabeth stepped into the room.

'What is going on? Mina, it is you?'

She tried to hug Mina but was pushed away.

'I am sorry, but until I have my questions answered, I will have nothing to do with you!' she said, backing away from the old woman.

'What questions?'

'I told you, Elizabeth; she wants to know about this Rachel and why I instructed Ethan to separate them. She is jumping to all sorts of conclusions.'

'What has happened to us?' shrieked the old woman, falling to her knees.

Mathias followed Thomas along the beach. It was good to get some fresh air and listen to the sound of the sea sucking and seething on the sandy shoreline. Strands of blackened seaweed festooned the rocks like dying mermaids' hair, and the gulls screeched and squawked following the fishing boats setting sail for the day's catch.

Ruth met them at the small wooden jetty protruding into the cold, grey sea. Several fishing vessels were preparing nets and unfurling large white canvas sails.

'We will be leaving for Jerusalem in the morning, and it would be good if you could all accompany us. There is so much to teach you, and you will benefit greatly from the journey. It will take about a week, with teaching and healing every day until we arrive in the city.'

'Why is he so intent on visiting Jerusalem? Is it not dangerous for him?' asked Thomas.

'The authorities are besetting us at every step, and he insists that it is time for him to go and cleanse the temple and begin fulfilling his Father's will,' whispered Ruth.

'How can he call our God Father?' asked Mathias.

'He is the Son of Man, who has come to set us free and usher in the new kingdom,' replied Ruth.

'I do not understand,' replied Mathias.

'That is why you need to be discipled. You must spend time with the rabboni, teacher, rabbi, Lord. These things must go beyond your head, into your heart and through to your soul until His spirit dwells in you richly. Without spiritual wisdom, this will all be meaningless.'

'But where do you get spiritual wisdom?' asked Mathias.

'It comes from fullness, as a gift of God.'

'We have a problem in that Rachel has been arrested,' said Thomas. 'I cannot leave her here in prison.'

'Pray. Ask the Spirit for knowledge of the Father's will, Thomas. We will be leaving from this jetty tomorrow at noon.'

Ruth bade them farewell and left them watching her disappear into the distance.

'What are you going to do?' asked Mathias

'I will have to ask the Spirit.'

'And how exactly does that work?'

'I do not know, Mathias. I have so much to learn.'

The two brothers walked back into the town. Thomas went to the garrison to see if he could speak to Portius. The officer was not available, but one of the soldiers allowed him to visit Rachel. He knocked on the door nervously.

'Can I speak to you without your shouting at me?' he asked.

'Am I that bad?'

'Most days,' he said with a laugh.

'They are taking me to Jerusalem, and I am frightened. I have been accused of conspiring to abduct Mina and forcing the authorities into finding Anna. Now we all have to be sent for trial in Jerusalem by the procurator who wants to make an example of Boataz and his men.'

'This cannot be possible! When will this ever end?'

'I am sorry I have been so mean to you, Thomas, but I fear that circumstances are always conspiring against us.'

'Us? You mean there is some kind of us, then?'

'Of course, and you know that. It's just so difficult...' Her voice was soft and tender and she tried not to look at him.

'I will come with you to Jerusalem and try to find some legal representation for you. There must be due process. There the authorities will have regulations that need to be followed.'

'Portius says he will do everything he can to ensure that I am not implicated in all of this. But he may not even be called up to Jerusalem as the whole case is moving jurisdiction.'

'When do they take you?'

'Tomorrow; we leave early under armed guard.'

Thomas sat down, put his hands on his face and rubbed hard.

'I can't believe this. It is a nightmare. Who has accused you of these things?'

'Boataz and the madam who helped me escape. She probably planned this from the beginning as a way of deflecting any charges against herself. I have been really naïve in trusting her. She gave me letters to take to the old woman who stored her nard for her, and these letters they say are written by me. But they will not be in my handwriting because I can neither read nor write. But what can I prove?'

'I have a good man of the law whom I can hire to represent you at any tribunal.'

Rachel sat down beside him.

'You do not need to do anything to help me. Mathias told me that you want to follow the Healer, the two of you together, to become his followers. Do not deviate from this. Follow your heart, Thomas. I do not believe this will end well for either of us if you go to Jerusalem and incur unnecessary expense and then have to witness what will happen to me. I do not believe there is any escape for me.'

'I will follow my heart; you are right,' he said.

Rachel tried to stay brave and suppressed her surprise at how easily he had agreed with her.

'I shall follow the convoy to Jerusalem and be with you,' he said.

CHAPTER 21

✦ ✦ ✦

A rough wooden floor or an iron ledge was all Rachel had to sit on when she was escorted by a cavalry unit from Capernaum to Jerusalem. They travelled in a convoy, thirty mounted men surrounding and escorting three prisoners in three square, wheeled boxes the eighty miles along crooked roads and terrible terrain. It took all day, and they arrived on the cobbled streets of the city at midnight. They were escorted to a large prison far from the shadow of the temple.

When she exited the box, she could see Gritz and Boataz being manhandled into the men's side of the prison. She was just as badly treated as she was dragged and then pushed into a prisoner's yard and hit on the head with a stick until she was driven into a small building and presented at a high desk.

'Charge?' asked a brutish-looking woman.

'Murder and civil unrest,' said one of the soldiers.

'This is ridiculous!' She was struck on the shoulder by the woman behind the desk, using a long pole with a wire hoop on the end.

'Cell 53,' she said, and Rachel was dragged along a long corridor and thrown into a cell of iron. The floors were filthy and the bed a mass of dirty, worn straw. She sat down, shaking, and drew her knees up beneath her chin. Numerous faces peered at her from the gloom of the other cells lit by a single oil-burning lantern suspended by a rope from the dingy ceiling. Thirty other female inmates, underfed and malnourished, lay listless and broken in the squalor and deprivation of the prison.

195

Rachel started to cry but suppressed the sound by biting on her hand. How was she to survive this latest madness of misfortune? The charges were appalling, and she could not fathom any way of surviving this trial – she felt utterly beaten.

To her surprise, she managed to slumber. Resting her head on her knees, closing her eyes and listening to the low murmur of the other women, she managed to drift off to sleep. She dreamed of the Healer walking through the crowd as ten men sought to stone her, causing them all to drop their rocks. He bent down and asked her to follow him.

When she awoke, it was deep into the night and there was some commotion outside her cell. A large woman in a dark uniform undid the door and beckoned her to follow her. She was accompanied by a soldier, who pulled her roughly to her feet and shoved her out of the cell.

They walked a hundred yards along the dim corridor, the air thick with the smell of excrement and urine, and entered a block with white-painted walls. One of the side rooms was open, and a slim man sat at the table waiting for her.

'Rachel, yes,' he said, sounding bored.

She nodded and sat down at the table, her hands shaking.

'You are charged with murder and insurrection, crimes punishable by crucifixion. If you plead guilty, we can commute the sentence to life in prison… What say you?'

'There has been a misunderstanding.'

'They all say that – so I will write down you are pleading not guilty, and then they will flog you and lead you up the hill where you will be nailed to a cross and die in agony. That is what you want?'

'I want justice. Surely I have a case that can be heard?'

His eyes were searching her and looking at her breasts, and she sensed his arousal at her plight.

'How about we have a good time and I will put a word in for you?' he said, leering at her.

'How about you back off?' she said, and he hit her across the face.

'Not guilty then, and I will add attacking an official of the empire to your charge sheet. Take her away.'

She was thrown into the cell and lay gasping at the pain in her body. She waited for daylight to appear in the gloom of a distant window, exhausted and bereft of hope.

✦ ✦ ✦

'What happened to you?' asked Boataz, staring angrily at Gritz, who still wore the remnants of Ode's fine, tailored clothes, now ripped and sodden.

'Ode the bookkeeper betrayed me.' Boataz was in the next cell, and thick iron bars and manacles contained his wrath, so Gritz explained how he had gone back to the estate and robbed the men of all their treasure.

'You thief! You damned thief…' The expletives were so loud and so offensive that a hush fell over the cacophony of the other male inmates.

'How did you know where I hid it all?' demanded Boataz.

'The old hag in the mountain, she used divination and magic to lead me straight to it in the well. I took it all and then went to Ode to convert some of it, but he recognised me as one of your men and turned me in to the Roman authorities. Now I will pay with my life for your stupidity, Boataz.'

'Don't you talk like that to me, you rat. I'll cut your tongue out before the night is over.'

'Why did you kill the household in Capernaum? Was that really necessary? Maybe a little coercion or an abduction could have sufficed. They were Roman citizens, and now we are charged with insurrection, punishable by death.'

'I can't wait to see you hang, you wretch,' bellowed Boataz, fighting with the chains around his legs and wrists.

'What was I thinking when I joined your crew?' retorted Gritz.

'What was I thinking trusting a thief like you?'

The shouting and hollering between the two men subsided when two guards appeared, wielding iron bars. Gritz sat down on his haunches far from Boataz, who sat on his bed, his head hanging down with his chin on his chest.

'He brought it on himself, that puny rat; he owed me dear.'

'All this for a stolen child? It can't really have been worth it.'

'I sold him the child, and then he got into debt. He came to me for help, and I lent him a small fortune, which he never repaid. What does that make me look like? What about all the other debtors? I rule by fear.'

'You said his father was loaded and we would get it back by just stealing the child – why did you slit their throats?'

'The look in his eyes – there was no fear – just a defiant glare of privilege. It was too much to bear, so I slit the shyster's throat and that of his wife. So what? They were Roman citizens, scum through and through, the lot of them.'

'It makes the difference between a quick death and one of drawn-out agony, that's what,' moaned Gritz. 'Why was there a woman in the third box?'

'She's the one who started this all off, the whore who stole the girl and returned her to her grandparents, and alerted the Romans in the process.'

'So why is she implicated, if she rescued the girl?'

'Because I said so, and the madam at Theims tried to trick me, too. I said Rachel was one of our accomplices, and they are eager to lock up anybody they can, so they have charged her, too. I cannot wait to see her crucified.'

'Do they crucify women?'

'If one slave kills his master, they crucify all the servants, male or female. And I understand their logic – rule through fear and retribution.'

'If she is the one you stole the baby from, haven't you punished her enough already?'

'No, I haven't even started.' He grimaced.

Maniac, thought Gritz, who felt some sympathy for the women whom Boataz abused through his brothels and gaming rooms. He wondered how he could help this woman escape Boataz's ire just so he could have the last laugh. He sat and listened to the din in the prison and smiled at the pleasure he had taken in telling Boataz to his face that he had stolen and lost all his fortune.

'You know I shall murder you before they do, don't you, Gritz?' growled Boataz throughout the night, waking him from his slumbers to spite him.

Early in the morning, Gritz was taken to see the prosecutor and caught sight of Rachel walking back to the women's wing. He remembered her on the day they had taken her child; he felt guilt and pain and recommitted himself to helping her in any way he could.

However hard he tried, he could not seem to wake Malachi, the scribe and lawyer, from his slumber. Thomas banged on the doors, threw stones up at the shuttered windows and waited until the shutters finally opened and Malachi appeared.

'What the heck!' he grumbled.

'It's Thomas. I need your help urgently.'

'What time is it? My wife will kill me... Shush, I'm coming down.'

The young lawyer opened one of the bottom doors and allowed Thomas to join him in the front room of the small but pleasantly appointed house.

'What is going on?' demanded Malachi.

Thomas asked if he could be seated and then explained his predicament, outlining all that he could remember about Rachel and her situation.

'So, why have they charged her?'

'Boataz the brigand says that she is an accomplice.'

'It is vital that we get those charges dropped. If she goes to trial on that basis, it is almost impossible that she will escape with anything less than a heavy jail sentence and perhaps life imprisonment.'

'Surely the testimony of Mina will suffice to clear her name?'

'Mina is a minor. She won't even be allowed to give evidence. Nor will they accept the evidence of a villain like Boataz. No, I need to examine the charges myself.'

Malachi got dressed and the two men travelled to the prison where they waited patiently for an interview with the prosecuting officer. After two hours, they were taken to a low-ceilinged room with white-painted walls.

'Good morning, kind sir,' said Malachi. 'We'd like to discuss the charges against a young woman called Rachel, who has been bought in from Capernaum.'

'I need to see your licence,' said the thin-faced man with a pock-marked face. He stared blandly at the documents Malachi provided and then looked through a pile of parchments to find to Rachel's charge sheet.

'I will give you ten minutes,' he said, sounding bored, and left them alone.

Malachi read the charges and then stroked his chin.

'These charges have nothing to do with Boataz. Mina's grandfather is making the claim that she threatened to extort money from him when he went to meet Boataz in a boat.'

'Asri! But that makes no sense. Why would he lie?' exclaimed Thomas.

'He tried to get her stoned, and now he's raised these trumped-up allegations – what has he got against Rachel? We need to speak to Rachel and Mina and this Asri to find out why he is doing this.'

'That won't be easy. Mina has joined the followers of the Healer with my brother, Mathias. How long do we have?'

'We have precious little time to have these charges struck off, but it will be weeks before they come to trial. But Pilate is making an example of all felons, so it may be quicker than that.'

The prosecuting officer returned to the room, and Malachi asked him whether he could see Rachel. The man stood, spat on the floor and held out his hand.

'Either you or she make it worth my while,' he said lewdly.

Malachi shook his head and passed some coins into the man's greedy hand. He then sent for Rachel.

After a short while, she appeared, bedraggled and filthy, in the doorway. She shuffled in under the weight of the manacles and the heavy bindings on her wrists.

'You look terrible!' said Thomas. 'Sit down. This is Malachi. He is a scribe and a lawyer I have asked to help us.'

Rachel shook with cold, and Thomas took off his cloak and draped it round her. He hugged her and she gasped.

'The charges against you have been bought by Mina's grandfather, Asri. He says that you extorted money out of him and you were present when he was threatened by Boataz on a boat – does this make any sense to you?'

'No,' she whispered meekly.

'What reason has this man to detest you so much?'

'Mina asked me to think of some connection between her and myself that would implicate her grandfather – but I can think of nothing.'

'Mina – I wish she was here. Why is she following this Healer?' moaned Malachi.

'She, like Mathias, is following her heart,' said Rachel with a quiet voice. She flashed her eyes up at Thomas and tried to smile at him.

'We will get you free, Rachel – I am sure we can get to the bottom of this,' said Thomas as warmly as he could.

Rachel was led away, and Malachi and Thomas walked back to the scribe's house through the busy city thoroughfares.

'You look as though you need a sleep, Thomas. Why don't you rest?'

Reluctantly, Thomas agreed and slept in one of the side rooms, oblivious to the sounds of Malachi's family of three boys waking up in the rooms above him.

When he awoke, it was mid-afternoon, and he panicked. Malachi's wife was sitting looking at him.

'Where is Malachi?' he asked.

'He is at work,' she said tersely.

'What is wrong, Sarah?' he asked.

'What stinking mess have you laid at our door? Yesterday, we were rejoicing my pregnancy, and today I am in fear of my husband's livelihood, if not his life.'

'What is this?' asked Thomas, confused.

'He has no experience of defending a criminal charged with murder and insurrection, and regardless of the outcome, he will be ruined if he takes this case. So, I beseech you, if you love him or care for him, you will leave this very day before he returns and not come back again until this mess is over.'

'But there is an innocent woman's life on the line here!' protested Thomas.

'And here there is an innocent woman, an unborn child, a father and three boys' lives on the line – so do not expect sympathy from me.' Her voice trailed off as she heard Malachi in the hall greeting the boys, who were jumping on his back and playing with him.

'Darling,' said Malachi, feeling her stomach as he kissed her. 'Thomas, how are you feeling?'

'Look, Malachi, I am sorry, but I think there has been a misunderstanding. It may be better that I hire someone else who has more experience than you. No offence intended.'

Malachi looked at his wife and then Thomas.

'There is no one else who will take this case, Thomas.'

'Why?'

'You cannot defend such a case without suffering some loss. If you win, you are a troublemaker, and if you lose, a fool.'

'Then I cannot hire you, my friend. I will have to do this on my own.'

'No, Thomas,' said Malachi, looking at Sarah, who was trembling.

'Say goodbye, Malachi,' she said angrily.

'Goodbye, friend,' said Thomas, extending his hand and leaving the house.

CHAPTER 22

✦ ✦ ✦

Mathias and Mina walked for days across the countryside, ministering to the poor and helping the sick. At each town, the Healer and his followers would seek to preach at the synagogue or out in an open space where many would gather to hear and receive his blessing. Not every town received them favourably, and sometimes they had to wait out in the open for the crowds to gather to them.

Early in the morning, the Healer would leave the camp and seek time on his own in lonely places. Mina would try to stir herself at the early hour to get a glimpse of him as he left for his own quiet time with God.

On morning, when they were but a few days from Jerusalem, she rose early in anticipation of his flight into the wilderness and followed him at a distance just to see where he went and how he practised communion with God, but Ruth, her gatekeeper, caught her intrusion and headed her back to the camp.

'What were you thinking of, Mina?' she asked.

'I just wanted to see how he communed with God,' said Mina sheepishly.

'I can show you how he communes with God – but first you must understand that, as a vessel, you must be filled with the Spirit of God. Imagine that you are a temple, and the glory of God descends to fill you – in that moment, and in that moment only, can you begin to dialogue with God.'

'But surely I will be burned up in an instant?'

'Only those who know God as Father can draw this close, and only those who know the Healer as the Son of God can recognise that Fatherhood.'

'What is this spirit?'

'The question is *who* is this spirit? It is the person of God made manifest within us.'

Ruth calmed Mina and then asked her to sit beside her, beneath a large tree. She held the young girl's hands and then prayed for her. Mina watched her face as a peace descended upon her mien, and the older woman spoke passionately, yet calmly, of the coming of God's spirit to fill Mina's new innermost being. Mina felt a calm falling over her mind like warm oil poured over her head and brow, touching her face and gently removing any doubts, anxiety and fear. She imagined a bright white light exploding in her very midst, causing streams of darkness to flee her being. The white light brightened and then expanded in a wide horizontal line, filling every dimension of her mind.

She felt lifeless, floating, like debris on a warm summer lake, the sun burning in the sky, and then she saw herself lying on a beach, soaked, looking up at the Healer who offered his hand to pull her back to her feet.

Ruth and Mina waited for an hour before the Healer returned, passing them on the road. He waited for them beside an outcrop of rocks, smiling at them. But they said nothing as they joined him and returned to the camp.

They helped pack up the camp and get ready for another day's walk towards the mighty temple city of Jerusalem. The sky was light and the walk airy; Mina's face tingled with the sensation of the breath of God warming her face, and playing with her hair, and pushing her gently along the road in a great meditative silence.

✦ ✦ ✦

It took nearly two days for Thomas to get back to Capernaum. The weather had changed, the wind howled and the rain fell, making the roads slushy and passage difficult.

He burst into Asri's residence, pushing past the servants, and demanded to see the master of the house. He woke Elizabeth, and it was only her cries of fear that bought Asri downstairs.

'What is this?' he shouted at Thomas.

'I need to talk to you about Rachel,' replied Thomas, desperate to speak to him.

The old man looked stubbornly at his wife and ordered the servants to put her back to bed and leave him alone with Thomas.

'How dare you break into my house like this? I will send for the soldiers!' he remonstrated, forcing Thomas closer to the door.

'Why have you raised charges against Rachel?' demanded Thomas.

'What is this that he is saying?' cried Elizabeth.

'Get her to bed!' shouted Asri.

He pulled Thomas to the door and hissed at him.

'How dare you! That woman is a whore. Now get out or I will call the soldiery.'

'Drop these charges! She has done nothing to hurt you. She saved Mina and this is how you repay her.'

'I had it all in hand. I just had to pay the ransom, and she goes and ruins everything by poking her nose into my business!' Asri pushed Thomas outside onto the ground and slammed the door. Thomas picked himself up and stood in the doorway panting, his hands on his knees.

'What ails you?' said a voice.

He looked up to find Portius and Servus standing behind him.

'He has raised charges against Rachel, accusing her of being in collusion with Boataz to defraud him. She is being tried for murder and civil unrest and faces execution.'

'When did these charges appear?' Portius asked Servus.

'These must have been lodged at Jerusalem; Asri is a man of great influence.'

'Thomas, go back to Jerusalem and leave this matter to me,' said Portius.

'What will become of her?' asked Thomas, but the two soldiers could say nothing to dissipate his fear for her life.

'What is it now?' bellowed Asri as Portius and Servus entered his room.

'Why have you made allegations about Rachel?' asked Portius. 'It seems you will do anything to get rid of her. Why is that?'

'She was part of the plot to embezzle me – it is a simple as that.'

'On what basis do you make this claim?'

'I do not need to explain myself to you – you are no longer involved. This case is outside your jurisdiction.'

'So was it you who tipped the authorities off in Jerusalem to get them involved so I would be effectively ruled out of the investigation.'

'You credit me with too much influence.'

'The one thousand denarii your manservant said you raised for Boataz's ransom – what did you do with it?'

'That is none of your business,' growled the old man.

'Quite the contrary. I believe you have been bribing officials to get this case moved out of my jurisdiction, and I will use all my powers to investigate this and assure myself that everything to do with you is above board.'

'You will regret this intrusion, Portius,' said Asri belligerently.

'How so?'

'I have friends in Jerusalem who will see you posted to some hell hole far from your family.'

'So, you threaten me?' said Portius, drawing nose to nose with the old man.

'I just give you due warning to leave this case alone; it has nothing to do with you anymore.'

✦ ✦ ✦

'Master,' said Mina.

'Why do you call me master?'

'Lord.'

He laughed. 'Yeshua will do, child.'

'Yeshua, I want to follow you but…'

'Ah, there it is, that little but… a little word that comes filled with self-doubt and deceit.' He was smiling at Mina, so she continued.

'But, Yeshua, I do not know you…'

'You did not choose me; I chose you and will appoint you to bear much fruit.'

'But I understand so little,' she protested, but her fears were melted by the glint in his eye and the smile of acceptance on his face.

'It is good that you understand little, for the little that you have will be like grit in the oyster; it will grow into a precious pearl once you know my business. Then you will not call me master but friend.'

'What is your business, Yeshua?'

'To put a grit of sand in every oyster I choose...'

'But how can I do that?'

'You will learn to be a disciple and then teach others to do the same... but you must stay in me and I in you. Now, child, come closer.'

He put his hand on her head and closed his eyes.

He bent his head and whispered into her ears. She did not understand what he said, but he smiled and then put his finger to her lips.

'Tell no one but the woman you call Rachel. I have a party of men going ahead of me to Jerusalem to prepare the way. You need to ride with them and pass on this word for the hour is nigh.'

'Is she in trouble?'

'Go, child, and wait for me there.'

Three men on horseback rode over to the Healer, who helped Mina up onto a saddle behind Andrew.

'What is happening?' asked Mathias, surprised to see Mina on horseback.

'I have to go and see Rachel. She is in big trouble,' she said anxiously.

'I will come with you,' offered Mathias.

'No, Mathias, walk some more with me,' said the Healer. Mathias looked at Mina, who half smiled to acknowledge the bond of trust between them.

The horses were ridden hard along the pathway, down onto the main road to Jerusalem, with Mina holding onto Andrew for dear life. They rode through the afternoon, through the rain and the wind, reaching the city outskirts in the middle of the night.

✦ ✦ ✦

Thomas was exhausted; the sun was beginning to rise as he galloped into the city. The sunlight glinted on the soft yellow and orange hues of the sandstone buttress and walls around the great temple. He dismounted, tied his horse up in the shadow of the tower of Antonia and knocked on the door of the agent's office.

'Master Thomas, come in, come,' said a friendly voice in the dim light. Tobit, his father's longest-serving agent, smiled and hugged him warmly.

'Tobit, I am sorry, but I need to draw funds to pay for various expenses – I need to hire a lawyer.'

'You look terrible! Come in, come in. There is a bed and a change of clothes out the back… come.' Tobit pulled Thomas into the office and out through a hallway lit by the light of the rising sun streaming through a parlour window.

'Here, rest and I will sort out the funds.'

'It is not as easy as that. My friend Rachel is being charged with murder and insurrection. I'm not sure anybody will defend her.'

'Rest!' said the large, elderly man with grey hair and beard and shining brown eyes.

Thomas slept for two hours before being awakened by Tobit's return.

'He has something to say,' said Tobit, making way for Malachi to enter the room.

'I am sorry, Thomas, but Sarah – she was so troubled, I did not want to upset her.'

'Malachi, I do not want you to come to any harm. It is fine – I can do this on my own.'

'If we can get the charges dropped, then it won't come to trial. This is our best hope; then no one will be implicated.'

'But how do we do that?'

'How did you get on with this Asri? We must find some way of getting him to drop the charges.'

'He will not change his mind or give any explanation why he has made these outrageous claims.'

'We need to get Rachel out of that prison cell. It will cost, but we can pay for her to be taken to a better cell,' said Malachi.

CHAPTER 23

✦ ✦ ✦

'Master,' said Tobit, 'you have a visitor.'

'Mina!' cried Thomas, hugging her.

'I must see Rachel. I have a word from the Healer for her.'

'What word?' he asked.

'I cannot tell anyone but Rachel herself.'

She explained the circumstances leading up to her flight into the city and the urgency of her need to tell Rachel what Yeshua had told her to say.

'Let's go,' said Malachi, and they mounted their horses and rode through the streets thickening with people milling around the temple in preparation for Passover.

At the prison, they asked to see the prosecuting officer and were taken to the interview room where they waited for several minutes before the officer skulked into the room.

His eyes lit up brightly as they explained their desire for Rachel to be moved to a more comfortable place.

'This is not an inn,' declared the officer.

'What will it cost for her to be moved? Ten, twelve, thirteen denarii?' asked Malachi.

'Fourteen and she can sleep in my bed!' laughed the officer with a disgusting leer.

'Fourteen, then; here,' said Thomas, handing over the money.

'When is the trial?' asked Malachi.

'Pilate wants to make a spectacle of them at Passover, so very soon,' said the officer, carefully counting his money.

'When you say spectacle, do you mean crucifixion?' asked Malachi.

'Yes, we have the possibility of four,' gloated the officer.

'Can we please speak to her?' begged Mina.

The officer held out his hand and Thomas pushed more denarii into his fleshy, sweating palm. He left the room and returned half an hour later with Rachel in chains. She looked deplorable, and Mina gasped in horror.

'Why have you bought her here?' Rachel asked angrily. 'She has been through enough.'

'Yeshua sent me with a word,' protested Mina.

Rachel sat down, filthy and aching, on the low bench beside the table. She was shivering, and bruises marked her ankles and wrists where the manacles had cut into her flesh.

'What word, Mina?'

Mina went over to her and hugged her. She stroked Rachel's hair and then bent over and whispered in her ear.

'What?' Rachel seemed greatly disturbed by the single word Mina had uttered.

'That is what he told me to say to you.'

'Birthmark – he told you to come all this way and say birthmark...' Rachel's eyes flitted across Mina's face, looking confused and wounded.

'What does this mean?' asked Malachi.

'I have a birthmark,' said Mina.

'You have a birthmark!' cried Rachel. 'So do I. It is shaped like a sickle, and Anna had the same mark.' Rachel shook and put her hand over her mouth. 'It cannot be....' She fell to her knees crying, and Mina went over to her and helped Thomas lift her back onto the bench.

'But what does this mean?' said Mina.

'It means that you are Rachel's daughter,' said Thomas.

'But my mother and father...'

'They must have known what had happened, and maybe they didn't pay what was due to Boataz.'

Mina withdrew to the corner of the room and shook. Rachel stared at her and trembled.

'You are my mother!' exclaimed Mina.

'And you are my daughter,' retorted Rachel.

Mina walked over to Rachel and the two embraced.

Portius had travelled on his own into Jerusalem and had taken a direct route to the procurator's office. Pontius Pilate was away on business, which gave Portius ample time to interview the officers in charge of the case against Boataz and his accomplices.

'What I do not understand is why the case was referred to Jerusalem when we were in the middle of putting the charges together ourselves,' he said to the elderly head of internal affairs.

'The first thing we heard about it was when a prosecuting officer came to us with the story of the insurgents and the murder of Roman officers and citizens. It was quite a shock; why did you not keep us informed of these matters?' said the elderly gentlemen.

'My investigations were quite delicate, and I could not afford to lose the chance to capture the fugitive Boataz. Who is this prosecuting officer and how did he get all of this confidential information?'

The elderly man gave him the name and Portius left the house for the prison. He arrived just as Thomas and his party were leaving. They collided in the cold entrance to the prison.

'Portius, it is good to see you. Have there been any developments?'

'I am following certain leads; what about here?'

'We just found out that Mina is Rachel's daughter. They share the same birthmark!'

Portius smiled wryly.

'So, the old man Asri, who has made these allegations against Rachel, knew they were related – he purchased Anna and must have known where she came from and the name of the mother. He knew the birthmark would be discovered, so tried to have her killed, first by stoning and now by execution. Thank you.'

'Does this help?' asked Thomas hopefully.

'We shall see. Now I am staying in the temple tavern; if you hear any further news, leave a message.'

Thomas and his party left the prison, and Portius pushed through the door and asked for an interview with the prosecuting officer, Cato of Iberia.

Cato entered the room eating an apple, his uniform dishevelled and his hair unkempt. He stared at the Roman officer in his military uniform and gulped.

'What can I do for you?' he asked, sitting down opposite Portius.

'I am Portius, the examiner of the district of Galilee, and my case was pulled from my jurisdiction because of your evidence. I am not happy!'

'These are serious crimes, and we should have been alerted to these incidents as soon as they occurred.'

'How do you know Asri?'

215

'He is a family friend,' replied Cato, trying to straighten his neck scarf.

'He passed on all of this information, but you have no authority and could do nothing unless you raised this case with Pilate's office. You took some risk.'

'It was my duty.'

'Was it your duty to accept such a hefty bribe?' added Portius darkly.

Cato looked nervous and fiddled with his necktie.

'Says who?'

'Drop the charges for this woman, Rachel – she is completely innocent – and I shall spare you,' said Portius.

'She is guilty! I have witnesses from both Asri and Boataz.'

'It is you who are guilty, my friend, and I will not leave a stone unturned until I prove it.'

'I need some new evidence. I can't just overturn it.'

'I can prove conclusively that Rachel is the mother of Mina, Asri's granddaughter, and he did everything in his power to kill her before the truth was revealed to his wife that his son and daughter-in-law had purchased a stolen child and faked the pregnancy and birth.

'But you will accompany me as I interview this Gaul – he may be able to confirm all of this.'

Cato gulped. 'I need more than your theories. Let's interview this Gaul and see whether fortune is smiling on us both.'

Gritz was bought into the room, in worse condition than Rachel. He had been severely beaten and his forehead was covered in cuts and bruises.

'Sit down,' ordered Portius.

'What do you want of me?' asked Gritz, his eyes swollen and nearly closed.

'The prosecuting officer here can relieve your circumstances and afford you a comfortable cell free of beatings if you cooperate with our enquiries,' continued Portius.

'Relieve my circumstances? I am a thief, not a murderer, and Boataz is a madman.'

'We can lessen the charges – not that that will change the sentence, but it will help you live the remaining days of your life in more comfortable and predictable circumstances,' said Portius.

'Free of interrogation?'

'Free until you are tried and found guilty,' growled Cato.

'What do I have to do – confess? Because that is not going to happen.'

'No, we merely need some information about Boataz and the harlot, Rachel. Why is he indicting her and claiming she is part of his plan to extort money out of Mina's family?'

'Because Boataz is a maniac. He will destroy everyone that crosses him. That is his mantra – hurt those who hurt you twenty times harder.'

'So how did this woman cross him?'

'She escaped with the child, Mina. From the brothel he had placed her in.'

'If we go back sixteen years, do you remember this same woman having her child taken from her?'

'Yes, of course; I told him not to be so mental. The child he took from this harlot was probably sold to a couple in Capernaum, the same family Boataz butchered. But he had to play games and drop the child back in the same place she had been snatched from; fate intervened and reunited them. Does she know this Mina is her child?'

'She does now,' replied Portius.

'He is spiteful, so he concocted this tale that Rachel was implicated in the extortion, but that is just not true. She is innocent.'

'And would you repeat this at the trial?' asked Portius.

'Of course.'

'Then Cato here will escort you to a more favourable cell.'

The knock on the door disturbed Tobit, Malachi and Thomas's discussion with Mina. It sounded emphatic and military, and Tobit looked nervous as he went to open the door.

Portius entered with Rachel draped in a long, thick military cloak.

'Rachel!' cried Mina, running to be with the woman.

'What is this?' asked Malachi.

'The charges have been dropped – she is a free woman,' said Portius, bowing to Rachel and then leaving the house.

'I just need a bath and a sleep,' pleaded Rachel.

'Of course; I will get the servants to prepare a room for you,' said Tobit.

'Thomas, can I go and buy her fresh clothes?' asked Mina.

'Of course,' he said, handing her some money.

CHAPTER 24

✦ ✦ ✦

The followers had entered Jericho, and the streets were lined with people cheering and clapping. Mathias walked gingerly along the street, marvelling at the great reception the Healer was drawing from the crowd. The sycamore trees were fully leaved, and the wind lifted the branches to show people who had climbed up into the trees to get a better view.

The Healer was walking alone in front of the followers and suddenly stopped and looked up into the tree. He called to a man by name, and the man climbed down to stand at his feet. He was very short but looked extremely wealthy – his presence drew hisses and boos and shouts of 'Tax collector!' from the crowd.

'I must stay at your house tonight, Zacchaeus,' said the Healer. The crowd booed and bayed and some shouted abuse at the Healer for mixing with such a rogue as a tax collector. The man stood in the full gaze of the Healer and he trembled. He tried to cover his eyes as if the sun were too bright for him.

'Lord, I will give half my fortune to the poor and repay all I have extorted four times over... Just, pray, forgive me.'

The Healer put his hands on the man's shoulders and declared, 'Today salvation has come to this house – for the Son of Man has come to seek and to save the lost.'

The crowd cried out with cheers and exclamations of awe and wonder as Zacchaeus the tax collector escorted the Healer to his palatial home.

Such was his gratitude towards the Healer that he laid on a full banquet for all fifty or so of his followers plus many of his friends. Mathias sat next to a large, thick-set man who was a fisherman by trade and who spent much time in the company of the Healer.

'My name is Simon. I hear you are Jezreel's son. Did you ever learn to fish yourself?' asked the rough-looking fisherman.

'No, my father ran the business, but my brother wanted to be a scribe, so we had nothing to do with the business until he passed away last year. We have appointed agents. Yourself?'

The man ate into a leg of chicken, pulling the flesh from the bone with his bare hands.

'I am a fisherman; this is all new to me,' he said, picking up a nectarine and scrunching it into his mouth, the thick juice flowing down his beard.

'May I ask you a question?' asked Mathias.

'Sure,' said Simon, going back to his chicken.

Why does the Healer call himself the Son of Man, and why does he say he has come to seek and save the lost?'

'I am a simple man, so I have a simple understanding of things. He is my Lord, my master, my friend; I do whatever he commands because I love him with all my heart. You may have to find someone cleverer than me to answer anything more than that.'

'Who are the lost?'

'All those who do not know him as the shepherd; they are shepherdless. He has come that they might be rescued from the darkness of never seeing or hearing the shepherd's voice. All have strayed and fallen short of the glory of God, yet not everyone who hears him accepts him as Lord.

'The road to hell is wide and long, the road to heaven narrow. He chooses those who he calls and appoints to go out and make disciples.'

'He has not called everyone?'

'No, only those who hear his voice and follow are called – some start out well and fade, some are choked by the world, others could not care less about spiritual matters and reject him.'

'But the miracles?'

'Many who are healed do not follow him, and many who witness them do not budge an inch. These miracles just demonstrate his love for the people. He puts himself at great risk in what he says and what he demonstrates.'

'Risk?'

'The authorities are taking a keener interest in his affairs. He is challenged at every teaching. And they do not take kindly to him.'

'Why not?'

'They are keepers of the law, of rules and regulations, dressed up in priestly garb; their heads are full of legalistic drivel. They seek to ensnare him so they can punish and silence him. And if they do, all our lives will be threatened.'

'But what authority do they have over the Son of Man?'

'I do not have a clue. All I know is that going to Jerusalem is a bad, bad idea, but he won't listen to reason.'

'How can I grow in my understanding of all of this?' begged Mathias.

'Stay close to him; it is simple, really.'

After the meal, the followers rested on the many cushions that had been scattered around the room. The men and the women were separated by the large table where Yeshua, Simon, two women and another man sat talking quietly.

Mathias found it hard to turn off his mind. He had seen so many amazing things since he had followed the Healer, yet he understood so little he felt as if he was an imposter. He thought of Rachel, Mina and his brother, and tried to pray for them using the pattern of prayer Andrew had introduced to him. He was not far into the prayer when he fell asleep.

In the morning, Zacchaeus had prepared breakfast for them, and the Healer was talking to a party of women who had come in from the street. Mathias could see they were women of ill-repute and marvelled that he conversed so freely with them.

The road from Jericho to Bethany was long and tiring and free from crowds, although the followers had temporarily swelled to over a hundred before people started to return to their homes.

A young man, fresh-faced and tall, attached himself to Mathias and asked him many questions that Mathias just could not answer.

'You need to speak to some of the men at the front,' exclaimed Mathias to the young man.

'Why are you following him then?' asked the young man.

'Because I believe,' stuttered Mathias.

'Believe what?'

'That he came into my life for a reason; that he chose me and appointed me as a disciple to learn his ways and obey his commands.'

'So you are responding to a calling?'

'Yes, of course.'

'Do you think he would call me?'

'I do not think you would be here unless you had been called.'

'But how will I know for certain?'

'Because you know you belong here and do not want to go anywhere else.'

The Healer did not teach them anything until they arrived at Bethany and sat around the house and garden of a brother and two sisters who appeared precious to the Healer. Ruth came and found him and sat with him.

'Who are those people?' the young man asked.

'That is Lazarus, and his sisters, Mary and Martha. They are special friends of Yeshua; they go back a long way.'

The Healer stood on a slight incline and addressed the followers, with the brother and sisters sitting on the ground in front of him. He spoke of his heartache that the authorities in the city would reject him. His voice trailed into silence and then he wept over the people of Israel, over the nation. He said the temple system was dead, the priesthood corrupt and the law used to burden the people. He would see the destruction of the temple in three days, a statement which drew alarm from Simon the fisherman, who shook his head and muttered complaints the Healer ignored.

When they returned to their journey over the brow of the hill at Bethany, they looked down at the Mount of Olives and the soft, undulating hills leading down towards the mighty fortress city of Jerusalem, set on a hill across the valley. Again, the Healer wept at the sight of the city, and Simon and some of the women comforted him. Mary, Martha and Lazarus had joined the party now, walking down towards the gates into Jerusalem.

To Mathias's surprise, crowds had gathered along the streets to see the Healer. The men who had been sent ahead were waiting beyond the city gates with a colt, which the Healer mounted. The crowds cheered and the followers pushed in behind the Healer as he rode the colt through the people who were now waving palm branches and throwing them in front of the colt as it slowly proceeded along the main road into the city.

A low hum was heard in the crowd as the pilgrims' song 'God bless the One who comes in the name of the Lord!' started to be sung all along the procession. The followers, walking steadily in rows three deep behind the Healer, were showered with palm branches too.

The party stopped at the temple, the massive edifice rising high into the air and supporting the imposing Tower of Antonia, from where Roman soldiers watched the city for any sign of riot or unrest. The Healer dismounted from the colt and he, his followers and most of the crowd went into the outer courts of the temple.

Yeshua walked everywhere, observing the traders of birds, sheep, lambs and other animals mingling with the money changers as hundreds of people filled the temple, ready to purchase an offering for their sins at the exorbitant prices charged by the traders.

He quickly withdrew, and Mathias and the followers went with him, via the back streets and alleyways, out of the gate through which he had entered, over the Mount of Olives and back to Bethany. He seemed upset and agitated and went into the house with Mary and Lazarus, while Martha supervised the lighting of a large fire and the preparation of food for the evening meal. Darkness fell and the fire burned brightly as Mathias sat with Ruth and pondered the day's events.

'Why did he seem so upset at the temple?'

'The temple is his Father's house of prayer, and the traders and money lenders have polluted it just because the priests want to grow rich and comfortable on the sacrifices. The whole system is corrupt, and it is too much for him to bear. He has come that we might be living temples, and a new priesthood, with a new covenant.'

'How can we be living temples? What about the sacrifice and the law?'

'He will fulfil the law and be our ultimate sacrifice!'

'But how?' asked Mathias.

'We do not know. He speaks sometimes in riddles, but the meaning will be made clear to us at some point in the future. All we know is that he will fulfil everything that is written about the suffering servant.'

'Has he not come to remove all suffering?' asked Mathias.

'No, he has come to show us how to suffer well in obedience to the Father.'

'Surely they will kill him if he continues telling the authorities such things? Simon is very worried about him.'

'Simon believes it is time for the Healer to rise up and lead the people in the overthrow of the old system; he's keen for a revolution, with the Messiah's rule and reign, but Yeshua will have none of it. We are all just waiting to see what happens now we are here in Jerusalem.'

'Do you think he will be careful?' asked Mathias.

Tobit had been making arrangements for the Passover meal, and the top floor was filled with low couches and cushions. The room was big enough for twenty people.

'Who are you inviting?' asked Thomas as they waited for Mina and Rachel to wake up from their mid-afternoon sleep.

'You and your guests, master,' said Tobit.

'My guests?'

'Yes, before you arrived, three men came here on horseback and said I needed to prepare a room for Passover. When I asked by what authority this request was made, they said master Mathias and Thomas require a room for twenty for the Healer.'

225

'The Healer? Yes, of course, that is fine. Please ensure we have the finest food and wines available; he is an esteemed guest.'

Thomas felt torn between waiting for Rachel to rebuild her strength and finding Mathias and re-joining the followers of the Healer. He felt ecstatic that the Healer would be using the room in the agent's house for Passover.

At four o'clock, the house lit by candles, Rachel appeared in a new dress, her hair washed and oiled, her skin shining and her spirits lifted. Mina followed, dressed like a picture of loveliness.

'The Healer is coming here for Passover, Mina. Do you imagine we will see Mathias?'

Rachel recognised the longing in his voice and begged him to go and find his brother and pay his respects to the Healer. But he refused, excusing himself to go and help Tobit decorate the upper room.

'I am so grateful to the Healer,' said Mina, 'but how did he know that the birthmark would be the breakthrough in discovering the truth about us?'

Rachel was tense and could not understand why she felt so gloomy and morbid. Mention of the Healer annoyed her, and she could not work out why. She felt angry with him, yet twice he had saved her life.

'I have given my life to follow him,' said Mina.

Rachel bit her lip. She could not bear the thought of losing Mina again but did not want to alienate her. Everything was still so new between them that it was almost more awkward now than it had been before.

'What does that mean – given your life to follow him? You have barely come of age!'

'He is so different to anybody I have ever met.'

'That is hardly a ringing endorsement; you don't exactly know many people.'

Mina laughed. 'Why do you get so cross when it comes to any mention of the Healer?'

'To be honest, Mina, I don't know, but mention of his name seems to make me panic inside, somewhere where I have no control.'

'But why? He has done you no harm, this Yeshua, Lord, Son of Man.'

Rachel was breathing heavily and could not control the sudden sense that she was about to vomit.

'I don't feel well,' she cried loudly, causing Thomas to come back into the room.

'What is the matter?' he asked, looking worried.

'I can't breathe,' said Rachel, standing up and then suddenly falling on the floor where she started to convulse.

'Get her tongue,' said Mina, jumping to Rachel's aid.

'Lord God, calm this woman, we ask you in the name of Yeshua,' prayed Thomas.

Rachel slumped over as if dead, and Thomas and Mina carried her into the bedroom and laid her on the bed. She seemed to have a temperature, and they could not wake her up.

'We must get the Healer,' murmured Mina.

'I will search for him,' said Thomas.

Outside, Thomas stared into the cold evening sky. The clouds were thick and portentous, and the stars were hidden. He had to find the Healer and went straight to the temple to get news of his whereabouts.

He soon learned that the Healer had visited the temple and driven out all the money changers and animal traders. He had denounced the system, rebuked the priests for their usury and condemned the temple as a den of thieves. The city was abuzz with the expectation that something dramatic was on the verge of occurring that would rock the establishment and perhaps drive out the Roman conquerors.

He learned of the Messiah's entry into the city on a colt. Everybody he spoke to seemed filled with wonder at the potential of the man. But no one seemed to know where he was currently located until he spoke to an old woman who said he had gone to the house of Lazarus in Bethany.

Thomas ran as fast as he could through the city and up onto the Mount of Olives where, at last, he could see torches and a fire illuminating a large house and garden.

CHAPTER 25

✦ ✦ ✦

The first person Thomas recognised was Mathias, who was sitting on the garden gate watching the fire blaze against the dull evening sky. The two men embraced and Mathias was desperate to know what had happened to Rachel.

'She is a free woman, but she is very ill. I am terrified that something is badly wrong with her. Mina is tending her while she sleeps, but it is urgent that the Healer comes and sees her.'

Mathias spoke to Ruth, who, in turn, spoke to Simon and asked whether Thomas and Mathias could go into the house to speak to the Healer.

'We are ready to go,' said a voice. Thomas turned and saw the Healer standing with his bed rolled up on his back, his winter gown around his shoulders, holding a long staff. 'Simon and John will come with us. I believe you have prepared a room for us?'

Yes, master, but it is Rachel, the girl...'

'With the birthmark. I know. Take me to her.'

Thomas felt slightly dizzy as if the air had changed in texture and orientation. He wanted to bow before the Healer with an overriding sense of being undone, or unclean, of being unready. He struggled to stand as the Healer walked past him, and he fell to his knees.

'Master, forgive me for I have sinned,' he cried.

The Healer came over to Thomas, put his hand on his head and smiled.

'Come, one day you will know me as friend, child.'

Thomas got to his feet, helped by Simon and Mathias. He staggered along with the group, supported by the diminutive figure of Mary, who whispered prayers of peace over his life. Thomas knew he had to make a choice between following the Healer or Rachel, and his heart was torn and greatly disturbed. He just could not let go of Rachel; it was too much to bear and he broke down.

'I have to follow him,' he whispered to Mary, who slipped her arm through his.

Mathias walked with Simon and John while Thomas led the party back through the streets and alleyways to the house of his agent Tobit. He shook as he banged on the door to alert Tobit to his arrival.

Mina opened the door and gasped. She bowed to the Healer, who asked Mary to go in first and inspect Rachel's condition. Yeshua sat in the front room with Simon, John and Mathias, his eyes closed.

Mary reappeared in the room and nodded her head.

'Yeshua, she is ready for you.'

The Healer rose to his feet and asked Simon and John to accompany him. They entered the room and shut the door.

The old woman struggled to wake Jinan. He had been sleeping for hours.

'Wake up, you fool! Get the horses ready; we must go to Jerusalem.'

Madam Thamina sat by the blazing fire, clutching an alabaster jar filled with all the nard she had purchased over twenty years of infamy. All the tears, the beatings, the horror were wiped away by the beautiful coolness and smell of the precious perfume imported from India. She had to escape to Jerusalem now the Romans had set fire to her brothel and allowed all the girls to escape to freedom.

'Why did you lie about the letters?' asked the old woman.

'I was frightened that I would be implicated in the abduction of the child,' replied the madam.

'So, you blamed the only person who actually fought for what is right?'

'Do not chide me, mother. We need to get out of here before they change their minds and decide to press charges. I do not feel good about any of this.'

'You ran a brothel for twenty years, and now you have discovered a conscience!' The old woman cackled.

Jinan awoke and ran out to get the new wagon and horses ready. The interior of the wagon box was made comfortable for the madam and the old woman to sit in and had a wide weatherproof covering. The boy drove the horses carefully through the muddy terrain in front of the hovel until they reached the firmer terrain of the main mountain road.

The seventy miles between Theims and Jerusalem would take a complete day if they did not have to stop for the madam to powder her face and realign her makeup.

'What will become of me?' he asked the old woman as they descended the mountain side.

'You will be fine so long as you do not run away again,' she growled and then laughed through her rotten teeth.

The journey was windswept, cold and wet, and the boy struggled to stay awake, fighting back his fear of seeing the strange creatures and visions of demons that he had seen the last time he had left the mountain.

The old woman had told him that a great light had broken out in the darkness and evil was fighting back. That he lived in strange times unlike

231

any other, when the very bowels of hell had been emptied out upon the land.

But soon, when the light was extinguished and the evil one was victor, all would turn back to its terrible normality.

When they arrived in Jerusalem, they went straight to the rented lodgings Madam Thamina had secured close to the temple, and the old woman whistled through her broken teeth at the luxury of it all.

'Phew, this must have cost you a pretty penny, or a vial or two of nard,' she said with a laugh, stretching out on an ornamental settee covered in ornate silk sheets.

Jinan unpacked the wagon and took the horses into the stable to feed them. He did not feel deranged but continued glancing into the shadows in fear of seeing some phantom leaping about on the surface of a normal person's reality.

The madam and the old woman sent him out to get supplies so he could cook for them, and he bought fine meats, succulent vegetables, fish and many spices and preserves.

He often thought of Rachel and Mina and the rest of the party now that Boataz had been apprehended. It was two o'clock in the morning by the time he had washed all the dishes and locked all the doors to retire for the night.

✦ ✦ ✦

Rachel came to and found the Healer sitting on the bed beside her. He smiled and asked her to drink some water.

'What happened to me?' she asked

'You had a fever; you were burning up and then you convulsed,' said Simon.

'Who are these men?' asked Rachel nervously.

'These are Simon and John. We have come to prepare the upper room for the Passover feast. They can leave us.' He nodded at the two men, who left the room to tell the others that she was free of the fever.

He stood up and looked around the room.

'How are things working out with your daughter? You know you will have to go slowly; you both need time to adjust.'

She gathered the sheet up around her neck and watched him as he moved casually and gently around her.

'How did you know about the birthmark and why did you help me?' she asked.

'Because the Father has given you to me – not that you know it yet, but the time will come when you will realise what a wonderful gift you are to me. I like all these little carvings; they are quite cute, do you not think?' he said playfully, showing her some carved animals on the shelf above the fire.

'I can't just be given away like a chattel,' she protested, still angry with him.

'It's not like that, and deep down inside you know it. But we have to deal with your resentment, your great antipathy. Do you like this?' he said, holding up a carved lion.

'My great resentment?'

'You resent the fact that I am going to forgive you your sins, going to wash you clean, because you think that means I am condemning you.'

'You are judging me... and I find it really patronizing.'

He laughed and sat next to her and slapped his hands on his knees.

'You do? You really find me patronizing?' He could not stop laughing. 'But I know what you mean – sort of,' he said in a whisper, smiling at her. 'You have neglected your God, despised Him because of the great horror you have endured, but he has, in his loving kindness, brought you to this place of refuge and reconciliation.

'Your sin is your resistance to his love, to any love – for in Him, there is no darkness. He is love.'

'So, I am condemned because of my resentment towards a God who allowed my suffering, my corruption, my abuse?' She felt her lips snarling. 'Why did he allow this to happen to me?'

'Satan rules this world with an iron grip, and I have come to smash his dominion, but many will hear and few see. It is he who hates the children of Eve; he is a thief and a murderer. But I have come that you may have life and life to the full.'

'But I have to repent of my sins?'

'You have to follow me; it is your calling. Repentance is a necessary habit, but it must start with your complete rebirth. Anyway, the time is coming when you shall hear, and see, and find great joy. It is but a while away.'

'I am sorry, but I just don't believe you. But thank you for saving my life... again.'

'I have come to save your soul, and there is work to be done yet, child.' He laughed and laid his hand on her head.

She felt an incredible sense of peace and lightness. He left the room and Mina entered.

'You are back!' She smiled. 'How do you feel?'

'Elated.' Rachel looked up at Mina and asked her to sit on the bed next to her. She had put off speaking to her, but the Healer was correct; she needed to proceed slowly but with the intention of regaining her daughter.

'Less of me – how are you feeling? I have gained so much, but you have suffered so terribly. How are you doing?' She picked up a brush and started to untangle the knots in Mina's hair.

'I am fine. It's all just a bit much at the moment,' replied Mina.

'We need to just carry on like we were, getting to know each other and proceeding slowly. Perhaps we could find somewhere to live together.'

'Is that going slowly?' Mina said, pushing Rachel's hand away from her head.

'I told you I am going to follow the Healer. I will live in his midst and follow him wherever he goes.'

'But you have ample time for that. Surely it would be good for the pair of us to get to know each other in the safety of our own place?'

'Rachel, you are not my mother...' She looked upset and bit her lip. 'Not yet; it will take time. But you must trust me and support me.'

'What would she have said?' asked Rachel sadly.

'Who?'

'Your mother. What would she have said about your following this Healer?'

'She would have flipped and locked me upstairs – but you are not like that, are you?' said Mina, kneeling on the bed and starting to brush Rachel's hair.

'And is Thomas going as well?' asked Rachel tersely.

'Everything will go well with us all... It's just you don't know it yet,' said Mina with a smile.

'So you are happy that he has forgiven you your sins? This man of miracles – he can just do that, yes?' asked Rachel, straining every sinew to talk about the Healer without sarcasm in her voice.

'Yes,' said Mina nonchalantly.

'What man can forgive another person's sin? I understand what he says about sinning against God, being defiant, but how can we have sinned against the Healer that he can forgive us? It is all too much for my little head.'

'You need to lighten up. When are you going to stop being horrible to Thomas?'

'Horrible? How dare you!' said Rachel coyly. 'I am spoilt goods; he is better off keeping well away,' she continued.

'You can't just keep saying that; you are stuck in the past. Besides, he doesn't think that, does he?'

'I do not know what he thinks.'

'Then why do you not ask him and stop being so stubborn? I can see why I get in so much trouble, Mother!' said Mina with a grin.

✦ ✦ ✦

'You can't go on like this,' said Mathias, shaking his head.

'She just won't speak to me,' Thomas protested.

'Well, knowing you, you probably said the wrong thing the moment you opened your mouth.'

'But it's just not that easy. I want to follow Yeshua, but my heart is so torn.'

'You have no relationship with Rachel; perhaps you shouldn't talk to her but leave her alone,' said Mathias.

'We have a connection, a bond and an understanding, but she just won't verbalise it.'

'We do not know what is going to happen with us. He caused a near riot down at the temple yesterday – throwing the tables over, driving out the merchants and traders – how he did not get arrested I do not know. And then he taught on how the whole temple system has become corrupt, an institutional den of robbers and thieves. Simon considers him too reckless and in danger of his life. Every day, the scribes come and try to trap him – but his wisdom outwits them every time.'

'What are they doing up there?' said Thomas, looking up at the ceiling where Simon, John and the Healer had retired.

'They are preparing the room for tomorrow's Passover feast. A select few will eat with him and celebrate the Passover meal. Have we the correct number of chalices?' asked Mathias.

'Tobit has arranged it all. Tomorrow we have a cook coming in to prepare the unleavened bread and the haroseth; we have apple, walnut and cinnamon, and lamb.'

Mina came over to them and pulled at Thomas's arm.

'You must talk to her; she is free now… Go in and see her,' she chided.

Rachel was sitting up, brushing her long, black hair. The bruises around her wrists and face had gone. She looked radiant, and Thomas asked whether he could sit with her.

She nodded and Mina came and sat opposite them, working the needle through an embroidery that she had started.

'I hear you are a follower now,' she said churlishly.

'Can't we start with how you are?'

'I am fine. You?' she said, trying to avoid Mina's glare.

'Not really. I do not know where I stand with you, and it upsets me.'

'You are too forward in thinking that I care one way or another.'

'You know that is not true, and I shall ignore your false bravado.'

'False bravado – I would call it self-protection.'

'Protection from what?'

'From being used and abandoned!' she said, raising her voice.

'What are you talking about, being used and abandoned? You know I have feelings for you. Who said I would abandon you?'

'Your heart declares it every time you set eyes on the Healer. All you want to do is run after him like a little pet sheep.'

'That is uncalled for. You are just causing an argument for argument's sake.'

'Mina is just as bad… She will be off with you; you can keep each other company along the journey to God knows where. This man is a trouble-maker; he will get himself and all of you killed. I have heard what he did in the temple. He is deranged to take on the authorities in such an overt way. I know what it is to be under the yoke of stern masters, and these people will kill him.'

'I must follow him, but I want you to come with us,' remonstrated Thomas.

'Us. Is that it, then? I am to be left on my own with nowhere to go?'

'Tobit has instructions to find you a house where you and Mina can live; it is up to her what she does.'

'She is sixteen and needs some guidance, not an invitation to get herself killed following a madman.'

'What is your problem, Rachel? How many times has he got to save your life before you see the truth of who he is?'

'I cannot follow someone who wants to forgive me of my sins – it is too much.'

'And your stubbornness is too much!' Thomas said with a raised voice.

'Then go! Go and follow your master and stop annoying me!' she said, throwing the hairbrush at him. He shook his head and stormed out of the room.

Mina clapped her hands.

'Brilliant, just brilliant!'

Rachel scowled, looked at the door and bit her lip.

CHAPTER 26

✦ ✦ ✦

Jinan followed the old woman through the streets crowded with Jews from every part of the empire. Many spoke in foreign languages, and the bustle intensified as they got closer to the temple. She was walking, back bent, head down, scratching along the ground with a crooked stick that helped her walk, cursing and shouting at anybody who got in her way.

He had never seen a building so huge and imposing and kept close to the old woman for fear of getting lost in its immensity. She seemed to know her way around and went straight through the outer court, into the deep shadows of the inner, slowing when she approached an old man who sat counting his money.

'Joshua, is that you?' she said, and the old man looked up. His face was skeletal and the sockets of his eyes deep in the gloom of the shade of a huge portico. He leant forward and Jinan could see his hair was grey and scant and a long scar crisscrossed down the right side of his face. His teeth were, if possible, worse than the old woman's, and his body stank. His hands were wrinkled and shrivelled, the skin black and damaged in places, his nails yellow and filled with dirt.

'Well, bless my soul!' he said with a laugh. He stood up and the two hugged.

'Sister,' he said.

'Brother,' she replied.

'What brings you here?'

'I have an instinct for unrest and believe there is a great battle to come...'

'If you have come about the evil one, then I must tell you I have washed my hands of all of that.'

'Evil one! My master has been kind to both of us. Look at all your riches, but you live dressed as a pauper.'

'I have no riches. I have given it all away to the poor. I am just counting here to put this in the offering, and then I am off to follow the Healer.'

'What Healer?' asked the old woman angrily.

'You have not heard? We shall all be drinking the Elijah cup tonight! The Messiah is amongst us!' He smiled and wiped his dry lips with his thin fingers.

'Messiah, where is he?' she growled.

'The Healer has performed great signs and great wonders, healing the sick, giving sight to the blind and driving out your fellow's demons! Ha!' he said, putting all the coins into a bag.

'Tell me more...' she demanded, and Jinan listened in wonder to the stories the old man told of the powers of the Healer.

'Yesterday he drove out the money changers and the traders, as it is written in Zechariah: there will be no...'

'Yes, I know exactly what is written, but you say this man comes from Galilee. Nothing good comes from there.'

'But the great light has broken in the darkness, and how your darkness is reviled and agitated! I have not lost the gift of foresight; I have seen what is happening.'

'This man will be killed like all the rest of the cranks,' threatened the old woman.

'Crank, you say? Yet he raises the dead.'

'By what power can he raise the dead? Poppycock!' she growled.

'He healed a man and forgave him his sins… Now that is music to my ears – my sins, my scum, my life of misery have been washed away and now I am a free man.' The old man smiled, his face flushed with joy.

The old woman spat on the floor and swore at her brother, who just laughed, picked up his bag and made off to the treasury to pay his dues. His sister followed closely behind, scolding him and cursing his treachery towards her dark Lord.

'Who is this man,' she asked bitterly, 'that he could defy my master?'

Jinan followed them both into the treasury where a queue of people was waiting to give an offering to the Lord most high. To the surprise of the old man, the Healer was standing near the head of the queue, alone, and free from a crowd.

'There he is!' he whispered to Jinan.

'Go on, young man, approach him and he will set you free like he did me! You don't want to be bound to that old hag all your days!' he said in earshot of the old woman, whose ears pricked up.

She sniffed the air and squinted like an animal evaluating danger; she stared at the Healer, who had his back to them. He seemed to be watching a poor woman who stood at the large golden box at the treasury to make her offering. When she returned and passed him, he caught her by the arm and smiled. Jinan looked at his face, and something inside him felt revulsion. He started to tremble.

'That's it, boy, show your colours: my magic versus his so-called powers. Go to him and see him for the charlatan he is. He will be gobbled up and spat out by my master, just wait and see.'

'What do you mean?' complained Jinan, who felt as though he was going to vomit.

'Go over to him and ask him to set you free – for he will not be able to contend with the power of the Lord of this world, mark my words.'

Jinan did not understand why he was beginning to shake, but he walked towards the Healer, who focused on his advance and crossed his arms to watch.

'Go, and demonstrate the power of darkness!' howled the old woman, causing a commotion in the lower court and disturbing the patiently waiting queue.

Jinan tried to walk over to the Healer but his legs did not want to move. He trembled and started to mutter profanities. The Healer walked towards him. Jinan's feet seemed glued to the floor but he shook uncontrollably. He fell to the floor and started to convulse. The old woman came over to him, raised her stick and started to mouth strange incantations that seemed to calm him. But when he looked up and saw the Healer, his mind screamed in pain.

'Leave us, Son of Man, for we are many!' screamed the boy.

When the Healer knelt down and put his hand on the boy's head, the convulsions and screaming rose to a frenzy. Then the boy slumped as if dead, and one of the Healer's followers leapt from the crowd to tend to him.

The old woman cursed him and shook her fist in his face.

'My master will kill you,' she started to say, but he put his finger to his lips and silenced her. She held her throat and stuttered and gargled but could say nothing.

Ruth helped the boy to his feet. He felt faint and dizzy, but his head was clear and empty of the incessant noise in his ears. He felt euphoric. He looked up at the Healer and thanked him.

'You saved me!' he exclaimed as the old man patted him on the back and laughed.

'Didn't I say as much? Now come, come with me, boy. I can teach you much in the trade of iron works....'

Jinan followed the old man and left his sinister old mistress standing speechless, watching them go. She tried to remonstrate with him but could say nothing. The Healer and Ruth walked past her and left the temple.

She stumbled with her cane, coughing and wheezing, and pushed back through the crowds. Once outside, she sucked in through her gappy teeth strong inhalations of fresh, cold air.

It took her some time to find her way back to the house rented by her daughter, who was arranging flowers in a pot when the old woman entered the room.

'Where is the boy?' she asked innocently. But the old woman said nothing.

'What has happened to you? You look as if you have seen a ghost.'

Her voice returned slowly, first hardly audible, a rasping sound in her throat, then thickening into words the madam could hardly make out.

'Let me get you a warm drink of milk,' said the madam and administered it, with a spoon of honey, to the old woman's hideous, white-spotted tongue.

'He has gone,' she said at last.

'Jinan has gone?'

'And your Uncle Joshua. I went to see him in the temple, but he has changed.'

244

'The old skinflint changed? He is the most miserable piece in the land!'

'He has been saved,' she said in a sad, solemn tone. 'My powers were nothing, nothing…'

'What do you mean, he has been saved – from what?'

'He, the Healer, he has taken away his sins. The fool believes that he is now spotless, like a new-born lamb, washed clean by the say-so of this Healer.'

'Uncle Joshua says his sins are washed clean! By what madness is this?' asked the madam, sitting down on the settee, awe-struck by the news.

The old woman proceeded to regale her with the details of the encounter with Joshua and the Healer, continuing with the account of her battle to keep Jinan in the power of darkness.

'He just raised his finger and silenced me,' she said brokenly. She turned around on the settee, tucked her feet up and went to sleep.

The madam could not believe what she had heard. But something stirred in her. Uncle Joshua and Jinan were now free, free men, forgiven and starting anew. She sat at her mother's feet and thought it over. The story of the Healer excited in her a sense of deep dread. She felt cursed by the old woman, who had cruelly kept her devoid of any affection all the days of her life. She felt hurt by the paucity of sound advice the woman had given her – encouraging her to enter into the business as a madam had been the worst mistake of her life. All she had left was her fortune in a jar of nard.

✦ ✦ ✦

They walked as fast as they could across the city, Thomas and Mathias determined to spend some time with the Healer. He was in Bethany, staying at the house of Mary, Martha and Lazarus. The fire had been lit, and the followers had increased with a number of new people who had encountered the Healer that day and decided to follow him.

John approached Thomas and invited them to follow him. The Healer was at the house of Simon the leper, not far from Mary's house. Ruth was standing at the gate and opened it for them.

'I met a woman today who said she would come tonight if I waited for her. She was out of her wits with worry and was most anxious to see the Healer.'

'Don't stay too long; come when you have finished,' said John, who looked tired but patted her on the shoulder.

The house was far grander than Mary's and many candles lit the windows. People were arriving on horseback and in fine carriages. The men had trouble pushing through the throng and gaining entrance to the main hall of the house. The servants were busy filling glasses of wine and replacing the sweetmeats on hand for the many guests who sat around a very long table.

The Healer was sitting at the side by the windows, and Simon the leper was speaking to him intensely. The elder man with a shock of white hair, dressed in a clean white robe, looked up and beckoned to the men to join him.

Thomas could not help but bow to the Healer, who smiled at him.

'Come, sit down, Thomas, my friend,' he said, his eyes twinkling. 'You have prepared the upper room well for us. We shall go there after this, and I would like you and your brother to eat with us.'

'Thank you, master... I mean friend,' said Thomas, his heart beating faster in his chest.

Thomas could tell by the standard of attire that the crowd was a mixture of poor people, prostitutes, tax collectors and officials from the synagogue, who had obviously been asked to attend the meal on pain of death if they did not go. The priests seemed nervous and interrupted the light conversations around the table with deep theological questions, which the Healer batted off much as one would swat a fly.

They were eating a light meal of mid-afternoon refreshments when Ruth appeared at the door and asked the Healer if she could introduce him to someone in great need. He smiled and beckoned her in.

A large woman, dressed in outlandish robes and bright red scarves, bedecked with golden bells and bracelets, her face plastered with white makeup, entered the room carrying a large alabaster jar.

Ruth pointed out where the Healer sat; the woman fell to her knees before him and poured the contents of the jar onto his feet. Instantly, the house was filled with the perfume of precious nard. She undid her turban, took off her scarves, rings and bracelets and started to weep. Her long, grey hair fell onto the Healer's feet, and she rubbed the nard from his toes to his ankles, uttering heartfelt cries of deep remorse.

The room was quiet but for the whisper of the prostitutes, who shared that this woman was the madam of a brothel.

'What a waste!' cried one of the Healer's followers, a thin-faced man called Judas. 'That is a fortune wasted,' he moaned.

The Healer lifted the woman's hands and looked into her face.

'Your sins are forgiven; go now in peace,' he said, then placed one hand on her head and prayed for her. She let out a gasp and then praised him. Ruth came over, helped her to her feet and led her from the room praising God and the Healer who had washed her clean of sin.

The room was a hubbub of disquiet. Judas was moaning about the wasted income, the priests were incandescent with rage that he should dare forgive anybody and others sounded offended that he would mix with women such as these.

The Healer looked up and the room became quiet.

'She has anointed my body for the tomb. It is time to go.'

He thanked Simon the leper and bade farewell. Thomas and Mathias followed him from the house.

✦ ✦ ✦

'What has happened to me?' said the madam, shaking, her makeup running down her face.

'What is your name?' asked Ruth.

'I am Madam Thamina of Theims.'

'No, today you have been made new. What is your first name?'

'Eliza. My name is Eliza.'

'You shall be called Eliza the Anointer from this day hence. It is time to follow him as he goes into the city. We are celebrating Passover this evening with some of the other women in the house. Please come with me,' invited Ruth, smiling and holding the woman's hands.

'I would like that very much,' said Eliza the Anointer.

CHAPTER 27

✦ ✦ ✦

The cook was busy in the kitchen preparing the haroseth of sugar, apple, walnuts and cinnamon. Five large silver chalices represented the cups of sanctification, plagues, redemption, completion, and Elijah, the herald of the messianic age. These were filled with expensive wine and taken on silver platters upstairs to a room lit by a myriad of single candles. Unleavened bread was being made, and Mina prepared a small meal for Rachel and herself to have in the downstairs dining hall.

A thin-faced young man in his twenties kept popping in and out, asking the cook who was paying for it all. He seemed nervous and somewhat anxious to avoid any unnecessary expense.

'Thomas is paying for all of this,' said Tobit, supervising the servants and ensuring the room was correctly prepared for the Healer and his guests.

'He could have spent less on the wine and given more to the collection,' said the thin-faced man, shaking his head. 'Such a waste of money,' he kept protesting, bobbing backwards and forwards between the hall and the street below where he was waiting for the Healer.

'Cheery soul,' joked Mina, and the two women shut the double doors on all the commotion in the kitchen. They went over to the Menorah and lit the seven oil lamps hanging from its branches. The light was warm and mellow, and the two sat on a low settee and rested. The cook would bring in the meal once the upper room had been attended to.

'That was a good heart-to-heart you two had there – Thomas must be quietly confident that he has won your affection,' said Mina.

'Stop it,' said Rachel lightly. 'I told you I am spoilt goods.'

'Don't talk about yourself like that,' replied Mina.

'Well, it's true.'

'It's not,' said a voice, and the girls jumped, startled by the presence of the Healer standing in the room, his face obscured by darkness but his tone gentle and encouraging.

'Sorry, I did not mean to startle you, but Rachel, I just wanted to say that the next time you see me, all will make sense. You did not choose me, I chose you – and I must go and make a way for you,' he said gently, then left the room, closing the door carefully behind him.

Rachel felt confused. Why, when the Passover was upon them and the Healer had so much on his mind, had he bothered to say that to her? What did he mean, he had chosen her but she had not chosen him? She recalled his saying she was a gift from the Father to the Son, but it all made no sense. She had a lifetime of horrific memories that devoured her if she ever stopped to think deeply about anything. For the last month, she had been driven by instinct and instinct alone to survive and to find her daughter. Now that was over, she felt she was in a place of quiet, rebellious ruin.

'Why does he say things like that to me? Why can't I be like you and Thomas or Mathias and just get it? I have such a sense of rebellion in me whenever he talks to me.'

'But why?' asked Mina

'I can't get past the superficial, and I am frightened that I am ruined, physically, emotionally and definitely spiritually. I am fragmented and blasted. I cannot seem to function in any other way than fleeing from Boataz. His is like a shadow over my life, and I cannot believe that I am free of him. I think something bad is going to happen at every moment – that I will lose you again.'

'But you will lose everything if you do not deal with your past, Mother,' said Mina kindly. 'The Healer has not taken my grief or shock away, but somehow, he has put something inside me that is bigger than that grief, something immense, in the form of an unfathomable ocean of love from him and for him. Maybe you are frightened of love.'

Rachel started to cry.

'You were the only lovely thing that ever happened to me, and they took you away. Do you know the pain? How do I love again?'

Mina came to sit next to her and hugged her. They listened to the sounds on the stairs as the guests of the Healer started to file up into the upper room.

One of the servants came into the room with the components of the Passover meal: four small cups of wine, unleavened bread, bitter herbs and a large leg of roast lamb. Mina arranged the food and wine on the floor at Rachel's feet.

'What do you do with all this stuff?' asked Rachel.

'You were never taught?'

'No, the rabbi came and taught us many things once a month, but no one listened to him. We all felt forsaken by a god who sent this man to goad us with his sense of nobility, justice and order.'

Mina blessed the four cups of wine and then washed her hands and those of her mother.

'Why all this washing?'

'Because what we do is sacred... of course.'

✦ ✦ ✦

In the room upstairs, the Healer washed his hands and then washed the feet of his disciples. Thomas was stunned that he took the time and care to wash everyone's feet, smiling and talking softly as he did it. When it came to his turn, he felt so humbled, so grateful, as the Healer's hands, which had delivered so many people from suffering, washed the dust of the day from his feet.

'This is discipleship, Thomas: to wash away the dirt of the day ready for the next day to go wherever God wills.'

Downstairs, Mina took up the cup of sanctification and drank of it and then passed it to Rachel, who asked what sanctification meant. Mina smiled and lifted the cup and said, 'God said, "I will bring you out."'

The Healer raised the cup and said, 'I will bring you out.' Thomas looked at Mathias, and all the men were awed that he should say something so bold: that he, the Messiah, was fulfilling the Passover story.

She took the middle of the three pieces of unleavened bread, broke it into two and showed her mother how to eat the bread with a sense of thankfulness to God.

✦ ✦ ✦

He broke the bread and said that his body would be pierced for their transgressions and then broken. The curtain of separation between the people and the Holy of Holies would be torn in two.

✦ ✦ ✦

She asked her mother to recount the Passover story, in which the people who were in slavery in Egypt marked the beams over their front doors with lamb's blood to ward off the angel of death that would come and slay all the first-born boys of Egypt.

Rachel squirmed at the story and asked why God was so awful. Mina tried not to smile and reverently said that Pharaoh had been given a choice to let God's people go or face judgement. In the end, death and loss were the only antidotes to Pharaoh's stubbornness.

✦ ✦ ✦

Upstairs, the room was filled with questions about what the Healer had said, but he just sat back and let his disciples answer them for him. Many had followed him for three years, and he was pleased to hear how they debated.

'The time has come when you must speak of my Passover offer to many people – few will respond and many will reject you, but you must wash each other's feet in love and push on to find the few that God has given to me.'

253

✦ ✦ ✦

The second cup – of plagues – was lifted to Rachel's lips, and the two women sipped the wine in turn.

'Have I too suffered plagues sent by God to assail me?' asked Rachel.

'No, we live in darkness, in a fallen state. There is an enemy of your soul who dominates this world – he has assailed you, not God.'

'But if God is in charge of everything?'

'He will not overrule the will of someone like Boataz, who does his master's bidding. It was he who abducted you and imprisoned you, not God.'

Mina washed her mother's hands, wishing that she could wash away all the pain that she had suffered and heal the dreadful wounds in her heart and soul. They ate the bitter herbs, and Mina explained that these were symbolic of the bitter herbs that the Hebrews had cooked the lamb in.

'There is bitterness at the very heart of the story of escape. Death and loss are central to the whole story of the people escaping Egypt and becoming the people of God.'

Rachel and Mina ate the meal of lamb in silence. Rachel loved her daughter's faith but counted it as a childish naivety that she hoped would never be tested by bitter experience. She hated the thought that death and loss lay at the heart of this story of redemption and resented this God who killed innocent children.

'What are you thinking?' asked Mina.

'All this talk of bitter suffering is too much – and I do not want you to suffer any of it.'

'The Healer is the suffering servant; he will take onto himself all our iniquity.'

'Then may God have mercy on him,' whispered Rachel.

✦ ✦ ✦

Picking up the cup of plagues, the Healer whispered, 'I will free you from being slaves...'

The Healer spoke of a blessing that had been fulfilled that very hour: a new covenant, a heavenly agreement, would be struck in the coming hour in which his body would be the bread and his blood the wine.

He broke the bread into pieces and offered it around. When they had eaten the bread, he asked them to do it often in memory of him. The room fell quiet. It seemed to Thomas that the very candle lights ceased to move. He was astounded at the import of the Healer's words – he was declaring himself the fulfilment of prophecy, of scripture, of the hopes of a nation – of the hope of the world. He was claiming he had come to complete the work of God – as his Son.

The Healer lifted the cup of redemption and closed his eyes. His hand trembled as if the weight were too much to bear.

'I will redeem you...'

✦ ✦ ✦

Mina laughed at how serious Rachel appeared and then went to the door, opened it and looked out.

'What are you doing?'

'A child goes to the door to see if Elijah has come to precede the Messiah.'

'Well, did you see him?'

'No,' she said simply and sat down beside her mother.

'Well, how can the Healer be your Messiah then?' said Rachel churlishly.

Mina pushed her mother playfully and laughed at her.

'Why do you get so annoyed with him and Thomas?' she asked.

'Do we have to? Just get on with your celebration of death and mayhem.'

'Is it because men have hurt you so badly?'

Rachel put her hand on Mina's head and stroked her hair.

'Does there have to be a reason for everything?'

'Yes, Mother, there does.'

The men sang songs of praise, but there was a hint of sadness in Thomas's voice. He sensed that the Healer would be that suffering servant who would be pierced for his transgressions, and he felt crushed by the fear of losing him.

'Do you know any songs of praise?' asked Mina.

'I cannot read or write, let alone remember any psalms.'

'Well, let me sing, and you can hum or just join in as best as you can.'

Rachel marvelled at the young woman's lovely voice and she sat looking at her daughter, so pleased that she had been safely cared for all these years. She thanked the girl's adopted mother and father and wished that they were still alive so this child would not have suffered their loss.

Her thoughts kept being interrupted by a worry about the future: how would they survive? How could she provide a roof over her head and food on the table? A single woman of no means had no way of feeding herself outside of a loving family.

◆ ◆ ◆

He picked up the fourth cup, the cup of completion, and said he would not drink of it again until they met in heaven. He placed it carefully on the table and then smiled.

'Many of you have been with me from the outset. But soon I must return to my Father – and you, my disciples, will have to continue without me. But I must go so that my Father will send the Holy Spirit, who will remind you of my words and teach you just as I have been teaching you. You need not fear any loss for, by his power, you will abide in me and I will abide in you. For I am the true vine…'

Thomas listened for an hour to the Healer's master lesson on how the disciples would cope without his physical presence. The many questions from the other disciples were tinged with sadness and fear and panic, but his soft reassurances calmed the room.

'How can he be the Messiah and the fulfilment of everything that has been written and then say he is going back to his Father in heaven? I do not understand,' Mathias asked Thomas.

'The Holy Spirit will be abroad… He will unite us with the Healer in our innermost being,' whispered Thomas.

'I do not understand what he is saying,' replied Mathias.

Thomas found comfort in the fact that the more senior disciples sounded as confused as Mathias.

'You did not choose me; I chose you and appointed you to bear fruit. But I no longer call you servants because you know my business as friends.

Remain in me and I in you and you will bear much fruit. Remember, without me, you can do nothing.'

'What is this fruit, master?' asked Simon.

'To love God with all your heart, strength and mind and obey my commandment to go and love others as I have loved you.'

'To bear the fruit of love,' said Simon quizzically.

'The true vine bears abundant fruit of love – but my Father must cut back and prune the vine to ensure that love is its product.'

Thomas noticed Judas, the keeper of the purse, looking nervous and agitated. He had barely eaten anything and appeared so preoccupied that his eyes wandered the room whilst everyone else's gaze was fixed upon the Healer. At one point late in the evening, Thomas noticed that he had left the room.

They drank from the fourth cup of completion, and Mina explained that this cup represented God's will to take them as his people. She prayed a blessing over Rachel, Thomas, Mathias and the followers of the Healer. Rachel watched how Mina's face changed as she shut her eyes and contemplated talking to her Maker – she seemed to strain, her eyebrows furrowed, her expression one of earnest repentance. The prayer meant so much to her, and Rachel could tell how important the Healer and his band of crazy people were to her. It made her sad to think that Mina loved others so openly and so naively.

When Mina had finished, Rachel asked her about prayer.

'Do you think he listens to you?' she asked.

'I believe so.'

'I prayed at first, when I was abducted and they threw me into that hell hole. Every day I asked him to free me, but he never heard my cries. In the end, I believed he hated me – how could he be so indifferent to my suffering?'

'I am so sorry,' said Mina.

'When they took you, I was in a rage with your God, and I suppose that anger has not left me.'

Rachel looked in surprise at Mina, whose face was stained with tears, and she realized that her words were an offence to the child, too much to bear.

'I am sorry, I should not speak to you about such things. I think it is lovely that you have your faith.'

'That sounds patronizing,' replied Mina, holding her mother's hands. 'We live in a fallen world. It is no paradise, and we have an enemy, a Lord of darkness, who will do everything he can to ruin us – some with money, some with indifference, some with hardship and others, like you, with cruelty. But God has made a way to suffer well.'

Rachel put her arm around Mina and cuddled her. She kissed her on the head and whispered that she would try with all her heart to do what her daughter said. But deep down, she knew there was no hope for her, and she felt a terror that she would be a burden and a curse to her child.

The candles were thickening and the light burned a soft, mellow hue of yellow and orange in the room. A stillness had fallen on all of the men's hearts as they listened intently to the Healer as he prayed for them before they left for the Mount of Olives.

He spoke to the Father as if there was not a single doubt in his head that he was the Son of God. Thomas could not close his eyes but stared at the expression on the face of the Healer. He was so serious, so animated, so beseeching and so calmly intent on communicating with his Father. There was a deep joy in his words, yet a sense of things ending, which made Thomas ache with sadness and fear.

CHAPTER 28

✦ ✦ ✦

Mina and Rachel had retired to their rooms by the time the men left the upper room to step out into the cold night and wander through the streets of Jerusalem on their way to the Mount of Olives.

'What did he mean about the new covenant?' asked Mathias as all the men began questioning Simon, John and the other senior disciples.

'Where is he going?' asked another.

'How can we follow him if he is leaving?'

Simon shrugged, too upset to answer anyone. John did his best to answer the questions.

'Let us calm ourselves and wait and see. The kingdom is coming this very day, and we must be ready. The master wants us to pray for him as he prays to the Father. So come, be still and wait upon him.'

The chatter did not subside but continued in a whisper. Mathias asked Thomas many things that he also struggled with, yet he reassured his brother as best he could that the Healer would not abandon them.

'Mathias, he said the Holy Spirit would be sent so that we could remain in him and he in us. He is not leaving us, but he will commune with us still in some deeper way.'

'But he said he is going back to his Father – what does that mean?' whispered Mathias.

'We will just have to wait and see. Surely, we are at the beginning of something glorious – if what he says is true, then he has fulfilled the old covenant of Moses and David and begun a new covenant between his people and God.'

'This is all too much,' mused Mathias.

On the Mount of Olives, the Healer withdrew into a garden to pray and asked John and Simon and the other senior disciples to pray for him and watch over him. The party sat down on the damp ground and all started a quiet prayer of thanks. So long was the wait that both Thomas and Mathias fell asleep.

They were awoken by cries from a crowd of people bearing torches. Simon and John sounded the alarm, and the followers woke up and jumped to their feet. Roman soldiers headed the group, followed by a row of senior temple priests. Thomas could see Judas standing in the midst of them.

An old man shouted out, 'Who among you is Yeshua?' his voice angry and belligerent.

The Healer stepped forward and lifted his hand.

'I am he,' he said resolutely.

A shrill, ear-piercing note exploded in Thomas's ears, and he, the followers and the great throng around the priests all fell to the ground, unable to move until the Healer lowered his arm.

The Roman soldiers staggered to their feet, and the priests helped each other up from the ground, the mud now clinging to their rich robes. They pushed Judas forward and he gingerly crossed the divide between the two parties. He walked over to the Healer and kissed him on the cheek.

With that, the soldiers seized the Healer, and the priests charged forward crying, 'Get the rest of them.'

Panic ensued as Simon drew a sword and the followers wrestled with the priests.

'Quick, run!' said someone, and Thomas and Mathias started to run, gripped by panic and fear. They pushed off the grabbing hands in the melee and ran as fast as they could out of the garden and down the Mount of Olives into the city.

✦ ✦ ✦

'I cannot wait to see you suffer this death,' growled Boataz in the opposite iron cage.

They had both been found guilty of murder, abduction and civil unrest and had been sentenced to crucifixion. Gritz had no relish for seeing anyone killed in such a barbaric way. He shuddered inside, exhausted by the beatings, the interrogations and the appalling weight of the fear of such a cruel death. Unlike Boataz, who spent what time he had left cursing everybody who had crossed him – and gloating over what he had done in retribution – Gritz spent what time he had left thinking deeply of his life back in Gaul.

They had been taken down to the prison cells where the Roman soldiers would prepare them for execution. Bored and ruthless, they took much delight in goading Boataz, prodding him with the end of a spear until he danced like an irate bear in the middle of his cage.

Gritz wished he had never robbed, but he could not fathom a course in his life that would have been any different. Now the consequence of his choices in life was appalling. He sat down and ignored the taunts of the bored Roman soldiers, wishing he could have found at least one path in his life that did not lead to total misery and destruction.

The guards were disturbed by a third prisoner brought for their entertainment.

'Hey, lads! They have bought us the King of the Jews,' shouted the presenting officer, laughing loudly. 'You won't believe what's on his charge sheet – he is a madman who thinks he is the rightful king of the Jews who will destroy the empire!'

The other men stopped goading Boataz and set about humiliating the prisoner, who appeared calm and at peace as they hit him and pulled him about. Gritz looked at the poor fellow and wondered what on earth he had done to be punished so severely.

'He has blasphemed God, it says here, and sets himself up as some Messiah King.'

'How many people has he killed?' asked one of the guards.

'None. He hasn't harmed anybody, but he has hurt the vanity of the damned priests, by the look of it.'

Gritz could not believe that the system could be so lousy as to condemn a man to crucifixion who had not committed a crime apart from living a delusion.

'Leave him alone!' cried Gritz as the men kicked and punched the man, who merely smiled back at them.

'He has done nothing wrong but upset a load of hypocrites!' cried Gritz.

The soldiers laughed and bowed mockingly towards Gritz.

'Of course, forgive us for our lack of respect, your majesty,' said one of the men.

'It seems this man has a follower in our midst. Let us show our appreciation for your king, Gritz,' said another.

They tied the man to a chair and then dressed him in a purple cloak. They took a heap of briars they would use to scold a man and twisted them into a crown that they forced onto the man's head. He groaned as the thorns bit into his flesh, and then the men set the chair in front of Gritz and they mockingly worshipped the new King of the Jews.

'Stop messing about!' said one of the officers. 'Go and get the crossbeams and the hammers.'

The men left the man sitting facing Gritz, who tried to reach through to lift the thorns from his head.

'Idiots,' he whispered, sitting back down on his haunches.

'They had every right to bow down at my feet – but I do not demand subservience, merely communion,' said the man. His voice sounded warm, wise and somehow comforting.

'So, you are mad then,' said Gritz.

'No, I have come to do my heavenly Father's bidding, and it is his will that I lay my life down for you, Gritz.'

'Gritz, you say. So you are my friend now?' said Gritz, imagining that somehow this man had overheard his name being read out from the charge sheets.

'I am the way – the new way for you and for everyone else who wants to escape the cruelty of the world.'

'Escape? They are about to crucify you – do you not know what that is?'

The man smiled and nodded and then closed his eyes as if he were praying.

'Flaming maniac,' said Gritz and pushed his back against the iron cage, trying to get the man's words out of his head. New way, he thought; this man had come to mock and afflict him. How he wanted a new way in his life! But it was all too late.

'It is not too late,' said the man, startling Gritz. What magic is this, he thought. 'What do you mean?' he asked.

'It is not too late for you to give up your old life, to surrender to my offer of a new way of life, to suffer well, knowing that you will have eternal life in my company – for I have chosen you, Gaul, to accompany me.'

'Accompany you where?'

'I am going to my Father, who has prepared many rooms for my followers – come with me.'

'What are you talking about?' moaned Gritz, annoyed that the man had disturbed his last hours of contemplation with such maddening thoughts.

✦ ✦ ✦

The pounding on the door awakened Rachel and then Mina as Thomas and Mathias were let into the house by Tobit. The men were flustered and agitated and went into the lounge area where they paced up and down in panic.

'What has happened?' asked Rachel, seeing the fear on Thomas's face.

'They have taken him!' said Mathias.

'The Roman soldiers and the priests – they have taken him to be tried for treason,' blurted out Mathias.

'It is true; everything is ruined. We were on the cusp of something incredible, and now they have ruined everything,' cried Thomas.

'Calm down, Thomas. Tobit, get some wine and light the fire, please,' said Rachel, trying to coax Thomas to sit beside her.

'Who took him?' asked Mina, sounding as if she were about to cry.

'Listen!' said Rachel in a loud voice, causing everyone to stand still. 'If the Healer is who you say he is, then nothing can stop him, so please, you are upsetting Mina; sit down and be quiet!'

Thomas and Mathias looked at each other and nodded and went to comfort Mina, who led them to sit with her on the settee.

'Right, calmly, from the beginning, tell us what happened,' demanded Rachel.

'He fulfilled the Mosaic law and then set up a new covenant,' started Mathias.

'We can jump to the point where he was arrested,' said Rachel hopefully.

'No, Mother, let them speak,' said Mina gently. Thomas and Mathias spoke of the Passover meal in the upper room, of all he had said, of all he had promised, of his prayer and how he had left for the garden.

'So, you all fell to the ground when he said, "I am,"?' asked Mina.

'Thomas, please, I am frightened now – what if they followed you? What if we are all to be arrested? I told you no good would come of this!' cried Rachel.

'Mother,' said Mina, holding Rachel's hands to comfort her, 'he is who he says he is, and as you say, nothing can prevail against him until the new kingdom comes. Do not fear; this is what I desire – to follow him.'

'I am terrified,' cried Rachel.

Thomas sat next to her, pulled her into him and put his arms around her. She did not resist but trembled.

'Rachel is quite right; whatever happens is meant to be.'

'He said he was going to return to his Father in heaven.'

'Is that what he said?' asked Mina.

'Yes, it all sounded so final, as if he would be taken away, as if he was going somewhere where we could follow, but I could not understand,' said Thomas.

'Maybe he will reveal who he is to the priests and they will finally see and bow down to him. Maybe he will be appointed the chief rabbi and high priest,' said Mina.

'You are all so naïve! They came to try him for driving out the traders in the temple and to reprimand him for all his threats about the temple being destroyed and his rebuilding it in three days. He is not exactly prudent, your Healer, is he?' said Rachel, who felt sleepy yet still frightened. 'They will lock him up for a long time.'

'As Mina says, they will, at last, encounter him in all his power and might. Nothing can prevail against him,' added Mathias.

'Whatever happens, this man will be an outlaw, and you must not continue to follow him – you will be putting all your lives at risk,' she said resolutely.

'Whatever happens, we cannot abandon him,' said Mina.

'Excuse me, darling, but the priests and soldiers turned up and that is exactly what they all did – they abandoned him and fled. I suggest you just keep on running until he is a distant memory. Now I am tired and will return to my bed. I suggest you all get a rest.'

The candle flames fluttered, causing lurid shadows to leap about the room as Rachel left. Thomas and Mathias sat motionless, frozen by a sense of foreboding. Mina continued to ask them questions, but the late hour and fatigue seemed to have captured their tongues and they just stared into the darkness.

✦ ✦ ✦

Boataz was abusing the man with the crown of thorns on his head, laughing with the officers and soldiers, who hit the crown repeatedly with long poles until blood trickled down the man's face.

'Why can't you leave him alone?' growled Gritz. 'You can see he is just a madman!'

But they continued to mock the man, who did not flinch but had a half smile on his face as he looked at Gritz.

'Why do you keep looking at me? Save yourself the pain and give in to them, man!' bellowed Gritz as the soldiers paraded around him, pretending that he was the king of the world, worthy of their applause.

'Follow me,' he said with a half smile and a look of love that Gritz had never seen before.

'Follow you where?' demanded Gritz.

'My Father's house has many rooms. I have prepared a room for you.'

One heavy blow knocked his head severely, and he shook with the pain but regained his composure and smiled at Gritz.

'For heaven's sake, can't you just stop!' Gritz bellowed at Boataz, who was shouting and rattling the iron cage in manic anger.

A Roman officer appeared in the doorway and shouted at the men to stop. The men all stood to attention, including the other officers.

'What stupidity is this? Get that prisoner ready. He is to be presented to Pilate; clean him up!'

The senior officer waited as the men took off the purple robe and the crown and then threw a bucket of water in his face. They untied him from the chair and wiped his face with a towel. The prisoner stood looking at Gritz.

'Save yourself; appeal to Pilate for clemency. You should not be here,' cried Gritz, but the man said nothing as he was led away. Boataz slumped back into his cage, and Gritz sat again on the floor, closing his eyes. He could vividly see the man's face – the peace to endure the mocking and the determination to call Gritz to follow him had a strange effect on his mood. He could not get his call to follow him out of his mind. How innocent this man had appeared in the face of the abuse and hurt! How calmly he had persevered through the many blows raining down upon his head. What madness was this that he had been called to follow?

The house was awakened by a knock at the door, which Tobit answered. Ruth entered the room and waited for Thomas and Mathias to wash and get ready for the day. They joined Ruth and Mina in the main sitting room and waited for Ruth to speak.

'They have tried him and found him guilty of blasphemy,' she said in a croaking voice.

'What does that mean?' asked Mina, who was hugged by Rachel at the news.

'They will crucify him,' said Ruth, her voice wavering.

'This is not possible,' said Thomas, profoundly shocked.

'How can he allow this to happen? He is the Messiah King!' exclaimed Mathias.

'The high priest has condemned him, and they have taken him to Pilate to be executed.'

'Please, no!' cried Mina.

'But we have Aquilina, who is a servant of Pilate. She is doing everything she can to warn him of these priests' infamy. At ten o'clock this morning, Pilate will appeal to the people to free one of two prisoners – the bandit

Barabbas or Yeshua. We must gather as many as we can to influence the outcome.'

'But the people love him! They will surely cry out in his favour?'

'We cannot trust the priests. They will flood the area with their own people. We urgently need to get into that square, so please come with me.'

'This is too dangerous,' cried Rachel.

'Mina, you will have to stay here,' said Thomas.

'You cannot stop me from being there in his crisis!'

'It is too dangerous. They may recognize us, or the crowd could turn ugly. There have been many deaths at these events before,' said Mathias.

'I don't care. He needs us right now,' remonstrated Mina.

'Well, I do care!' said Rachel, holding Mina's arm. 'Please stay with me. I will be too frightened if you go.'

Ruth intervened; she came over to Mina and cupped her face in her hands.

'Pray, Mina; a number of us are praying for him. I can stay here with you if that helps?'

Mina looked at all the worried-looking faces and then nodded.

'I will stay here with you,' she said at last.

Thomas and Mathias left the house, ready to join the followers in the square in front of Pilate's residence. The streets were filled with people, and as they drew near to the square, many of the roads were blocked by temple guards of the high priest. People were being turned away unless they wore the phylactery and robes of the pharisaic tradition.

'They are controlling who goes into the square! How are we to get in?' said Mathias.

Thomas looked at the scene and asked Mathias to follow him. They walked back down the road and into an alleyway that ran along the back of the packed houses on the road. They tried a number of doors until they found one that opened and pushed through the dimly lit lower floor and out the other side, stepping out of the house and onto the road where they joined the long line of people streaming into Pilate's square.

Mathias and Thomas pushed through the crowd to get closer to a raised platform erected in front of Pilate's residence. A large purple canopy had been mounted over the stage where ten Roman soldiers in shiny breastplates and helmets stood guard. The square was surrounded by soldiers with blood-red cloaks covering their metal armour and short swords.

The atmosphere on the square seemed tense. Thomas kept a lookout for any other followers but could see no one whom he recognized. The place was packed with Pharisees and Roman citizens.

'This is not good,' whispered Mathias. As they stood and waited, Thomas thought of Rachel, of her antipathy towards the Healer, of her hardness towards himself, and he prayed for her. He so longed for her to join him in following the Healer and knew that her intransigence towards the Healer would become a bigger problem than her poor sense of self-worth. He felt guilty at this particular time that he hankered after union with Rachel when the Healer's life was so in danger.

'Would you like to join us?' Ruth asked Rachel.

'I would like to sit and listen,' replied Rachel suspiciously.

Ruth and Mina knelt on the floor. The morning sun streamed through the window, lighting their features with a soft yellow glow. Rachel wondered at the power this Healer had over these two women, who were almost rapturous in their exclamations of love for the man.

She had never loved a man like that. Men were repulsive to her, a cause of self-hatred and deep loathing and, worse, a deep fear of being hit or harmed. Yet she knew that her circumstances had warped her ability to love and be loved, and she feared for her future. She had no education, no skills, no means to support herself and her daughter unless she found a man who could provide for her. But who would dare take on a woman of harlotry?

She knew the answer but could not let herself be free to love anyone apart from Mina.

The young woman inside her screamed, but she steeled herself and tried to concentrate on the two women's prayers.

They spoke of sin, of rebellion, of a broken, empty temple system, of a great king who would come and save them all. And Rachel thought of the scapegoat, of the poor animal that would be cast into the desert to die, bearing the sins of the nation in its being. Such poppycock and effrontery that a priest could cleanse a brutal man's seared conscience with such a trite ritual. She wondered why God would be any different – why he didn't just put his hand upon some wretched animal and put it to death for the sins of mankind.

She hated man and his sin, his probing, pawing, slavering sin that could be washed away so easily, leaving all of his victims bereft of innocence and loveliness.

✦ ✦ ✦

They prepared the scourging post by throwing buckets of water over it and then scrubbing the floor with brooms. He was chained tightly to it, with his wrist manacled closely to the five-foot stump of wood. They took off his clothes and he stood naked before them, his back arched and exposed to the two soldiers, who picked up two long whips encrusted with hundreds of jagged bone talons.

Gritz had seen this before, many times before, in the arenas in Rome, and it had never bothered him as this did. He tried to cry out for mercy for the man, who was like an innocent child before them, but they just told him to shut up as they prepared to take this man within an inch of losing his life.

The first blow opened up the man's back. He moaned in pain as the whip was dragged down his back and then ripped off, causing flesh and blood to splatter the backs of his legs and feet. Blow after blow followed during a rhythmic cadence of exertion, moaning and crying until the man's body was a raw, bloody mess.

When they unchained him, he fell onto the floor. Some of the whip lashes had extended around his neck and onto his face, and his cheeks were ripped and spread with blood. His whole body was maimed where the stone and bone scrapings had torn open the top layer of his flesh. He knelt down shaking, his body going into shock that could kill him.

He fell on his side in pools of his blood; then they pulled him to his feet and dragged him out of the prison yard.

✦ ✦ ✦

The crowds started shouting and yelling as a small figure in a purple uniform appeared on the stage. Pontius Pilate addressed the crowd and then looked behind him as a bloody mess of a figure shuffled into view. The figure was unrecognizable, its body bleeding and its face a mass of blood.

'I give you a choice this day – do I crucify Yeshua of Nazareth or Barabbas the bandit?'

He looked at the blood-red figure glistening in the sunlight when he mentioned Yeshua, and Thomas felt nauseous. The Healer had been mutilated by his scourging; there was hardly anything left by which to identify him.

'Shall I save Yeshua?' cried Pilate.

Thomas and Mathias and a few other voices shouted as loudly as they could beneath the great shadow of doom that overpowered them.

'Or shall I save Barabbas?' shouted Pilate. The whole crowd went into a frenzy of shouting and whooping and applauding.

Someone pushed Thomas in the back. He turned and heard two Pharisees shouting at them to leave the square. The crowd started to turn ugly, and each of the followers of Yeshua who had shouted out for him was ejected from the square and beaten.

Thomas and Mathias lay on the road until Simon and John and some of the other followers helped them to their feet.

'They will take him to Golgotha and crucify him. Tell Ruth to meet us there,' ordered Simon.

Thomas and Mathias limped home, feeling battered and bruised but horrified at what had happened to the Healer. They could not say anything when they were led into the house by Tobit and sat in the anteroom listening to the prayers of Ruth and Mina in the adjoining room.

When the praying had ceased, Rachel came out to find them sitting on the floor being tended to by Tobit and the servants.

'What has happened to you?' exclaimed Ruth, kneeling down beside the two men. She was soon joined by Mina and Ruth.

It took a few minutes for either of the brothers to say anything. Mathias deferred to Thomas, who, with tears in his eyes, told them how the meeting in the square had progressed.

Mina and Ruth started to cry. Rachel tended to Thomas, dabbing his lips.

'We are to go to Golgotha where they will crucify him. Simon wants us to be there.'

'Mina is not going to witness such a perverse act of cruelty.'

'I need to be there, Mother,' she protested.

'No, Mina, you are not going,' said Rachel vehemently.

Thomas rose to his feet and held his broken ribs, groaning.

'Mina, he would not want your last memory of him to be as disgusting as that. It will be truly horrible,' he said, squeezing Mina's hand.

'I don't know if I have the stomach for it,' said Mathias, rubbing his bruised eyes.

Ruth bade them farewell and left the house, bereft. Reluctantly, Thomas and Mathias went to follow her, but Rachel held Thomas's arm to stop him.

'If you leave, I will have nothing to do with you, do you understand? You have a choice: to stay with us or to go!'

He pulled his arm away, looked forlornly at her and whispered, 'I understand.' He and his brother left the house.

Mina shrieked at her mother and slumped onto the settee.

Gritz, Boataz and the Healer each had to carry a heavy crossbeam on their shoulders. They wore leg chains that were connected to one long chain joining them all. Gritz helped the man who had been scourged to bear the weight on the torn flesh around his shoulders. The prisoner groaned under the weight of pain.

'How are you doing?' asked Gritz, trying to make out the man's lips from the mess of his face.

To his surprise, the man smiled, showing his broken teeth and cut gums.

'Follow me,' he said, almost gurgling, 'as I return to my Father. Come with me !'

A soldier shoved Gritz to get him walking, and the prisoners shuffled through the bloody pools out into the daylight. Each step caused the wounded prisoner to gasp in pain. Gritz tried as best he could to help the man whenever he stopped and drew the cruel attentions of the soldiers, who whipped him with a stick into continuing his shuffle.

Outside, the streets were lined with people. Gritz had never seen so many people at a public execution, but only a few were cheering or shouting. The sight of the bloody prisoner brought a solemn and reverential hush as his shadow fell at the feet of the crowd.

They shuffled through the city and up onto the dreadful hill of Golgotha in silent pain.

✦ ✦ ✦

Jinan and the old man had heard the news resounding around the temple that the Healer had been tried, found guilty, scourged and then led, that very hour, to die a terrible death upon a cross. They had been working metal in the old man's workshop when they were alerted by a gloating priest, who was going around telling everyone, 'They have got him!'

The old man put down the tools, wiped his hands on his apron and motioned for the boy to get their cloaks from the workshop door.

Wanting to be with Mina, Rachel began climbing the stairs but Tobit pulled her back.

'You won't find her there,' he said, pointing out of the window where Rachel could see Mina escaping into the crowd.

'Please, Tobit, we must stop her!' cried Rachel, getting her cloak on and starting to run with Tobit through the busy crowds towards Golgotha.

The men were weeping and beside themselves, but the women stayed calm and tried to comfort them. Eliza the Anointer walked with Ruth around the garden, praying for each of the men who sat or lay on the grass, looking bruised and broken. Mary and Martha were already dressed and Lazarus held the gate open.

'It is time to be with him,' said Mary loudly, her words ushering the men to their feet.

CHAPTER 29

✦ ✦ ✦

The hill was surrounded by soldiers and priests, who were excitedly shouting out the laws relating to blasphemy. Thomas and Mathias were kept at a distance from the brow of the hill where men who looked like blacksmiths were standing beside three large beams of wood and three holes in the ground. The men looked like workmen going about their daily business, hammers in hand, ready to crucify three men.

Mary and the others joined them, and a dignified hush fell over the followers who were now cowering in the place of execution.

'What does this all mean?' asked Mathias. 'How could he be taken like this? I just don't understand...' he said, his voice breaking.

Simon put his hand on Mathias's shoulder to comfort him. The women had brought a large shroud to wrap the Healer's body in and a basket of oils to anoint his body. The sight of the objects sickened Thomas, who could not bear to watch as news simmered in the crowd that the execution party was approaching.

Mina had no idea where to go until she saw the crowds lining the road. She followed at a distance as the long rows of people began a winding crawl up a long hill through tall buildings and impressive houses, out past the city gates to a low hill they called Golgotha. Mina looked hard for any signs of followers, at last finding Ruth in the crowd.

'Mina! What are you doing here? You are too young,' said Ruth, putting her arms around the girl and leading her to where Thomas was standing.

'Mina, where is Rachel?' he asked.

'I left her – I just had to be here.' Thomas hugged the girl and then drew her into his side, placing his arms around her neck and shoulders as if to shield her from what they were all about to witness.

✦ ✦ ✦

Far down in the crowd, Joshua and Jinan watched in horror as the three prisoners shuffled past them. They could hardly recognize the Healer in his broken, stooped stumble as the last prisoner helped him, as best he could, bear the weight of the crossbeam on his back.

The crowd was silent as if the funeral procession of someone precious in their life had passed them by. A few Pharisees laughed and hurled abuse at the Healer and his fellow criminals.

✦ ✦ ✦

The crowds were difficult to navigate. Rachel and Tobit had to join the collapsing lines as they fell in behind the execution party and heaved up the streets through the city towards Golgotha. Rachel could see nothing of the prisoners but noticed, high above them, the crowds, pushed back by a contingent of soldiers, already gathering around the brow of the hill.

She felt panic and fear and sickness in her stomach. Why had she said what she had said to Thomas? Why was she always so stupid and so headstrong? And what of Mina?

Then she caught sight of the execution party, a brief glimpse of three men in chains bearing the weight of the heavy crossbeams. She felt sick at the thought of the death that awaited the Healer and angry that the authorities had destroyed the great illusion of change that the Healer had created in the minds of his followers. She felt such warmth towards Ruth and Thomas and Mathias and Mina that the thought of the ruin of their great hope was too much to bear. And then she thought of the Healer and what he had said to her and found it ironic that she was now following him to his place and time of death.

✦ ✦ ✦

The prisoner fell to the ground and Gritz tried to deflect the blows from the soldiers from the prisoner's shredded torso. The man had lost so much blood he was too weak to walk, and Gritz protested to the soldiers that he could not continue.

A poor fellow was grabbed from the crowd and ordered to carry the crossbeam. Gritz helped the prisoner to his feet, and even though his own crossbeam made his body ache, he tried to help the prisoner, by holding one arm around his waist, to recommence his painful shuffle.

They arrived at Golgotha exhausted and in agony. Gritz at last could drop the crossbeam and gasp for air. The three prisoners fell to the ground where their chains were removed.

The prisoner looked at Gritz and through the pain and suffering smiled at him.

'Ready?' he asked and Gritz shook his head.

'You don't give up, do you?' Gritz replied, quietly deciding to compose himself now the hour of execution was upon him.

The priests were baying for the prisoner's death and cheered when the soldiers delivered the scourged man to the executioners, who went about their business with great skill. They placed his crossbeam in a metal bracket on the main slab of wood of the cross and then laid him out. With leather thongs around his wrists, they stretched his arms to breaking point and tied them around two nails they hammered in the crossbeam. The prisoner groaned under the pain of being rubbed on the rough wood of the cross. The three workmen worked the body until it was so tightly tied to the cross the prisoner could hardly breathe.

They drove the nails into the two wrists with efficient synchronism and then undid the leather thongs. The prisoner writhed as the large iron nails bit into the flesh.

Pushing the legs down, they tied a thong around the ankles, repeated the stretching and then drove a nail through both feet. The prisoner gasped in agony, and the crowd of priests cheered as the soldiers and workmen hauled the cross into its hole and raised it into the air, with the prisoner suspended on its bloodied beams.

Thomas watched in horror as the priests danced up and down and laughed and hurled abuse at the Healer who was hung on the cross. He felt sick to his stomach and trembled. He tried to turn Mina away from the scene as she wept, tucking her face into his chest.

It did not take long for the two other prisoners, Boataz and Gritz, to be nailed and then lifted into the air beside the Healer. The two men gasped for air and started to rise and fall in agony as they tried to breathe. The

Healer seemed dead already and hung slumped, with the weight of his body pressing down on the nail through his feet.

✦ ✦ ✦

The old woman laughed. She had managed to get in amongst the priests and shook her fist up at the Healer, the so-called Messiah who fulfilled all prophecy.

'Save yourself, mighty king!' she shouted, and the priests followed her example. They laughed and shouted for this false Elijah to save himself.

'How dare you set yourself up against my master, who rules with an iron fist the affairs of man!' she scoffed. 'You who seek to ruin him have been ruined by his great might and authority.' The old woman began to praise and thank her master for his ascendency over the Healer and all of his followers. She laughed at how her brother Joshua and the boy Jinan would tremble in fear at her powers when she came to claim the boy as her own again.

✦ ✦ ✦

The momentum of the crowd spilling out of the city and pushing up the hill placed enormous pressure on the band of soldiers and priests surrounding the place of execution. They just could not hold out and were soon pushed back to the foot of the cross. Thomas and Mina were shoved away from Mathias, and he had to fight hard to ensure they did not fall on the floor and get trampled. They were pushed sideways in an eddy of people to the foot of the cross of Boataz, who was fighting hard to breathe and cursed the pain he was enduring.

Further down the hill, Rachel had been separated from Tobit and felt an increasing panic that she would be swept away far from the hill and Mina and Thomas. She pressed hard towards the brow of the hill, fighting the crowd at every turn.

Exhausted, she finally broke through into the packed ground around the foot of the three crosses.

The pain was so intense that Gritz had fainted three or four times as he fought for breath. The constant motion of his body fighting for survival, even though he wanted to die quickly, astounded him. When he slumped on his arms, his shoulders threatening to pop out of their sockets, his body pressed down on the spikes through his feet to lift him up to gulp air.

Boataz had spent the whole time cursing him and gloating over his demise and then had started to abuse the scourged prisoner.

'If you are king, then save yourself and us... you maggot!' shouted Boataz.

'Shut your mouth,' snarled Gritz. 'He has done nothing wrong, unlike you and I.'

'He is a worthless mass of flesh!' shouted Boataz.

In the madness of the pain, in the last dregs of anything that meant anything to him, Gritz rebuked Boataz for all he represented – and for all the crimes he himself had committed. He looked down at the melee and remembered the laughter and rebukes of the priests and soldiers and thought he would defy them all. In one last act of rebellion against authority, he cried out to the man whose smile could not be removed from his face, 'Lord, remember me when you come into the kingdom!'

Boataz stopped his cursing and laughed.

The prisoner who was scourged looked around at Gritz and through the agony smiled again.

'Today you will be with me in paradise,' he said, blood spilling from his lips.

At the top of the hill, Rachel crossed her arms and tried to warm herself in the fading afternoon light. She dared not look up at the cross for the men were naked and she cared not to see their agony. She looked around for anyone she could recognize and saw Ruth standing at the foot of the cross with an older woman and one of the other followers. She continued walking until someone cried out, 'Whore!' She looked up and saw Boataz hanging half dead on the cross. The word shook her to her core and she began to weep. Then an arm appeared around her shoulder. Mina held her hands and started to weep too.

Thomas pulled her away from Boataz, who was cursing her, and took her to where an elderly woman and Ruth were standing talking to the Healer, who had slumped down on the cross, occasionally heaving himself up for air.

The elderly woman was pulled to one side, leaving the man to continue speaking. Rachel could not help herself; in her filth and in her growing sense of panic and emptiness at bearing the sin of all of those men in her body, she glanced up at the Healer.

She looked at him in his naked death throes and started to weep. He had been whipped and shredded beyond recognition. Yet still his eyes shone with a love for her that pierced her very being.

'I have made a way for you and many others, woman,' he said, smiling, then coughed a large globule of blood and flesh out of his mouth.

'Receive my peace...' He writhed up in one great exhalation of air.

She looked at him as he slumped and something changed deep within her. She felt love, his love, rising not without, not penetrating or obtrusive, but gentle and all-consuming as he unlocked the young woman from her iron cage and led her out of captivity. A light seemed to burst out inside her, stretching for miles to the west and the east and the north and the south – burning up a myriad of strange bat-like forms that flowed out of her heart and mind. She looked around at the faces and back to her saviour and knew, in an instant, that everything had changed. Everything seemed so much clearer and so bright. She knew that she had been rescued, that somehow his death had counted as a sacrifice for all the sins that bound her. Her heart felt young and tender, and she wept for her Lord and master. She bowed down and then collapsed on her knees before the cross.

Thomas and Mina went to pick her up, but Ruth intervened and said softly, 'Leave them.' They withdrew, allowing Rachel to weep and sob and look up through her tears at the man who had set her free.

✦ ✦ ✦

The old woman found Joshua and Jinan standing in the crowd watching the proceedings, and she cawed with laughter.

'Joshua, you old fool, give me back the boy before I box his ears!' she cried. But the old man was looking at the woman who had knelt before the cross and he bent down with difficulty to get on his knees and close his eyes in prayer. Jinan looked not at the old woman but at the Healer who had rescued him, and he bent down too, closed his eyes and started to pray. As he did so, the old woman began to shriek as if boiling water were being poured on her head.

Across the site, the followers of Yeshua knelt in respect as their Lord's life passed from his body and he lay motionless on the cross.

When the soldiers had lowered the cross and the workmen had drawn the nails from his body, the women wrapped him in the shroud and lifted him onto a low wagon. They took him to a tomb not far from Golgotha.

Thomas walked over to Rachel and bent down beside her. He held her cold hands and looked at her face wet with tears; he could see an expression of deep peace.

'What will become of us?' he said, and she opened her eyes and looked at him.

'We shall follow him, of course,' she said with a young girl's smile.

CHAPTER 30

✦ ✦ ✦

They washed his ravaged body as best they could and anointed it with oils and herbs, under the watchful gaze of a Pharisee and a party of soldiers who had been commanded to guard the tomb. Eliza the Anointer wept as she washed the blood from his face and his ears, dabbing the cloth into the great gouges in his flesh. They bound him in the shroud and lifted him onto a ledge before they were ushered out of the tomb. They stood outside and watched the soldiers pull a huge, heavy stone over the mouth of the tomb. They remained there for an hour before being beseeched by Simon and John to return to Bethany with them.

Eliza, who had spent the last two days in the company of the followers of the Healer, was unrecognizable in her simple apparel and with her bright, shining face. The party came across her old mother, who seemed to be wandering around, groping and falling on the floor.

'What ails you?' Eliza said to her mother.

'I am struck blind, daughter,' she wailed. Eliza held her mother up in her arms and led her back with the party to the house of Lazarus. She felt pity for the old woman, whom the other women helped to walk blindly through the streets of the city back to the safety of the main house.

'Is this your mother?' asked Ruth with a hint of surprise in her voice.

'Yes, we have been estranged for I am afraid she is bound to her very core in witchcraft and a love for the darkness.'

'She has been struck blind at the cross for a reason. Let us minister to her.'

'She will not take kindly to your attention,' said Eliza nervously.

But the old woman was docile and broken. She walked calmly and with the humility of someone in great need of help. As they drew closer to the house of Mary, Martha and Lazarus, she began to cry out to the Son of Man for help.

Mary, the mother of Yeshua, and Mary of Magdala prayed for the old woman, who fell on the floor the moment they laid hands on her. Eliza felt pity for the old woman, and love for the first time, assuming that she had dropped dead at the force of love the women had poured into her. Instead, she found her mother sleeping as peacefully as a baby at her feet. They carried her into the house and laid her in a bed.

Outside, the men were dispirited and broken. Some wept whilst others sank into a listless mood of sorrow. Mary, the sister of Lazarus and Martha, walked out into the garden and addressed the men.

'Just as this old woman has been struck by blindness, so have you all. Death cannot hold him. Tomorrow is the Sabbath, but the day after, we shall go to the tomb and see him raised from the dead, just as we did my brother!'

The women applauded Mary, but the men shook their heads and fell asleep. Mary of Magdala spoke to Eliza about her mother and assured her that she would have been saved from the many spirits that afflicted her.

There was great joy amongst the women when Ruth came into the garden with Rachel, Mina, Thomas, Tobit and Mathias. Tobit and Mathias joined the men sitting silently around the fire, and Mina went over to the women with Ruth.

'Let's walk for a while?' invited Thomas and Rachel nodded. 'I am sorry that you will have nothing to do with me,' he started, but Rachel grabbed his arm and stopped him.

'*I* am sorry. I did not believe in him or you. I was just so frightened and confused, but now – I am reborn, Thomas, reborn!' She held his hands and he pulled her into him and kissed her on the head. She allowed him to hold her and sank into the warmth of his love – alive at last.

✦ ✦ ✦

Portius pushed open the door to the old man's room. He was dishevelled and smelt awful.

'Have you come to gloat?' he asked.

'No, just to tell you that your charge of perverting the course of justice has been commuted. You are free to go. You do have friends in high places!'

'Free, you say? Free! I have lost everything: my wife won't talk to me, I have lost my fortune, my son and daughter-in-law are dead, my granddaughter will have nothing to do with us… and you say I am free. It would have been better if you had thrown the key away.'

✦ ✦ ✦

Arriving home on his own, Barnabas felt empty and somehow sad. He missed the camaraderie of their adventure trying to save the harlot and her daughter. The servants had righted the house and set all the fires ablaze so he could sit in warmth. He had everything he needed – his estate, his vocation, his riches and his homestead – but he knew something was missing. When the others had gone to Jerusalem, he had left Capernaum on his own because he did not want to tarnish his reputation or hinder his progress as a successful merchant. Now he felt flat – he should have gone with them, and the thought agitated him until he could not stand it any longer. Who was this Healer, and what was the fuss about him?

He ordered a fresh horse to be saddled, determined to return to his friends in Jerusalem and find out.

❖ ❖ ❖

Rachel had slept with the women in the main house and had woken on the Sabbath to a day of rest. The men sat around the fire outside, continuing in a deep malaise of misery. The women, however, had, during the prayers in the early hours of the morning, avowed to keep their spirits up and their hopes alive of seeing the kingdom come, regardless of what had happened.

Simon and John tried, during the day, to rouse the men's spirits, but their own sense of suffering and loss undid whatever they said with a hint of hypocrisy. Neither seemed to believe a word that they said about the fight continuing and the message to be spread abroad that the Messiah had come.

If the Messiah had come, the priests had killed him easily enough. The men could not kick off their gloom.

'They are silly beggars!' exclaimed the old woman, her sight restored through the ministry of the women. 'He is up to something, that Healer!' she said with glee. Eliza was astounded at the change in her mother, who seemed to walk taller than she ever had before. She washed herself and made her bed tidily and tried to dress just like the other women, which she had never done before. Mary of Magdala and the old woman seemed to have a deep and mutual affection, the younger woman seeming to dote on the older.

'You will go in the morning and sort this all out!' the old woman said to the younger women. 'What a useless lot of naysayers we have out there!' She laughed, pointing at the men, who were unclean, poorly dressed, unkempt and smelling of smoke from the fire.

Simon and John were tending to the mother of the Healer, who was beside herself with grief, and the two men bent their heads in sorrow as they spoke to her.

'I dread to think what they are saying to her,' said the old woman, asking the younger Mary to go and speak to the mother.

Mary of Magdala helped the mother of the Healer to come indoors out of the cold and sit by the fire. The other women warmed her hands and feet, and Eliza put a shawl around her. Rachel and Mina sat at her feet and stared into the fire.

'Cheer up!' said the old woman to the mother. 'I tell you, it has not finished yet! He has to go and snatch the keys of death – and the enemy of our souls is then doomed. He has crushed his head, and the snake has pierced his heel. Don't you see that God has poured out all his wrath and anger for us all onto his shoulders? He has borne the iniquity of us all – the suffering servant king. What did you expect the Messiah to do? Live in a palace, stuffing his face all day with sweetmeats and glory? He is the scapegoat, the sacrifice for all our sins – and you will see, death will lose its sting!'

Mary, the mother of the Healer, smiled as best she could and looked into the face of the old woman.

'Is that what you believe!' she asked.

'No, it is what I know,' replied the old woman.

The old woman woke Mary of Magdala up early in the morning.

'It is time for you to go,' she said, her voice waking Rachel, who quietly watched as the old woman helped the younger woman to her feet.

'But I am afraid,' said Mary. 'What of the demons? I dare not risk it.'

'You are free of demons, and your house is not empty but full of his protection and might; no harm can befall you,' said the old woman.

'Come with me,' begged the younger woman.

'No, this is something that you must do alone.'

Rachel watched as the young woman slipped out of the house under the cover of darkness. She waited a few moments for the old woman to leave the room and then got up, put on a cloak and tried to follow Mary of Magdala, but when she was outside, she could not see where the young girl had gone. She walked around the garden amongst the sleeping men and stood at the gate looking down the road towards the Mount of Olives, the city on the hill beginning to waken from its slumber to the mist of a new day.

She looked up and saw Thomas walking over to her. He had washed and combed his hair and unmatted his beard, and his eyes seemed freshly shining as he looked at her.

'I could not sleep,' she said.

He smiled, put his arms around her waist and pulled her into him.

'I have something to tell you,' he said, but his eyes and lips said it all. She put her finger on his lips and said, 'Hush, let me say it first...' Then she kissed him on the lips.

Mary of Magdala was running back along the path, her voice rising ever higher in tone. Rachel ran down towards her to see what was wrong, fearing the woman had been attacked.

'Rachel,' she cried, 'it's empty! The tomb is empty!'

Made in United States
Troutdale, OR
07/11/2023

11137057R00181